THE YELLOW JERSEY

THE YELLOW JERSEY

Ralph Hurne

BREAKAWAY BOOKS
HALCOTTSVILLE, NEW YORK

THE YELLOW JERSEY
Copyright © 1973 by Ralph Hurne

ISBN: 1-55821-452-6

Published by
BREAKAWAY BOOKS
P. O. Box 24
Halcottsville, NY 12438
(800) 548-4348
www.breakawaybooks.com

Originally published in the United States by Simon & Schuster.

First BREAKAWAY BOOKS edition: June 1996.
Fifth printing October 2003
This edition has been slightly revised and updated by the author.

Riders referred to historically are real, but those who compete within these pages are imaginary, as is the Tour de France featured in Part 2 of the book.

In the lowlands I have no comrade, not even the lone
      man's friend—
Her who suffereth long and is kind; accepts what he is too
      weak to mend;
Down there they are dubious and askance; there nobody
      thinks as I,
But the mind-chains do not clank where one's next
      neighbor is the sky.

—Thomas Hardy, from *Wessex Heights*

Part One

1

Smile and Say Fromage

"If he steals my watch I shall strike him.

"*S'il vole ma montre je le frapperai.*"

"Now say it in English, and properly, please."

"If he steals my watch I shall strike him."

"And again."

I cross my eyes and repeat it and Susan smiles and puts down the textbook. Her mother, Paula, and I are planning to get married. Paula owns this high-class antique business here in Ghent and gradually I am being worked into it, but as only the Right Sort of People buy the type of gear Paula sells I am having to improve both my French and English. It's my own idea, don't think it's not. I haven't been nagged into it or anything like that. After all, one must adapt, and if a few elocution lessons now will later turn a passing customer into a regular, then it's all right by me. Most of the French expressions I know are oaths and terms of abuse and while Yank customers might find my English quaint, the English themselves would see it as having a touch of the Non-U. I'm developing the right sort of stance too; "weak-wristed" I call it, and I haven't yet got over feeling a twit when I do it.

Susan stands up and passes close to me. I pat her bottom and she shoots a guilty look toward the door. "Not now," she whispers. "When we're both married this will have to stop."

"Yes," I say, but she looks as if she doesn't believe me. Lately I've been making a bit of a pig of myself as far as birds are concerned. And I'm enjoying it. You see, for sixteen years I was a professional cyclist here in Europe and I wasn't able to be choosy about the birds I knew. I retired when I was thirty-five and went home to London to try and settle down. But things didn't work out, I didn't belong there any more. After nearly a year in England I landed a job back here in Belgium, as manager of a team I'd ridden for. Between ourselves, it isn't going too well. For a start the riders aren't much cop. There's one who's all right: his name's Romain Hendrickx and this Susan bird is sort of engaged to him. I say sort of because Romain's great drawback is his timidness both on and off the bike. He's a nice enough kid, a Luxembourger, and he could be a great racing cyclist, except that pro cycle racing is no place for the timid.

Susan is English and looks it, having one of those caved-in square-jawed faces. She reminds me of the sort the wicked squire would ravish in the barn, but in spite of this tea-and-muffin appearance she's really quite randy. And as I said, Romain is a bit timid. So that's where I fit in. Naturally enough Paula knows nothing of this small service I'm supplying to her daughter.

Paula herself is a different sort of person altogether. She's thirty-nine, full and round and warm, and to be honest I'm very fond of her. In a way I feel bad about carrying on with her twenty-one-year-old daughter, but it is in the family and doing nobody any harm.

"Do you want any more practice today?" Susan asks.

"No, I've got to get down the track in about an hour."

"Will Romain be there?" She's wearing a quilted house-coat with roses on it, even though it's a warm day. Susan's got it made here: goes to university, speaks several languages, never been hard up. And Romain—if undemonstrative—dotes on her.

I stand up and go to the window. There's a posh Mercedes below, outside the shop. No doubt the reptilia who own it are being flogged something by Paula. "Yes, Romain'll be at the track," I say at last.

"Will you be racing?"

Racing is a word she's got hold of and I'm never quite sure what she means by it. "Romain's so weak in a bunch finish. If I can't make him aggressive, then at least I must make him crafty."

"Don't make him too crafty, Terry, or he might find out about us. What really are his chances in the Tour de France?"

I shrug. "Just like with any other aspect of life—pure luck or the right contacts."

She gives a bit of a sneer. "Come off it, Terry. Ability must play a large part. Do you attribute a good performance to luck because you yourself never did much good in the race?"

When she goes on like this she gets my goat. "You stick to what you know, eh?"

"If it were luck or contacts then I could win it!"

I sigh heavily and slap my open palm against my forehead. "Allow me to qualify my statement. Among the possible winners entering the race, of which there are, say, twenty, and of which Romain is one, he could if things went either well for him or badly for the others, win the Tour de France. Okay?"

"I'm sorry, Terry," she says arrogantly. "I'll slip into my

hair shirt." The sunlight catches her black patent-leather shoes and for a second they flash. She moves very elegantly to the chaise-longue and sits down. At least it's what I assume to be an elegant walk. She does a bit of part-time modeling "for fun," so it must be okay. Come to think of it, she is a bit like these too-skinny-to-really-fancy bits you see in fashion magazines: the sort who, when they're not dressed like one of the Brontës and Escaping to the Sun, are involved in some absorbing creative work requiring sky-high I.Q. and yielding astronomical rewards. I'm waiting for the day when the Meek Inherit and a hairy, spotty bird with a club foot is shown modeling clothes.

"Seriously," she says, lighting up a fag about a foot long, "are his chances based mostly on luck?" She creaks into a smile signifying hostilities have officially ceased.

"I don't know," I reply honestly. "I wish I did. Theoretically he could win it. He's the best climber in the race and a climber can usually open a big gap and win by minutes. Being a Luxembourger, and as this year it's national instead of trade teams. Romain'll be in a mixed international team. The international team always has been the weakest. It's made up of two or three riders from the lesser cycling countries which can't field a full national team. The riders won't help each other as they will in a national team. It's a sort of coalition government. But then Romain's a climber, and a climber is usually way out on his own when he attacks, and so generally a team can't stay with a super climber, anyway. He's not too bad at time trials; in fact, Romain's good at anything when he's out on his own. Where he comes unstuck is in the bunch, and particularly in these big sprint finishes. And there'll be plenty of big sprint finishes this year. I think the race will be very close right up to the Pyrenees, to the Alps even. If Romain can get to the mountains without getting too mauled or losing too much time, he's got a fair chance. You see, if there were trade teams this year it would be better. Although our lot isn't much good, I could whip them into giving Romain more support than he'd get from an international team. But as you know, a Swiss has been picked to direct the international team."

Susan looks along her cigarette as if testing it for straightness. "And how much does the winner get? It's quite a lot, isn't it? Thousands, or something."

"All in—from contracts, personal appearances, say a few stage wins in the race itself, and advertising—about as much as a multi-national's tax fiddle."

She tips the cigarette up vertically and examines it from that angle. Her mother's business sense is barking at the back door. "Enough to make him financially independent for life, really, if he invested it correctly."

"Enough to give him courage to fix a wedding date with you."

"I knew you were thinking that. Have you thought that it could make him independent enough to turn his back on me altogether?"

"What, and take to a life of debauchery? Romain's not like that. I've managed to do it on a shoestring, but then I'm Terry Davenport—sensualist, bon vivant, radical, cyclist extraordinaire, light work done with horse and trap."

She smiles and slumps into a rather undignified position, sitting with legs apart and shoulders hunched. In the far corner of the room a buzzer sounds. This is Paula's signal that she needs help in the shop. Susan drops her cigarette into an ashtray and hurries toward the stairs. Obviously she can't go into the shop dressed like that and I hear Paula whispering to her on the landing. Seconds later she reappears and tells me that there's an American woman in the shop showing an interest in some old firearms. As there would be no language difficulty and firearms are my department, Paula requests the pleasure of my company downstairs. Anyway, I'm dressed for the part: dark brown button-down candy-striped shirt, dark green suede tie, Norfolk jacket ex-works from the Swinging City, tapered turn-upless green needlecords with a two-inch gap of silk sock before coming to suitably characterized (i.e., worn) Hush Puppies. It smacks of discrimination and "He knows what he's talking about," even if he doesn't.

I go all limp and saunter into the shop. The bird in question is holding a cased pepperbox pistol and studying it carefully. She's about sixty, done up like twenty-five, and I take it the notches along the sides of her spectacles represent hairdressers she's driven round the twist.

"Can I be of any assistance?" I inquire, molars bared, hands clasped behind back, trunk inclined forward from waist.

"Waal . . . waal, I was just looking at these pistols you have here. How much is this one?"

"That one is a very nice piece, madam. Yes, very nice. Cased pepperbox by Blissett. Very reputable London maker. Complete with all accessories, as you can see. That one works out at three thousand dollars. Of course, in that condition they're getting hard to find now."

"Umm . . ." Liberty, Free Enterprise and Mom's cookies clasp hands and dance a jig of indecision.

I point to a nice muzzle-loading .577 Rabone hunting rifle. "Of course, if you want to knock off the odd politician or two, this is more the weapon." (Try humor; nothing to lose.) "Lovely walnut stock; will clean up just like plastic." I broaden the smile a millimeter or two and wring my hands wretchedly.

The hard Belgian sun flicks on her Boston-made lenses as she looks me up and down. She puts the pistol case down with a clatter and stalks out. I wonder if I should tug the forelock and scurry after her, but like all old birds who can give a turn of speed when it suits them, she's gone.

I stick my chin out like Sherlock Holmes when he's just solved something. Looking about thoughtfully and yet avoiding Paula's blank glances, I stroll back to the sanctuary of the heavy velvet curtains that conceal the stairs to the flat above.

"How did you get on?" Susan asks me.

"I fluffed it."

"What was she like?"

"She looked like an old diseuse I once knew, except that this one had Great Society written all over it."

"Is there *anybody* you like?"

"Apart from people who have the power to stick one on me—authority in any form, hard women, loudmouths, politicians and the Swiss—I like everybody. Really, I'm pretty easygoing and unbiased."

"Sounds like it. My God, Terry, you can be a hard bastard."

She looks at me sideways and I raise an eyebrow. The hockey sticks have died in her eyes and a look which I prefer has come into them.

"You haven't got long if you're meeting Romain," she says.

◆

I don't bother to put my salesman's clobber back on, just denims and a dark blue shirt. Susan goes back to the quilted rosepatterned housecoat, which at least was quick. Not like in the old days. By the time you'd got the bird out of all that gear she'd aged so much you'd lost interest. I used to call on

15

a farmer's wife near Bordeaux when I was in the district. It used to take her about half an hour to get ready. Strictly round-behind-the-cowshed stuff, it was. It used to keep its wellingtons on, although once when her old man was out I went indoors and she fluffed all her hair up and wore a babydoll nightdress. Still kept its wellingtons on, though.

"I'm off, then," I say.

She comes over and kisses me. "Goodbye, Terry. This has definitely got to stop. It's not fair to either Mother or Romain. Now is it?"

"No," I say, picking up my jacket and holdall.

◆

I leave my Peugeot in the car park of the old Velodrome and go inside. As it's an enclosed building, used mainly for winter audiences, the lights are all burning. Round and round the big bowl are cyclists going at different speeds and trying different things. Trainers are at the track side and managers farther back, in the middle of the bowl. There're no big names here today. Anybody who is anybody is out on the roads getting ready for Paris-Roubaix and Milan-San Remo. As Romain is now, it would be useless entering him for classics like these. Milan-San Remo is usually one great massive sprint finish, while Paris-Roubaix (the tougher race of the two) is usually a sprint between half a dozen super-hard men who have managed to drop the whole field over the last cobbled stretch of the race. I just can't see Romain even finishing races like these. I advised the sponsors to try him in last season's final classic, the Tour of Lombardy, and he did quite well. I knew he could get away from the rest on the climbs, and he did. He was out on his own for miles, but the big names stirred the bunch up and overhauled him before the finish.

I'm sort of on light duties at the moment. Another manager is looking after the main team while I concentrate on Romain and some of the junior riders. The sponsors have got hold of the idea that Romain, with special training from me and nonparticipation in killing events, can win the Tour de France. Me, I'm not so sure, but then I only take orders. They won't hear of his riding in the Tour of Italy and with this I agree as it's rare for a non-italian ever to win this race. The Italian public somehow miraculously will a native rider into winning. My idea is to try him, but not push him hard, in the Tour of Spain and to use it as a training ground for the big French Tour. But no, thumbs down on this too. I've got a list of fast minor events that he's got to be entered for, all designed to improve his weak riding in bunch finishes and big breaks.

I see him riding round high on the banking. He keeps "jumping"—sprinting suddenly—and then easing up. When he sees me waiting he comes down the banking and gets off his bike. He's a tall fair gangling bloke of twenty-two, looking as mild and inoffensive as he really is. Earlier, as an amateur, he took a bad fall which broke his nose, but in spite of its wavy contour he looks nothing but timid.

He smiles pleasantly and takes off his crash helmet.

"How's it going?" I ask.

A trickle of sweat runs down from his hair. He speaks good English. (But they all do, don't they? Here's me after sixteen years stuck with such gems as "If he steals my watch I shall strike him.") "Not bad, Terry. I've been trying some quick jumps while I waited."

"Right." I duck down into the riders' rooms and change into a track suit. I have a track cycle permanently kept there. We mount and ride off together, keeping at the bot-

17

tom of the banking.

"Now then. There're only a few riders disputing this sprint: five say, including yourself. Two of them're sprinters, two rouleurs. The sun's behind you, the finish on a slight incline. You're dead tired. What tactic do you think you should use?"

"With two strong finishers there I'm not going to win, anyway."

"No, but a second place can earn you a thirty-second bonus in a stage race." I put my hand on his shoulder and we ride slowly.

He says, "I'd make a quick assessment of the other riders' condition, and if I thought I could make it, then I would try for a solo break before reaching the line."

I shake my head. "No. You'd be unlikely to drop all four of 'em, and with you leading out, any one of them could take you at the line. Mark the stronger of the two sprinters. Sit directly on his back wheel well before the finish in case someone else has the same idea. If the sprinters are in the same team, or if for any other reason there might be collusion, you'll have to assess which one is not going to try harder. So, mark your man and sit there. If the sun's behind, then, as you know, the shadows on the road will let you know when someone's coming past you. Obviously you can't cut him off sharply, but if—without looking round—you drift toward the shadow it's going to check him. For a second he'll think you're going to ride into him. But only do this near the line or he'll have time, and be ready, to try again. Watch for short solo breaks by the rouleurs, watch for their shadows. If they look like succeeding, come off the sprinter's wheel but ride wide and try to come up on the far side of the rouleur. If you merely nip from one wheel to another you'll take the sprinter with you, sitting on your wheel.

I suddenly drop back and grab his jersey. He knows what to do and I feel him grip at a point on the base of my thumb.

"Lower," I tell him.

He gropes, but misses the right spot and I let go.

"Too late," I say.

He looks choked and rides away up the banking. You get a lot of this jersey pulling in a massed sprint. If you're steaming along and somebody going slower grabs hold of you, it can nearly jerk you off your bike. Usually they let go immediately and try to look as if they didn't do it, but sometimes they hold long enough for their teammate to get away. A tightly packed mass of cyclists, almost touching, and steaming at about thirty-five miles per hour, is no place to start a punch-up. If you wobble you could bring the whole lot down like ten pins.

I fix a grin and ride up the banking toward him. He half smiles and sets off, winding up a good pace. I ride through a bunch of slow-moving riders and come up to Romain. "All right," I tell him. "Two laps, and I want you over the line first."

The year I spent in England off the bike did me the world of good. I had been getting a bit rusty when I officially retired. Since coming back to Europe I've been out with the team riding the same miles they have. Apart from Romain's ability to climb mountains they're a pretty poor lot, and I'm not being big-headed when I say I can still beat each and every one of them at the sprint—eight times out of ten, anyway.

Hang on, I'd better concentrate. We've only half a lap to go. I can see what he's going to do. He's going to stay as high on the banking as possible, then swoop down across the banking so that when he crosses the line he has the advantage of actually riding down a hill. As we come into the straight, with me in roughly the middle of the track, I put on a spurt and zoom upward toward him as if to cut him off. He knows I'd never ride into him, yet he's so nervy that my action checks him. Immediately he realizes his mistake and starts to ride hard down the banking for the line, which is now some fifty yards away. I, being slightly in front, do the same, except that I aim for a spot halfway up the banking about twelve yards beyond the line. This has the effect again of cutting him off without actually doing so, and I cross the line while he's still sorting himself out.

In a track race between the two of us I might have been disqualified for such riding. But on the track you're out there for all to see, like two moist prunes on a white china plate. On the road, in a bunch of riders, and carried out less pointedly, such tactics can pass unnoticed.

Romain looks fed up as he rides next to me shaking his head. "What should I have done?" he asks miserably.

"If it had been a straight race, would you have beaten me anyway?"

We ride off the track and come to a standstill. "No," he says and leans his cycle against the fence.

"I've told you before, there is no secret. The whole snag lies in your nature. You've simply got to give as good as you get. When I rode up the banking toward you, you should have kept going, then I'd have been the one to be checked."

He tilts his crash helmet to the back of his head and pulls a glum face. There is no doubt of his powers as an athlete, but he's so boyish and fragile. "Wait until the Alps in the Tour. I'll show them. I'll show them all. You won't know me, Terry. I shall be out there in front, alone. You'll see."

"I hope so for your sake, and for Susan's. Just don't start believing too much in your own propaganda. Men who can climb but do little else seldom win the Tour. I can't see you losing the King of the Mountains title and the loot that goes with it, but the Tour's not all mountains."

"Bahamontes won it. He was a super climber and probably worse than me at time trials."

Four riders are steaming round the Velodrome and the others practicing there have stopped to watch them. They are relaying one another in preparation for some team event, but they look hell-bent on breaking a world record. As they pass they gasp encouragement among themselves. They're amateurs, youngsters, probably the lot Belgium is sending to the Olympics.

"Bahamontes won it because he was directed by a superman, the others thought him incapable and ignored him until it was too late, and it was so bloody hot that only a Spaniard could survive in the heat. None of which applies to your case. Ever heard of Vervaecke, Vietto, Martano?"

His eyes search my face. "Yes, I know the names."

"Well, they could climb too, probably better than you can. And do other things well. Did they ever win? No."

"You'll see," he says cheerfully, getting on his machine and riding off. "I'll surprise you all."

◆

"What happened with the American woman this morning?" Paula asks me without looking up from the box of effects that she's just opened. A whole load of gear has arrived from an estate which was auctioned off. It looks as if Paula spent a bomb there.

"Oh, we hadn't got what she really wanted." I've just eaten a piece of cake and run a sliver of airmail paper between my two front teeth to clear away debris.

"What was she after?"

Aren't women bloody persistent, especially when they

smell blood.

"Colts, Remingtons—American guns, what else? Take away their Glorious West and what's left? They forget that virtually every battle in the West was a mere skirmish by European standards."

"I hope you weren't rude to her." For the first time she looks up. I'm not sure if this is a question or an accusation. Anyway, I'm not going to answer.

I start to look through a tea chest full of books. I suppose these were in lots and she had to buy much of this tot to get the good pieces. At the back of the shop, in an enormous shed, is enough stuff to make Steptoes' yard look like a tidy windowsill. A lot of it's good gear and I find it more interesting than the posh stuff she sells in the shop. Valuable china and silver candlesticks are all right, I suppose, but I'd rather have an old uniform, a Victorian steam engine or a swordstick any day. A lot of the stuff in this shed is rubbish, mind you. There're some 1930s wind-up gramophones and plenty of those Highland-Cattle, Monarch-of-the-Glen, Stag-at-Bay type pictures. And loads of old photographs. Most people laugh at them, but I can't. I wouldn't like to think people one day will be laughing at my photos (although I suppose they will). Anyway, in some ways they must have been good times to live. I don't think the Victorians were as daft as some today make out. People don't change much, they just wear different clothes.

The old junk trade appeals to me. This job of coaching Romain is all right, but if he doesn't win the Tour it'll be all my fault, or so they'll say. Then I'll be put back trying to get some teamwork out of the rest of the riders. They're mostly Swiss and a right dour lot too. They just look at you as if you were a bloody idiot. I think in a quiet way they're full of Herrenvolk and reckon they're the Master Race. They give me the pip. I sometimes fancy that down there in my fatty tissues I can detect the muffled limb stretchings of a baby ulcer searching for light. I never had any worries when I was riding.

What I'd really like to do is to continue giving individual coaching to any youngster who either wanted to pay or who I thought had potential. This would be a spare-time job. For the real income I'd like to go in with Paula, but to convert the upstairs flat into a sort of Collectors' Corner. She could handle the Right Sort of People downstairs while I dealt with all the bits and pieces upstairs. I reckon life could be very nice like that. I've looked into my Terry Davenport crystal ball and this is what I see: If Romain does well in the Tour he and Susan will probably get married. That gets Susan out of the way for both Paula and myself. Not far from here there're some very nice flats going up. Not rubbish, mind you; they're really suave. I've sort of mentioned all this to Paula and I think she's keen. She'll have to be. She'd be paying. The money I've got (about forty thousand quid) I'll simply give to Paula, although she'll have to return most of it again to pay for the conversion of the upstairs flat into a Collectors' Corner. These premises are old, which is all right for a shop but no good for living in. Next door there's a posh interior decorator's and the couple who own it must sit up all night chanting in Flemish. Either that or one of them's dictating his life story. No matter what time of the night I wake up, I can hear this bleedin' mumbling like a bumblebee. Thin walls, see.

Paula's blowing dust off some old books. She sees me looking and smiles. "Dusty," she says.

"Yes."

"Look at this, Terry. *The Prisoner of Zenda* and inside it's signed Anthony Hope Hawkins."

"Where? Let's see. So it is. There's probably some bloke in a basement near here signing great piles of these."

"Oh, no. This was in a job lot. Anyway, it doesn't add much to the price. What's it worth? Four hundred francs?"

"About that. It'd be a shame to sell it. I'd like to keep it."

Paula sighs. "If you had your way you'd keep everything. Still, if you want it you'd better have it."

"Ta." I pick up a saber and swish it through the air. "The play actor with his tin sword. Oh, yes, I can see it all: Ronald Colman, Douglas Fairbanks, Junior." I parry and lunge and Paula watches me, laughing. It's a nice laugh, not too anything. She must have been drilled early in life to be charming and sweet, and the lesson stuck. There's no doubt that she's made a great success of her shop, for she combines a good business sense with understanding and unflappability. Paula's a warm-hearted woman who needs to give, and there's not really much more she can give Susan. To be honest, she could do a lot better for herself than marrying me. But the other candidates, and I gather there have been many, are handicapped by being Haves. Paula must have a Have-Not because her nature needs someone to give things to. Also, because of the rather proper life she's led, with everyone being terribly nice, she's missed out a bit on the old slap-and-tickle, to which, reading between the lines, I think she's a bit partial. Once when Susan was out I took all my clothes off and chased Paula round the flat. Although she ran, it wasn't too fast and I think she enjoyed it all the more for the chase. It was like taking a ceremonial horse for a canter over the downs.

She's a biggish woman and not as skinny as her daughter. Although I've seen rows of dresses in her wardrobe, she always seems to wear costumes. She wears glasses for reading, and sometimes in the shop. There never seems to be a moment when she isn't doing something. The one asset which gives a woman lasting beauty is a lovely mouth, and Paula has this. It's soft and wide, and pink even without lipstick. For a reason I can't explain, I should hate to hurt her or see her hurt. Half these birds deserve what they get, and the Best of British Luck, I say. But not Paula.

She was married to a Regular officer who was killed in a pile-up shortly before Susan was born. Paula's hair is very long and she tells me she has never had it cut; she wears it up during the daytime and loosely plaited at night. There are a few gray hairs in it now, the same as I'm getting in mine.

Paula looks up from her dusting. She gives me a broad smile which I know to be a casual prelude to a more serious topic.

"They're getting on with those flats you told me about."

"You looked, then?"

"Oh, yes. I looked the day after you told me about them."

"Yes, they're nice. I like the big ornamental pond they're putting in the forecourt. There was a pond in the garden where I used to live way back. Well, I say pond; it was more of a swamp, really."

She sits on a tea chest and keeps looking at me, smiling. "I wish I knew what Susan's intentions were. Can't you have a little talk with Romain? Tell him about the birds and the bees and things. I know he's dedicated to racing, but he is a man. I know I shouldn't say this, but I'd be almost happy if he seduced Susan."

"Perhaps he has."

"No. No. I'm sure I'd know. To my knowledge they've never been anywhere where anything like that could successfully take place." She points to me with a book. "Terry, you're the expert. Tell him how to go about it!"

"Huh." I walk away looking at the copy of *The Prisoner of Zenda*. I don't like talking about things like this to Paula. "I heard of some old model railway stuff going for sale in Antwerp. I might drive up and have a look. It's gauge two tinplate."

I don't think she likes my changing the subject.

"Is that good?" Her smile has gone.

I try to sound keen. "Good? I'll say! It's worth a packet these days."

"How old is it?"

"Oh, 1920s, I expect."

"And that's antique!"

"No. More collectors' items."

"But I won't be able to display those in the shop. They'd be quite out of keeping."

I get it. She's pretending she's forgotten about my idea for turning the upstairs flat into a Collectors' Corner so that I'll have to mention it and she can talk about Susan again. "I was thinking of buying them for myself. Anyway, they're not much older than I am, and that should be antique enough for anyone."

2

Someday All This
Will Be Yours

ROMAIN AND THE MOTORCYCLIST are waiting for me as I ride into the square. The day is cold and damp, and so Romain and I wear track suits and have mudguards fitted to our cycles. The motorcyclist is an old bloke who's paid by the hour, and his job is to pace Romain. It's funny, but a paced cyclist can go a hell of a lot faster than an unpaced one, and the idea of using a motorcycle is that it gets a cyclist used to riding at a cracking pace—at a speed faster than he'd do in an actual race. Usually the trainer sits on the pillion and gives his instructions to both driver and cyclist. But me, I like to go along on the old cycle and sit in behind Romain. I've worked out a set of signals to give the driver should I want him to slow or accelerate. By suffering with Romain I find I can get the feel of things much better, and at this type of riding I've still got the edge on him, anyway.

To be truthful, it sort of does the ego a bit of good. Even though I know I could take him on the flat, I have to somehow keep proving it. Perhaps I have a secret death wish that's waiting for the day he goes past me and leaves me gasping, and then I'll know I'm really finished. I suppose this is why I'm reluctant to give up Susan and girls like her. I sort of need constant proof. I'm not being big-headed when I say I'm a young thirty-seven, and I'm usually taken for being about thirty-two. I feel really scared, sick scared, of the day when my proofs don't prove any more.

I tell the old boy, Alphonse, to hold as near as traffic will allow, forty kilometers an hour for the next hour. "Let's go," I say to Romain, and we set off through the outskirts of Ghent. Once we get clear and are heading down one of those straight poplar-lined roads, I tap Romain on the hip and indicate to him to use a lower gear. He looks glum and points at me to do the same, which I do, and he follows suit. The sudden shock of pedaling so much faster to get the same speed hits us a bit hard, but we get used to it. After an hour I signal to Alphonse to open up a bit, and for Romain to use a higher gear again.

We're really going now. One thing about the public here, they know what it's all about and they give us bags of encouragement. Romain's beginning to loll a bit and his elbows are sticking out. I shoot out a hand and slosh his nearest elbow. We're both gasping too much to say anything but he nods and sits better on his machine. I signal that we should turn for home and that I want the motorcycle driven in bursts, so that we have to keep sprinting to hold it. I maintain a close watch on Romain. His reactions are slow. You can tell from the exhaust note when the burst is coming, but half the time the thing's on its way before Romain has tumbled it. This means he loses contact with the motorcycle and has to fight that much harder to get back with it.

"Anticipate!" I yell at him and he seems to perk up, but once he slips badly and Alphonse has to wait for us.

We stay with the motorcycle all the way back to the team's headquarters, which is in an eastern suburb of

Ghent. Neither of us speaks until we've had a hot shower and Romain is receiving a massage.

"How was I?" he asks.

"Bit slow off the mark. Late night with Susan, I expect. There's nothing for it, Romain me lad, you'll have to marry her and get to bed early."

He smiles. "When I am rich and can give her everything."

I have a little grin and sit on one of the benches listening to the slaps and pummeling that Romain's getting from the masseur. I don't know if getting married would help him. He might get to bed earlier, but he certainly wouldn't get much sleep, not with Susan there. His head's full of daydreams about winning the Tour, but I think he's in for a shock. The longest stage race he's ever ridden was Paris-Nice, which is a five-day event. I admit he should have won it and was dead unlucky not to. But the Tour de France? I don't know. With Susan for a wife and a Tour that he didn't win behind him, he might pull his finger out. If he had a home to keep and a future to save for and Susan (who's no mug) to egg him on, he might one day win. For one thing he'd need a good team, which he hasn't got this year.

Back in the old days pros used to ride for one of the big cycle firms, and then when an international race like the Tour de France came along a number of the best riders, regardless of the cycle firms they rode for, were selected to ride for their country. The whole idea nowadays of a cycle team is to advertise. That's why the riders' vests and shorts are plastered with the various names of whatever they're advertising. The decline of the cycle trade and the high cost of running a team made the future of pro racing look a bit dicey in the mid-1950s. What saved it was the bright idea that a team did not necessarily have to advertise a cycle or cycle products. A rider's vest and shorts could advertise anything, and so all sorts of big concerns began sponsoring teams. They poured money into racing—big firms who made anything from patent medicine to electrical appliances to wine. They all had a go. Major cycle races are watched by thousands and are televised, filmed and photographed. It doesn't need much imagination to see that a race round, say, Italy or France would bring a sponsoring advertiser's name before the public in no uncertain way. And if one of their team won, a picture of him posing in the sponsor's colorful racing vest would be in all the papers. All this was a shot in the arm for cycle racing.

However, there are two schools of thought as to whether or not it helped the Tour de France. This race is, of course, the biggest event on the calendar and enthusiasm for it can reach fever pitch. The Frenchman likes to cheer his French idol, not a man riding for a wine company. The Italian wants to shout himself hoarse—not for a Dutchman riding for an Italian firm of spaghetti manufacturers, but for an Italian riding in an Italian national team. After all, nationalism is everywhere on the up and up. The Tour, many say, is above advertising. It is a bitterly fought international affair. There is an old saying to the effect that great riders don't make the Tour, the Tour makes great riders. The argument put forward by the sponsoring firms is that they spend large amounts on the teams and so keep pro racing going, yet when the Tour comes round they are denied their greatest public and their biggest chance to advertise. I think the riders themselves prefer the trade teams, because otherwise you get the effect of a united team backed by a commercial concern suddenly in the Tour confronting one another as rivals. As money talks all languages, the trade team system has had its way for many years now, with an occasional Tour using the national team system slung in to keep the other faction happy.

And that's what it is this year—national teams. The French, as one would expect, are fielding several teams: their main "A" team and several regional teams representing the southwest of France, Paris, etc. Should a regional French rider win the Tour, they forget he represented a region, and all that counts is that he's French. There are Italian "A" and "B" teams, likewise two Belgian teams. Of the rest there is one team of each for the Dutch and Spaniards. Because other countries can't field enough pro riders of Tour de France standards, there is also an international team. As he's a Luxembourger, this is where Romain comes in. The teams are of twelve men each, and so the international team will be made up of one Luxembourger, one Portuguese, two English, two Danes, two Swiss, two Germans, one Austrian and one Australian. The racing vests worn by the riders will be in their national colors. The Italian vest, for example, is green with broad red and white stripes around the chest.

To keep the moneymen happy, each rider is also permitted to carry the name of his trade sponsor, although the sponsor's name must not be too prominent. It can be displayed on the vest and around the legs of the shorts. So although the amount of visual advertising will be small this year, there is still a keen commercial interest. Say a member of the French national team wins, and normally he rides for the Artois sponsors. Advertising from this would be big and would go something like this: "Artois rider, Jean-Pierre Bloggs, riding in the French national team, wins the world's greatest sporting event, the three-thousand-mile Tour de France. A win for France! A win for Artois!" Something like that, anyway. And what's all this leading up to? Well, I'll tell you. Take the big trade team of Artois. For the Tour it will be split up because in it are Frenchmen, Belgians and Italians. But if the stakes are big enough and the price is right, nationalism doesn't mean a thing, and an Italian can help a Frenchman not so much by openly giving aid, but by not trying too hard at the right time to stop him. See what I mean? Romain will be like a lamb among wolves.

◆

I see her park this new blue Vespa outside the shop and then spend five minutes looking in the window. At last she comes in.

"What a lovely shop. Could I look around?" she says in English.

My poised subjunctives disappear in a happy flash. "By all means."

Susan's attending a lecture, Romain is down at the gym and Paula's grabbing some lunch. I put on a Harrods' floor-walker-type stance and stalk her at a respectable distance. "Is there anything in particular you're looking for? Perhaps I could direct you straight to it."

I think she's shy and the time spent looking in the window has been a period of moral rearmament. She acts as if I've put the hard word on her and stands there smiling awkwardly, swinging this brown corduroy shoulder bag. I feel terrible. I myself know there's nothing worse than being pestered when you just want to look. Unless of course it's not being able to get served when you march in and know exactly what you want.

She still doesn't answer, so I say, "I'm sorry. You did say you only wanted to look. Go ahead."

A confused look flashes across her face. "Oh, no, it's your job—" She turns away quickly and picks up an ornament, so

I give a cough and shuttle back to looking out of the window. Her rubber soles make a noise on the parquet floor and at last she moves round so that I can see her reflection in the window. She's wearing brown and fawn check trousers with slightly bell bottoms, brown suede chukka boots and a short white mac. I suppose she's twentyish, and she has the standard for long fair hair combed straight down from a center parting. I fancy she recently had a fringe because the front pieces of hair seem shorter than the rest and she keeps brushing them off her face. She's of medium build and has a modern face—you know, not particularly beautiful yet very attractive. You used to know where you were; they were either gorgeous or they weren't. Black and white, you know what I mean? Not any more. They're all ugly-pretty these days.

If you think I ought to be satisfied with two birds, let me leap to point out that after leading a monastic existence for sixteen years, twelve birds are my present idea of enough. Of course I've always had something on the go, but living as I did—traveling all over the place—what I had was taken only because it was there and required little effort. And on that basis all I usually got was load of old rough.

"Is this pewter mug Flemish?" she asks.

I turn and look to where she's pointing.

"Yes. All on that shelf are. Don't be shy; take them down and have a look."

She seems more at ease now and begins examining the mugs.

"You work in Belgium?" I ask casually. It never does any harm to chat up passing nubility.

"Oh, no." She puts down the mug and picks up another. Quiet sort. Well, I'll let it look. Three right on the doorstep would be a bit much, wouldn't it? But then Susan, my deportment and grooming consultant, wants out. So really

33

there is a vacancy. She'll either fancy me and I'll be all right, or she'll think I'm too old and just a "nice man." I miss not having something on the go, some little scheme. When things are stationary I feel as lost as a British tabloid without a feature on the Royal Family.

Funny things, women. Ever noticed how they must always latch on to something? First it's men, then the kids come along to claim their interest, and then when women are old they congregate with one another at mothers' meetings. I picked up with one who came in here a few months back. She and her husband were looking round the shop. It was a bit prim and frumpy but had a chest and a half on it, I couldn't drag my eyes away. Her husband was with her; short-back-and-sides and a briefcase (dodgy combination). He was choked with me because he knew I was ogling. I finally made out with it, but only once, and then I wasn't prepared. I had this China-made vest on which had stretched to mini-skirt proportions, and I felt a bit of a twit. It only happened the once though, as I said. Apparently she heard a voice far off calling to her telling her she was wicked, or something. I wouldn't have liked her husband. I noticed over his dresser he had the old "If there is any good that I can do, let me do it now" motto. Funny couple.

Other recent trophies include Marian, the ladies' hairdresser. It was big as Sylvester Stallone and all bra straps and lacquer, the sort where you can trace the outline of the suspender belt through its skirt. And go? Are you kidding? One night several of my fillings fell out. It was like Perpetual Labor in the Hulks. All that finally saved me was my collection of white feathers which I'd been saving for the end of the world. Its idea of dressing up was PVC and sunglasses, and what was worse, Her Best Friends Wouldn't Tell Her. Like all people with a breath on them, she had to keep sticking her face into mine every time she spoke. The last I heard of her she had a Boston Crab on some gypsum and clinker contractor down near Roubaix.

Shortly after Marian came Carol. She was a Belgian, and with a few genes less would have been a dwarf. Her husband was a surgical bootmaker who, for some undefined reason, found it more to his liking to bootmake elsewhere. A funny apartment they had. Apparently the Christmas decorations had been up for three years. The neighbors were always charging in and out; it was like an open asylum. But I'd labored in other vineyards and soon dropped that.

Oh, yes, and then there was this Englishwoman who was over here on some convention. Normally I wouldn't have got anywhere there, but I cheated a bit and got it tipsy. She smacked of Homes and Gardens, Townswomen's Guild and that lot. For reasons I can't go into, we had to use the bathroom and she sat on the edge of the hand basin. We were about to finish when she moved backwards a bit and sat on the tap, which was one of those press-down sort you get on ships. There was a tremendous hissing and a cloud of steam and for a second I thought it was her. God, how I've lived.

"This one's nice. How much?" She's holding out a pewter mug. I take it down and show her the price tag.

She looks crestfallen. "Perhaps I'll leave it. Thanks." She starts to walk away a bit sheepishly.

I hold it up between two fingers. "You really want it?"

She must think I'm going to offer hire purchase terms, because she silently mouths the word "No" and grins awkwardly. I step forward and give it to her. "It's yours. I'll buy it for you. All I ask is that I treat you to dinner."

When she smiles her eyes screw up and look as if they're closed, but you can just see two slivers of brightness shining through the lids. I'd expected to do a lot of "strictly

35

honorable" explaining, but she answers simply, "Thank you. There's no reason why you should give me the mug. It's just that I was looking for something Belgian for my old grandfather. I promised him I would. He was here in the war. I'll get him something else, something I can afford, but thanks for offering." She pushes a short end of hair from her face.

I spin the mug on my finger, like a six-shooter. "Okay. But what about dinner? Could you make it tomorrow night?"

She shrugs and hitches her bag onto her shoulder. "What time?"

"Seven o'clock?"

She agrees and I tell her where I'll meet her.

"My name's Bobbie," she says as she reaches the door.

"I'm Terry Davenport. See you tomorrow."

◆

It's not a very important race, just a weekend round-the-houses, and there are no big names present. The course is eighty kilometers, three times round a circuit between this village and the next. The crowds, as usual, are large. A couple of local firms have offered prime prizes. This helps to liven up the race, because on the two occasions the riders cross the line before the finish on the third lap there's a substantial prize each time for the first man over the line. The course is too flat and windy for a lone break to work, and I look through my binoculars at the fast-moving peloton, hoping to see Romain near the front.

He tried hard on the first lap, but the strong sprinters swept past him like a tide as he came up to the line. On the second lap he must have been in the middle of the bunch, because I didn't even see him. Although Romain is probably the best-known man in the event and in a big stage race would be head and shoulders above the others here today, this kermesse-type riding is a specialist's art and some men make a living by riding exclusively in these events.

But it's practice of this sort that Romain needs so badly. He has always known his weakness and, until coming into our T.B.H.-Aigle team, he avoided these closely fought events as much as possible, trying to make his name in those short hilly events in the Alps and Pyrenees. I think he hoped to win one of the hilly classics like Milan-San Remo or the Tour of Lombardy so that he would be a big name and draw good contract fees. Then he signed up with us and they sold him the old, old theory that if a good climber doesn't lose too much time on the flat stages, then he must automatically win the Tour de France. But the men who have convinced him of this are businessmen who are so fat they'd fall off a bike if they sat on one, and are backed by yes men who secretly know better but who realize which side their bread's buttered. I've mostly stuck my tongue in my cheek and kept quiet, and when they asked me definitely what I thought, I said that it was possible for Romain to win it, but by no means certain. The only sure way I know for getting him to win would be to graft my head onto his body. That, or stick the pair of us on a tandem.

Here they come, about sixty of them, and the tremendous whirring sound a large bunch makes as it swoops up to the line is drowned by the roar of the crowd. The road is only wide enough for about ten riders who have fought their way to the front and are going to let nobody past. It's easy to see Romain. He's bogged down right in the middle and is out of his saddle bouncing up and down as if climbing a mountain.

That's that, then. It's all over. He didn't even get placed.

Give him a wall and he could ride up it, but the minute he gets into finishes of the sort I've just witnessed his mind goes blank and he forgets everything I've told him.

Across the road I see Mottiat, one of the T.B.H.-Aigle big wheels, getting into his limousine. His face is as black as thunder.

Romain pushes his cycle toward me. His shoulders are heaving, he's covered in sweat and his eyes are blinking nineteen to the dozen. "I'm sorry, Terry. I just couldn't get near the front. To do so I would have had to ride over, not round them. Short of carrying a revolver and shooting my way through, I don't see how I'm ever going to make it."

"That's all right," I say and take his machine from him. It's no good moaning at him now, he looks so near to tears.

When he's showered and changed, he sits in the back of the van with the cycles, so I can't speak to him. I drive him back to headquarters and lock up the van and cycles. He's waiting by my car as I come from the building. "Could you take me round to Susan's? I feel like taking her out and having a good meal and some entertainment. A show or something. I'm sick to death of bikes. I want to go out and forget them."

"Sure." I unlock the car door and we get in.

It begins to rain a little and I switch on the wipers. As I take a right turn I glance at him. His eyes are watching the arc made by the wiper as it flops backward and forward.

"Cheer up," I say to him.

I feel him look at me. "Would you ride in the Tour with me and get me to the mountains?"

I laugh out loud. "At my age! Blimey, I'm so old I can remember rarities you never dreamt of: long-forgotten things such as Socialism, and words like 'please' and 'thank you.' Why, I can remember when dustmen collected rubbish and all London bus conductors were like Steve Martin. No, Romain, I'm past it."

"Plenty of men have done it," he says softly.

I laugh again and shake my head. "It never was my sort of race, Romain. I never had any luck in it. The heat whacks me. In any race north of Paris I had as much chance as the next rider, but down there in the south, in June—phew!"

He says nothing else for some minutes, then: "Is it really that hard?"

I breathe in deeply through my nose. "Well, you're all in the same boat. I suppose it's just that you get the feeling it will never end." Romain once rode in, but didn't finish, the amateur Tour de France, which is easier and about half the length of the professional race.

Last month he and I went down in the van to the Alps and Pyrenees for ten days. I drove him to and made him ride up and descend all the major cols in this year's race. Of course, he went up like a bird. He's not so hot at coming down, or "descending" as it's known, but this is something you can either do naturally or you never will. I'm not really worried about it, as most of the other possible winners are poor descenders. There's no athletic ability needed to descend, just an iron nerve and the ability to really control a bike. And in my own modest and unassuming way I must tell you I was one of the best in the trade. It's a useful asset in mountain racing, because often a man who can't climb too well is able, on the descent, to catch the climbers who dropped him on the way up. Often minutes can be gained without turning a pedal, just by sitting on your machine and leaving more nervous riders behind. And there's something to be nervous about. You can drop like a stone on unsurfaced roads with hairpin bends where a slight miscalculation can mean possible death and certain injury. A descending cyclist can reach speeds of sixty-five miles per hour, and at this speed brakes are useless and a puncture disastrous. Riders have been killed or maimed through descending accidents. The mountain roads are unfenced and often a sheer drop waits for a rider who miscalculates.

"I wish I'd ridden as many tours as you have," he says, brightening up. "If only I could be me, here, now, at my age, only with your experience. To think you rode against Merckx and Gimondi."

"Yes," I say.

"What were they like?"

"Mostly all any of us saw of them were their back wheels disappearing up the road."

"Were they better than today's cyclists?"

"I don't know. They were different. I suppose I think they were better, but everyone thinks his generation's the best. It's just natural bias, I suppose."

For a while he appears to be thinking about what I have said, then he blurts out, "Really the best way to contemplate the Tour is to think of riding twenty-one one-day classics, one each day for three weeks."

"No," I tell him, "don't think of it like that. It would be wrong. The Tour is one race, one bloody great long race. You've got to regard it as a whole, you've got to get the feel of it, to anticipate, plan ahead. If you start out thinking of it as twenty-one separate races all linked up, you'll come unstuck. You enter a one-day event with the hope of winning, but there are days in the Tour when, even if you could, it would be unwise to win. I'm not talking about the usual mad scramble for glory in winning a stage, or wearing the yellow jersey. For a rider like yourself who has the overall victory in mind, the Tour must be strategically ridden.

"Ideally, you yourself should 'do a Bartali.' Try to reach

the Pyrenees fairly well placed, say in the first twenty. Through the Pyrenees take all the mountain primes that go toward the King of the Mountains title, but don't aim yet for overall leadership. Once you've got the yellow jersey you're everybody's marked man. Think in terms of leaving the Pyrenees in the first six, say within four or five minutes of the yellow jersey. Attack in the Alps, but attack with increasing pressure so that you just win the first Alpine stage, clinch it in the second and slaughter them in the third. You must leave the Alps with at least three minutes in hand, more if the second and third places are filled by rouleurs who will cut down your lead on the flat stages back to Paris. By the time you leave the Alps a team such as the international will be so decimated that it will probably be nonexistent and you'll be on your own. The big national teams will still be fielding about nine men apiece, and they'll all be out to stop you."

He looks at me for a second, blinking. "You don't think I can pull it off, do you? Not really, not in your heart."

I wait until a truck as long as Southend Pier has passed us. "If I *knew* just one thing in this life, Romain, I'd be happy. I'll only say what I've always said, that you're a possible winner. There're no allowances made in the Tour for misfortune. Everything is shrugged aside with '*C'est le Tour!*' Only the death of a rider can put the mockers on it for a while, but next day it'll all be back into full swing, all the cut and thrust will be there. Because of its harshness it gives off this fascination. Many say that a lone rider riding against the clock in a time trial is competing in the real race of truth. But I disagree. I see a time trialist riding *contre la montre* as a specialist riding his chosen type of race. Others say Paris-Roubaix is the race that really decides, because no outsider has ever won it and even the Tour has been won by lucky unknowns. But I still disagree, because again it's specialists competing in the type of event to which they're best suited.

"Where did great riders like Anquetil and Kubler ever come in Paris-Roubaix? Nowhere. For me, Romain, the Tour is the real race because it is the nearest thing to life, outside life itself. It's just like the human cycle. You're born and you set out. For some, things go wrong from the start; others catch the good breaks and get well placed. Sometimes the deserving doers win, mostly they flog for nothing. Those with connections—that is, strong team support and good press publicity—have every advantage. These usually win, but it's interesting to see how sometimes Justice will put the boot in and upset things. The Tour even resembles modern life by having a blaring commercial setup tailing it; and all the riders, privileged and otherwise, are workers whose efforts to some degree are being exploited by a nonparticipant.

"I hate the Tour, yet it fascinates me. It can have wonderful moments, like when the commercial caravan and the cars are way back and a good team of men engineer a clever break and get away. To see them working as hard as politicians at election time—to see them relaying, pacing, pounding their hearts out to put more road between themselves and the others. And then you get the bad moments when things go wrong, or there's unfairness and corruption. Yes, it's really just like life. You set out in company with your own ability and fate. There are the good bits and the bad, the easy and the hard. You climb, descend, slog, rest. Very occasionally you win. And as sure as death you come back again to where you started and it's all over, and the names are recorded. Other than the winner, you all go unnoticed and unappreciated and are soon forgotten. Winners are always remembered. Why, I can tell you them all from when it started in 1903. But who came second, third? I can tell you a few, that's all, and they're all from recent years. If you win, Romain, they even put it on your tombstone."

I think my talking has made his emotions thump a bit. His eyes are watering as he says quietly, "I'll win."

"That's the spirit! Get stuck into those sprint finishes and you've got every chance. Meanwhile forget about today's race. Take Susan out, have a good time."

"Yes." He's smiling.

"Will you marry her if you win the Tour?"

He answers excitedly. "Of course. I'll be able to buy a house outright and have no need of mortgages, get a new car, furnish the house and invest the rest. And as you yourself have often said, if I never win another race as long as I live, I'd have—barring accidents—about thirteen years of fame ahead of me. For every criterium, every track meeting, the classics and the tours, the starting fee paid me by the organizers will be high. And the maximum amount shall be asked—for Romain Hendrickx, winner of the Tour de France!"

We chuckle a duet.

"And if you only win the King of the Mountains prize?"

He thinks for a second and I glance at his reflection. "Yes, I think we could still get married. It would mean renting a flat and keeping the same car. But I've got ten years ahead of me in which I could win the Tour. And why am I restricted to winning it once?"

"You're not. It's up to you."

"And luck, as you said."

I nod. One way or another it seems he'll get married, which means Susan leaves home, which means Terry's Collectors' Corner opens, which means I marry Paula and am financially set. If he doesn't make a pile in this year's Tour, the next chance he'll get to make any big money will be next year, and if he fails then . . . See what I mean?

They're not paying him much, which is reasonable because he's not racing much. He's got even less chance of winning the Tour of Italy or the Tour of Spain, and even if he did there's not the same amount of cash or glory attached. He could pick up a few thousand quid if he could win a hilly classic, but with the big gears they push today a climber has less and less chance of hanging on to a lead even if he gets it.

Paula can't evict Susan from what's always been her home, especially when she's still at university. I don't want to start married life with Susan under the same roof. The temptation would always be there, if you know what I mean. That's how it started, seeing her come out of the bathroom, catching glimpses through her bedroom door, looking at her underwear drying on the line. I'm an athlete, in every sense of the word, and a veteran like myself can always tell when a woman wants something. No, it'll have to end, but I want her married and out of the way before I can definitely say That's that. I've got this attic bedroom in a gable above the flat, but I keep only clothes in it. The last time I went there some bats flew out and I had to push my way through cobwebs. Both Susan and Romain know where I really sleep, but there's something oddly respectable about bedding down with a bird like Paula.

Another reason I'd like to see Romain do well is that he's such an inoffensive bloke, yet the game he's in is about as hard as they come. He hasn't got a spark of push in him; he just grins and blinks and you can't help but forgive him. As a prototype professional cyclist he's hopeless, yet he has this great potential in his legs. Right from the word go the Tour literally explodes and seldom lets up. There's always somebody whipping up the pace for some reason. There are prizes for the most aggressive rider of the day, a large prize for the rider collecting the most points by winning or being placed in the daily stages, and various prime prizes. Sometimes, when you think you're about to get a rest, a local boy on home ground will want to show off—and away you go again. Often the pace is cracked up into a frenzy by a favorite's team trying to make an opponent suffer and tire. Whatever the reason, it boils down to being virtually flat out most of the time. Many riders—professionals—can't even keep up, let alone try to win. It's bloody hard, I'll tell you, and it's a gauntlet such as this that Romain's got to run before he can fly in the mountains.

3

I Don't Care
If I Do Go Blind

SHE'S WEARING A SKIRT THIS TIME, quite short, and she's got nice legs. The white mac's undone and she's spinning her shoulder bag so that the strap winds and uncoils. She sees me.

"Oh, hello." Her hand goes up to her hair and catches a piece that's flapping in the breeze.

"Good evening, Bobbie. Is that your real name?"

"Of course."

"Let's go in, shall we?" I push open the restaurant door. I've picked one of these places where it's impossible to see in, just in case. She's definitely young, so I've shaved as close as possible without actually removing a layer of skin and have dressed as mod as my inner man will allow. I reek of Old Spice and have combed my hair forward a bit.

We order while a genial cherub scribbles it all down.

"What a marvelous place," she says in a hushed voice.

"Is it?" I'm genuinely surprised, because I'd picked it for its dark decor and the fact that it was well away from prying eyes.

"You don't know how marvelous it is. There's nothing like it back home. Oh, they try, but this is so *authentic*."

"Where's 'back home'?"

"New Zealand."

"Huh." I grin as I sip my martini. "You know, I'd thought of everywhere, but never there. I'd concluded you were born in Liverpool, moved to Norfolk, schooled in Devon and then lived in Stepney."

I can see only her eyes above the glass she's holding. "What, my accent, you mean?"

"Yes." I ask her to tell me about herself. It turns out she's the inevitable daughter of the inevitable sheep farmer doing the inevitable Grand Tour. You know; they come to Europe by the boatload looking for what they expect to be 100 percent Real Life, chrome plate and all. Most of them find that chrome is not only bright but hard, and they slink back to the Antipodes in varying states of conviction that there's something to be said after all for materialism, beer and sandflies.

It's nice to watch her speak. She's trying to be at ease but is finding it difficult. I rather think she fancies she's letting Back Home down if she's not bright on the conversation. She has a broad face, really, wide mouth and forehead. Makeup is deadpan, lipstick slight and silver. A few delinquent spots push arrogantly through makeup which covers an otherwise blemishless skin. It looks as if she's got a lot of small teeth, but I think this is because they are so uniform. The front piece of hair that seems to trouble her is definitely shorter and a sometime fringe, and its unruliness is aggravated by a widow's peak on her hairline. The light from the table lamp is catching one side of her face and I bend forward to catch what she says. I haven't been as close to such a young-looking person for so long that for a minute I'm fooled, but I tell you, I thought there was something wrong with her eyes. It looked as if she was a bit sparse on eyelash or eyebrow, but then it strikes me it's simply that she's so smooth.

She smiles at Cherub while he serves her, and when he's gone she continues: "And so I got off the ship at Genoa and bought my scooter there. I left most of my luggage on the ship and will pick it up in London. So many of my friends have gone straight to London and never got over to the Continent that I thought I would see something of it first. I've driven up from Genoa in a week—that's not bad, is it? —and I'd promised I'd get Gramps something from Belgium. He was with the Air Force during the war and was shot down off the Belgian coast. Now all I've got to do is go on to Ostend and catch the ferry to Dover."

"And when will you do that?" I try not to sound too interested.

She squeezes lemon over her sole. "Tomorrow, I expect."

That's all I need; but there, I've been racing all my life. I'm just thinking of the subject myself when she asks, "Do you own that antique shop?"

I find I'm answering before I've even worked out the line of bull I'm about to give. "Sort of; you could say I'm a sleeping partner." Her face registers nothing. "Actually I'm a professional racing cyclist, although I don't suppose that means anything to you."

"Oh, it does," she says, leaning forward. "I have a boyfriend back home who went in for cycle racing and I used to watch. Do you ride in that Tour de France, and things like that?"

I flourish my wine glass. "I have done, many times, but I'm getting on a bit for big races like that." This is the bit where she should ask me how old I am. But she doesn't.

"Yes, when you reach thirty-two the old Tour strikes you as being a bit long."

She smiles and goes on eating.

"Does it make any difference? My being thirty-two, I mean?"

"No," she replies, shaking her head, making it sound as if it doesn't matter whether I'm fifteen or seventy.

"It's a pity I didn't see a cycle race while I was here, then I could have taken some photos for this boy I know."

"We'll have to see what we can do, then. It could easily be arranged, but you say you're leaving tomorrow?"

Her mouth is full and she shakes her head, making her long straight hair swirl around her face. "I don't have to leave tomorrow. It's just that I've seen around Ghent and there's no reason to stay."

"No, I suppose not." We eat in silence. "Of course, if you did stay on a bit longer I could fix it for you to get a grandstand view with all the pictures you like. And you could give me a little cheer."

"Yes, you'd be in the race too, I expect."

"Naturally, it's my living."

She looks thoughtfully down at her plate.

"How long before there's a race? I couldn't wait more than a couple of days."

There will be plenty of racing at the weekend, but that's four days away. I have a quick think. The day after tomorrow there's the beginning of a festival at Bruges and I feel sure there's a motor-paced kermesse early in the evening, but who's in it and what it's all about I don't know. I take the plunge. "Day after tomorrow. Is that too long?"

She thinks; I can see she's not wild about the idea.

I continue: "It's an evening affair and part of a festival at Bruges, which is a very nice place."

This has interested her. "That would be worth seeing. I've read about Bruges in my guidebook. All right, then."

"Fine. I'll give you details tomorrow."

By Thursday night she'll either be gone in a huff, or

50

another chapter will be boldly and fearlessly written in *Captain Davenport's Lascivious Wanderings among Primitive and Savage Peoples*. And if I have to actually ride I'm sure a little graft and corruption can be arranged there.

She's very attractive, with no side or phoniness. Her initial act of being chatty begins to fall away, and I start to see her as a serious young person. She appears to belong to the worldwide group of youngsters who are very concerned about political corruption and the Third World—all those sort of things. Her arguments are well thought out and she delivers them in a way that appeals, speaking slowly and moving her hands slightly to give emphasis. I remain noncommittal and give few opinions, and even if I agree with her I show it only in the mildest way. I know she's trying to find out what I think about things, and an obvious tactic would be to agree with her on everything. But the day I have to resort to agreement on Great Issues so that I can screw then that'll be the day I quit.

We get away from world problems and she starts asking me about England. She's got the Image all right, but who am I to disillusion her? I don't think she actually sees herself dressed up like Carole Lombard and running hand-in-hand down the King's Road with Mick Jagger, but from what she's said I do see how it must be to live in a place where Life is imported and pretty well everything comes out of books and magazines. But there, perhaps it's me. Perhaps she won't be disappointed.

Her hand plunges into the brown corduroy bag. "Would you like to see a picture of my parents?" She brings out a photograph of a group of five people. Straightaway I spot her, with a fringe and the rest of her hair blowing out like streamers on an electric fan. That's Dad with the circa-1950 gabardine mac and hat with turned-town brim. Mum's nice looking, fat legs and a "frock." The sister is about nine feet tall and dressed in a gym slip, which Bobbie tells me is the local hockey get-up. Sister's boyfriend is wearing a black vest, shorts and boots without laces; apparently he works on the farm for Dad and is posing like a recently emancipated slave who still isn't sure whether or not Dad's going to work him over with his malacca cane.

"Yes, very nice," I tell her. "Bobbie, how old are you?"

"Nineteen," she says, straightening up as if to say So what? "Listen, I like this." In the restaurant there are several loudspeakers from which popular songs are being softly relayed. She cocks her head to one side and sways slightly to the rhythm. I've heard the tune before and must admit it's quite nice. So she's nineteen. Susan, only a few years older, is middle-aged by comparison. I can just see Bobbie in Greedsville, all the chattings-up it'll get from gorgeous Modern Man, how earnestly and sincerely they'll agree with her before they belt her. She doesn't even know what it's all about. It makes me feel like a fat spider in a jar. Yet if it's not me this time, then next week it'll be somebody else. Look at her lovely face, nostrils slightly flared as she listens to the music, innocence straight off the ship.

When the tune's stopped I ask her if she'd like to drive round for a while, and she says yes. I pay and we leave. Here we go, then: round 2,058.

◆

Her eyes are closed and it's hard to guess what she's thinking. I'd used the car. Well, I had to. By the time I'd found a hotel she might have cooled off and changed her mind. When I bought this model I made sure it was a station wagon with a fold-down seat.

I gently push aside some strands of hair from her face and tuck them behind her ear. There's only a faint light from the dashboard, but I see her open her eyes—those green wide-apart slits.

It hadn't been hard. Upbringing and fear had yelled no and body had screamed yes. I didn't force her; I never do that. And yet I feel a bit of a bastard. If I could've been sure she'd have stayed as she was, always, I would have left her alone. But on her own, in London? I ask you. She had only said yes, really, because she's a human being and couldn't help herself. I was gentle but firm. When a virgin says no to me it's like those 'Let Drusila Dysentry Solve Your Problem' columns coming to life with their sensible answers.

"My God," she whispers.

I hug her close to me. "Feel bad about it?"

Her head shakes. "Not really. I don't know yet."

"I'm sorry. I am, really."

"You don't have to be."

"It was inevitable."

"I know."

"And I'm sorry it's so disappointing the first time."

She doesn't answer.

How marvelous this would be, I tell myself, if I were nineteen with her. She couldn't get any closer and yet, really, she's as far from me as, say, a star. I was doing this with girls of nineteen before she was born. I imagine I can visualize the sort of person she's going to be. I could tell her now but she'd say, "How does he know," and not believe me. If time could stand still for me and jump ten years for her, I don't think anything could be more perfect. But I've ridden a lot of my Tour and she's just setting out on hers. I know about dust and rain and heat and mountains, but she's only read about them. She's very lovely and going to be even lovelier.

In some ways it would be all right as it is now if time never moved beyond tomorrow. But she'll outstrip me, I couldn't keep her, not until some of her Tour has been ridden and she knows what it's all about. I have this feeling that one day she'll turn out to be the same type of person I am.

Before we leave I switch on the cab light so that she can comb her hair, and it's then that I notice some blood on my hand. She starts to apologize and looks through the corduroy bag for a paper handkerchief. I have no choice but to spit on the handkerchief and wipe my hand, because she watches me anxiously, still saying how sorry she is. I laugh it off, but for some reason beyond me I wish she'd turn away so I could leave my hand as it is.

◆

I don't sleep much, and it's not conscience that keeps me awake. I try various methods of trying to sleep: counting an endless daisy chain of queers, imagining what it would be like to vote Tory, watching the gray square cobbles flash past under my wheels as I win Paris-Roubaix with a five-minute lead. I convince myself that it's simply because physically she's hard to fault, and even though I believe myself I still can't doze off. Perhaps Youth has nothing and knows nothing, yet somehow it wields the Big Stick.

Paula turns and her arm falls across me; I lie quite still so as not to wake her. On the other side of the wall the bumblebee is still bumbling, and if I thought my hand wouldn't go through the wall I'd beat on it.

I've always found "those sort" of accents grate on me, the same as mine must do on them, yet her voice was in keeping with her appearance, sort of simple and clear. It was a bit deep for a girl, but it went with her broad features. She had a way of going up the scale when she asked a question, and of pronouncing words such as "six" as "sux" and "kids" as "kuds."

I'm going to feel a bloody fool in the morning. Things always look different then. It's just that you lie here and your mind races on and won't stop, and you get flashes of dim dark thoughts you never knew you had.

At breakfast I come bounding into the living room, trying to look as fresh and perky as possible, and the first thing Paula says is "You look a bit rough, Terry. Didn't you sleep?"

I drop into a chair, relieved that I can act as I feel. "Not really. If that bumblebee next door doesn't give it a rest soon, I swear he'll catch a bunch of five. "

Paula looks fine. She'll never let you see her looking a mess. With her it's a way of life, not a thing she's keeping up until we're married. She's the sort of bird who will spend two hours in the hairdresser's rather than let you see her in curlers. A while back she had the flu and I saw then that she can even be ill with dignity.

Susan, who's the dead opposite to her mother, has on this quilted housecoat thing and pink fur slippers, a complexion like a boiled potato and hair like Harpo Marx. She's one of these people who are either A or B—done up like a dog's dinner or like someone the hippies have rejected.

I get up and help Paula serve the breakfast. Susan keeps looking at me and I wonder if she's suspicious about last night. When I think of Bobbie all my mind comes up with is a static picture of her face. I had dozed off about four o'clock and woken around six, and in that time I lost the diamond clear impressions I had of her. Even the pop tune which she'd liked and which had hammered out a background to my night thoughts now seemed hazy and flat. I feel both rotten and mildly relieved.

55

Romain will be out behind the motorcycle again today. Normally I would go with him, but apart from my thumping head I have to meet Bobbie at ten-thirty.

Susan turns up her transistor. This usually grates on me, but today I don't mind, because it means that talking will be out. Paula goes and gets the post and comes back into the room shuffling a pack of letters. "Susan, turn that thing down a bit, will you?"

It's an old Beatle record, and obviously Susan is recapturing an age long gone. She pulls a face as if she's being fitted for the iron boot and makes a slight adjustment to the volume. It makes me think of a toffee-nosed bird I went out with in England. She said she simply *deplored* pop music but didn't mind the Beatles too much; after all, they were well-educated boys.

"This is very interesting," Paula says.

"What is?" I ask.

"I said this is very interesting!"

"Yes, I heard you. What's interesting?"

Susan sighs and turns the set down a bit further.

"It's from that estate in Strasbourg. You remember I made an offer of—Susan, will you either turn that set off or take it to your room or somewhere."

Susan snatches up the set and storms out, up the stairs to her bedroom. This is one of the reasons why I don't want to start off married life with two women. I'd like to kick Susan's arse when she's like this.

Paula looks upset, so I pull her toward me and she sits on my lap and puts her arm round my neck. We kiss.

"You're a lot of woman," I tell her.

"I know. But am I enough?"

I don't like to look at her, so I take the letter from her. "Ample."

After we've kissed again she says, "Yes, you remember that estate where I offered nine hundred thousand francs for the glass, china and silver? Well, they don't want to split or auction it and have accepted my offer! I never thought they would. I'd just paid out a lot on that last shipment from England and to tell the truth I was a bit overextended then."

"And now?"

"Well, I still am, I suppose. Most of our new stock has been on display only a week or two and not much has moved yet. Also I recently invested quite a bit. Nine hundred thousand francs is a bargain, but I don't know whether I ought to run my shop money too low.

I give her a bounce as if she were a baby, and she almost loses her balance. "It'll all sell, surely?"

"Eventually, yes, but I can't display everything at once, as it makes the place look too cluttered. The stuff would realize double its outlay but might take a year to do it."

She reaches out and picks up her coffee cup.

"Can't you bung it all in the shop and shift it quicker?"

Paula punches me gently on the nose. "You and your 'bung it all in.' I don't run a junk shop, Terence Davenport. A place has got to look right." She sighs. "Normally I'd buy it, but—"

"But what?"

She wriggles her behind and lays her head against mine. "I've got to keep some ready cash for this flat. Or had you forgotten?"

I had, too. "Forgotten? No, of course not."

She's pouting playfully, so I shoot my hand up her skirt and she lets out a shriek, then covers her mouth with her hand like a naughty child.

"Look," I say, "there's my money. You've got enough junk in that shed to start a Collectors' Corner, so let me transfer my loot to you, then you can buy this estate. Well, we're going to get it all back, aren't we? It's only an investment."

She lets her head drop forward and gives herself a double chin, then looks at me sideways, all sort of loving. "That's very nice of you, darling. I know you earned that money in the hardest possible way and that it must hurt just to sign it away for a lot of old stuff which doesn't really interest you. But as you say, it's an investment. Think of it if you'd rather as going toward the flat."

Her hair is still in one enormous plait. I work my fingers between the strands and jerk her head backwards so that I can kiss her. "You're a bit of all right, Paula, but you're still a businesswoman, and in the cold light of morning like to see the color of my money." Paula wriggles free and stands up. There are tears in her eyes. "How can you think that, Terry? I love you and would marry you if you were broke."

"I know. I'm sorry. I didn't mean it like that."

"The money's got nothing to do with it. If you were in debt I'd marry you. If you think that about me, then keep your money. Do what you like with it. I'll still marry you and pay for the flat!"

My head's really thumping now, like rubber truncheons in a Paris police station. "Paula, I didn't mean it like that. I didn't sleep and I don't feel up to an argument. Look, make me an aspirin sandwich and I'll be back in a flash."

I go up the stairs and catch a glance of a very sour-looking Susan reclining on her bed hugging a silent transistor. "Is the board meeting over yet?" she calls out, but I don't answer and slam the door to our room. From a drawer I take my check book and make out a check to Paula for most of my money. I had to do it sometime, and now that it's done I should be set for life. All I've got left is about eight hundred. When I think of the miles and the years and the suffering

58

that have gone into that check, that little slip of paper. It'll pass through the bank's hands and an eyebrow won't even be raised.

There's money in pro cycling if you're a star, a super champion. But for the average pro there's not much, and the unfairness of it all is that the difference between the stars and the rest is so slight. It can be the thickness of a tire, or a second or a minute, or six wins out of twelve instead of nine out of twelve. In my day I've beaten all the big names in cycling. Perhaps I've only done it the once or twice and they've screwed me more times than I've taken them, but I was never far behind, only the few yards that make the difference. You'd think for one man to earn a fortune and another a living wage, that the former would be home in bed while the latter was still finishing. But it's not like that. The difference is that the highly paid man has an eighty percent chance of winning a certain race while the poorer one, blokes such as myself, has a fifty percent chance. I never had the education or the opportunities, so I suppose things couldn't have been very different, but if I had my time again and just a few ordinary breaks, I'd have gone in for being something like a house agent or an accountant or a lawyer or a dentist. There's money for old rope, if you like, and here's hoping the junk trade will be too. It's about time I made a bit of easy money.

When I get downstairs I find Romain waiting for me. I fold the check and put it into the breast pocket of Paula's blouse. She smiles and says nothing.

"Look, Romain, I won't be going with you today. I've got to see Big Wheels about things. Don't just ride along behind the motorbike, get the driver to keep accelerating."

"Will the bosses want to know how I'm doing?" He's

wearing his track suit, light gray with green lettering outlined in white. Across his chest and back is the lettering T.B.H.-Aigle, with just the T.B.H. bit around his arms, between elbow and shoulder. T.B.H. are the team sponsors, and in case you haven't heard of them they are big manufacturers of electrical appliances. The "Aigle" bit is the make of cycle, and they are the side of the business actually concerned with the team and its results.

"No," I tell Romain, "I don't think the bosses will be worried about you today."

Susan has heard Romain's voice and she comes into the room smiling. There's no transistor, so I take it Everything's Going to Be All Right and that the Dow Jones is steady.

She kisses Romain. "Good morning, darling."

Because Paula is there he writhes awkwardly in his seat and picks up a magazine. Both Paula and Susan are acting amicably and the paranoiac tic that has been twitching along the edge of my karate-hardened hand dies. A punch-up, yes; jabbering women, never.

"Listen to this," Romain says, folding back the page of his magazine. "It says here that a forty-four-year-old man kept staring at this young girl in her bathing costume, and that a fight started when the girl's boyfriend went up to the man and said, 'Dream, dad, dream.'"

Susan laughs with false heartiness. She's getting at me; I know the symptoms. "Poor girl. I know how she must have felt. You're always getting these middle-aged men looking at you and wishing they were fifteen years younger and had some hair."

I'm all right still for a drop of thatch, but I'll defend my mates. "Bald men are supposed to be more virile," I say, looking straight at her.

Paula puts a tray of coffee cups on the table. "Don't you

believe it. It's a story put around by bald men."

Romain and I laugh and her ladyship sniggers.

Later, when Romain has gone and Paula's in the shop, Susan calls me into her room. Books and papers are spread all over her bed and I take it she's studying.

"Are you having a lesson this morning, Terry? We could sort out the difference between the imperfect and the conditional." She smiles sweetly.

"How stunning. No, I'm off out soon. I've got time to give you a lesson, though."

"Wrong time of the month."

"There are other things."

"Not today, thank you."

"Pity. I feel like hurting you."

"Hurting me? Why? Because of what happened earlier on?"

"Yes, you spoiled cow. I'd like to—"

"Don't tell me. You can be so uncouth. Sometimes you're so coarse it makes my toes cross. Do it if you like, but I don't want to hear about it first.

A quick change of mind. She starts to take off the housecoat. I wait until she's naked and then walk round the bed. "Lie on your stomach." As soon as she has, I catch her a swipe across the backside and she leaps up off the bed.

"What the hell are you doing?"

"That, O spoiled one, is your lesson for the day."

On first impulse she seizes a book and brings her arm back as if she had the best right hook in the business, but when she sees I'm laughing at her the arm comes down and she stands there, starkers, grinning her head off.

I lift a forefinger. "You asked for that."

"Yes. I'm sorry."

"And honestly, I haven't got time. I'll be late if I don't fly straightaway."

Now I can leave them both content. It's nine-forty-five and all I've had to do so far to achieve bliss is sign away my life's savings and slap one behind. Perhaps I can hit a happy medium with Bobbie.

◆

I manage to find a park for the car. For ten minutes I sit with a *Paris-Match* on the table before me. Le Pen is on the cover and I pass the time penciling in rotten teeth, an eye patch, and a lighted candle on the top of his hat.

I watch her circle the blue Vespa in front of the café, trying to find somewhere to put it. I wave to her and she sees me, then she points down the road and roars off in that direction. A few minutes later she walks toward me through the deserted tables and chairs on the boulevard outside. She comes into the café and I get up and lead her to a quiet corner away from the glass front where I've been sitting. I take her navy duffle coat from her and lay it on a chair. Her face is flushed and every time our eyes meet she looks away. She's wearing shoes like my Great-aunt Agnes used to have, but they're a bit Minnie Mouse-ish and I don't think she feels at home in them. The dress she's got on one of those little short frilly things that only a young bird with a good figure can hope to get away with. And she can.

I milk and sugar my coffee and she takes hers black and bitter.

"Any regrets?" I ask her.

She screws her face up to look as if she's thinking. "No, I don't think so. If I have, it's too late."

"I suppose you expected it to happen?"

Her eyes open wide. "No! I had the shock of my life. I didn't know what to do."

"You didn't think I'd do anything?"

"No! It never occurred to me."

I shake my head and drink some coffee. "Here," I say, picking up a packet from the chair, "I bought you something. I know you can't carry much on a scooter but I hope you can squeeze this in."

I give her the packet and she opens it and takes out a record.

"Our tune," I tell her.

She looks really pleased, as if I'd given her a pearl necklace. Next time I'll try her with a cocoa tin and a stone.

"You shouldn't have! I wish I could play it."

It must be paradise where she comes from. Any youngsters whom I've had any dealings with lately seem so immovable, so cynical. I reckon that on their thirteenth birthday they trade in their babydolls for a strip of microfilm which they tape to their top plates, giving a list of the forty best abortionists, the Top Ten and a head-on-and-profile of Joplin.

I lean toward her and put my hand on top of hers. "Bobbie, I admit I am a roué and I admit I calculatingly seduced you, but I don't want you to see it only like that. I do care for you. You're real and untouched and natural, and while you might not be the photogenic sort, you've got one of the loveliest grow-on-you faces I've ever seen."

She looks at my hand, then at me, then my hand again, but says nothing.

"I'm very fond of you. To be honest, I hardly slept for thinking about you." I mean this, but as I say the words I can't even imagine why I'm saying them or where they'll lead. I suppose at the back of my mind I think this burst of honesty will sweep her off her feet.

She looks up at me and a cold twinge tells me deflation's at hand. Perhaps I'd expected tears or sobs, or something, but her eyes are first quizzical then blank.

"I ought to leave today," she says.

"But the race, the cycle race."

"No, I ought to leave. I can't get involved."

"Why can't you?"

"I don't know. Because, I suppose."

"Because what?"

Her face screws up and her eyes go into slits, as if she's struggling to find the right words. "Well . . . I want to find out what life's all about. No, more than that . . . Oh, I don't know how to put it!"

I squeeze her hand. "Try."

She pushes a strand of hair from her face. "Somehow, I don't know what it is, but I can't feel anything. It's not only with you, it's with everyone. I know I ought to love them, or hate them, or be glad to see them, but . . . but I can't."

I know she's not kidding. Her face is really wretched and she starts to cry. "I suppose I ought to see somebody about it, a doctor or a psychiatrist, but first I want to see life to find out if it will change me."

I sit back and stare at her. Her hands are clasped on the table and are working nervously. "You say you've always been like this?"

"Yes."

"What, with girl friends as well?"

"Yes."

"Didn't you like what we did last night?"

"Not particularly. It was all right at the time."

Oh, Gawd. Out, Terry-lad, out, I say to myself, but clattering hoofs tell me there's a bloke in shining armor coming up fast. "Dry your eyes," I tell her.

I give her a minute to compose herself. "What do your parents think of all this?"

"I've never told them. I've never told anybody."

I seem to collect Firsts. "What are your parents like?"

"All right, I suppose."

I sigh and have a think. "Last night—up until a few minutes ago, in fact—you seemed to be so interested in things."

"Well I am! I love talking to people. I love talking to you. It's just that I can't get close, that's all. Last night I gave way because I thought it might help change things. But it didn't. After what you did I ought to feel something, but for all it's done to me you might as well have asked me the time."

My coffee cup gets pushed to one side as I take hold of her hand again. "You try too hard. You're straining for emotion. Perhaps it'll come if you forget about it."

Her head's shaking. "It won't. I've tried it."

"Oh, come off it, Bobbie, a lovely girl like you. You're so uninhibited and intelligent. Besides, you were all right last night, believe me."

"I only did it to please you. I've got to do things like that if I'm to find out."

God, it's hot in here. Again there are tears in her eyes. I'd better give it a rest. "There's a lot of love in you somewhere. and we're going to find it. A person like yourself who's so concerned about the world can't lack feeling."

"No," she says vaguely, sitting back. "No." Her head turns and she stares across the café.

"Anyway," I say, "see this cycle race. Don't go yet. I meant what I said about being fond of you and I want to help if I can."

She forces a smile. "I'm beyond aid."

"That's better. Nineteen and so serious. When I was your age and you were hooked on rusks, I could only afford a day in Brighton provided I cycled there. Yet here are you traveling across the world, a new scooter, a family who'd obviously rescue you if you came unstuck. Bobbie, you've got it made."

There's a strong tone of contempt in her reply. "Have I?"

"Of course you have!"

She looks as if she's going to open up a bit; her jaw moves slightly as she thinks. "Really, you're the one who's had it made. However hard your life has been, it has been real. Mine? Nothing has ever happened. 'Nothing' to you is just a word, but for me it constitutes my whole background, my whole existence. My father drinks a lot, which back home is the norm. I don't hold it against him, because Nothing made him do it. I'm not being unkind to my parents, but if I told them that this big Nothing had made them what they are, they wouldn't even know what I was talking about. All they know is sheep, northerly winds, southerly winds, sheep, drink, a day at the races, booze, sheep. For my father salvation lies at the bottom of a beer bottle. I know that people's lives the world over are subject to monotony and ritual, and many have poverty thrown in, but somehow my life has been—"

"Nothing?"

"Yes."

"Well, things should change for you now. They started last night."

"That's the point. I still don't feel anything. I don't even feel that I'm going to feel anything. Oh, I'm sorry to go on like this, Terry, because I know you mean well. My life between the ages of twelve and eighteen wasn't a period of six years, it was six thousand. I think Nothingness, in those six years, killed anything that may have been in me. When they got a TV, I thought that it would give my parents a glimmer of what things were really like. But you know what? They didn't like it. I don't know whether it forced a shaft of light into them which hurt too much, or whether they just didn't understand it. There's little doubt that eighty-five percent of the programs are rubbish, but if anything, they preferred these and dismissed the few good ones. TV is only a small point, I know, but it's a good illustration. The great Nothing triumphed again; it was everywhere, in everything. Terry, do you like poetry?"

"You're joking. Only dirty ones. Do you, then?"

"Some. Mostly I like writing it. I think if I hadn't I'd have gone out of my mind."

"I'd like to see some."

"But you don't like it."

"I'd like yours."

"Maybe, then." She closes her eyes and sighs. "I'm sorry to have bored you with my troubles."

"You'll stay a bit longer? Please say you will."

The eyes open. "All right, but only if you promise to win."

"I promise. . . . You feel better now?"

"Yes, a bit."

"Look, there's a hotel near here, no questions asked. This time there should be more in it for you."

She looks at me with a faint sad smile.

"Well?"

"All right."

◆

Between now and the race tomorrow night I'm going to have to move quickly. I can't race without a license, and I can't get a license without a medical. For anyone less involved with the trade than myself, it would be impossible. But I know the top men concerned and so I should get the license through in time.

I keep a pile of license application forms in my office, so I stop there first and fill one out. Then I make the right calls to the right people, who, when the astonishment has died within their fatty tissues, say they'll push it all through.

Once this is done I visit dear old Doktor Maës. He's a German and has always been the "cyclists' doctor." I shouldn't be surprised if he isn't wanted for war crimes. He has a brusque efficient manner and I'll swear I once saw a uniform hanging in his office. Even on the nameplate his title is spelled *Doktor*, and is done in that cruel sort of writing that they used for stenciling slogans on bombs and writing *Achtung* outside minefields. I'll never know whether he was a top needle at Dachau; all I know is that he seems a good doctor and with a slap to my biceps and an ideological glint in his monocled eye he pronounces me a "perfectly fit human specimen."

I hand in his report with my application form and go to the gymnasium to look for Romain. He's a bit of an amateur gymnast and likes to combine work in the gym with his cycling. It doesn't do him any harm and does him a lot of good mentally. Myself, I'm of the old school and would rather devote training time to cycling only.

He breaks off, thinking I just want a word with him, but I tell him I'll wait until he's finished. I watch him on the parallel bars. He's a skinny sort of bloke, really, but a lot of the great ones were. Many people think an athlete must look like a Greek god, but this isn't true as far as cycling goes. It's what's inside that counts. Nobody will ever know how little Gaul could pedal as fast as he could without blowing up, or what gave the tiny Ockers his tenacity. The things that go toward making a great cyclist are big lungs and a slow-beating heart. Bartali's secret was a slow heart; it used to thump about once every hour and when it did it gave him enough strength to ride up the side of the Eiffel Tower. Size doesn't matter either. What does count is strength in relation to weight. You get all sorts, such as the late Gerard Saint, who was like a streak of nothing, or Robic, who was so short you couldn't see him in a bunch.

"What's up, Terry?"

"Put your track suit on," I tell him.

He starts to wriggle into it.

"Will you do me a favor, Romain?"

"Of course." Out comes a comb and he starts to comb his hair.

"Tomorrow evening there's a race near Bruges. It's just a crowd puller—thirty-five kilometers only, four laps round the houses, the first three laps scooter-paced and the last lap solo."

"They won't let me ride in that."

"No, I know." What he means is that the sponsors don't want him competing in anything that's motor-paced. All right for training when there's just the two of us and no carving up, but a rider goes so much faster when paced that should he come off he could do himself a lot of damage.

"Well, what about this race near Bruges?"

"I know it's against orders and if you say no then it's all right with me. But I'm riding in it and I want to win. I'd like you there to pace me on that last solo lap and to help me all you can. Will you?"

He mouths words which won't come. "You're riding! But you haven't got a license! Why, Terry, why are you riding?"

"Listen. Sit down and I'll tell you. I got talking to a couple of blokes and they more or less said that not only am I well past it, but that I never was any good. I told them to put their money where their mouths were, and to cut a long story short I'm committed to a pretty heavy bet. I know I shouldn't have done it, but I was so choked at the time. It's a minor race, away from Ghent, and when you've done your bit I want you to pack it in so that your name doesn't appear on the finishing list. The chances of anyone from our lot even being in the area are remote."

I then tell Romain about the license and the medical. and he asks me who's riding in the event.

"Most of them are locals. They'll be out to impress, but however good they are, motor pacing's too specialized for them to get far against us. The two snags are Geyer and Loncke."

Romain runs his hand round his head and pulls thinking faces. "Loncke's good. I've never seen Geyer."

"No, Geyer's a bit far afield. He doesn't come up into Belgium very often. I know him quite well. As the first prize is only two thousand dollars and a load of gift junk, and as my bet is well in excess of this amount, I think for five big ones and a quiet word in the earhole Geyer would pull out. Which leaves Loncke."

"He's good," Romain tells me again. "Could you offer him money?"

"I don't know." I'm beginning to think it's a lot of loot to impress a bird, even if I did win the race. Actually Geyer would be the more dangerous of the two, especially on that last solo lap. I think I'll risk Loncke.

"Which only leaves your answer," I remind him.

He blinks for a second and then stammers, "Of course I'll ride. It goes without saying."

"Good. And thanks. I'll have old Alphonse to pace me and I'll get someone out of town for you. Alphonse will keep his mouth shut."

"I'd better get on the phone and enter for the race." This has just occurred to him and he jumps up nervously.

"Sit down."

"But the event!"

"Sit down. I've already entered you."

◆

It's been such an active day that I've forgotten to eat. The last thing I did before leaving Romain was to impress on him that I don't want Paula and Susan to know about the race. Tonight I'll have to get to bed early and leave it alone, and tomorrow morning I'll put in about forty kilometers behind Alphonse's scooter. That'll leave me several hours to rest in the afternoon and we can drive to Bruges about four o'clock.

She should be here in half an hour, but I'm too hungry to wait, so I order a sandwich. I've arranged to meet her in the same place I first took her. Paula's got piles of books out the back and I had a quick look through them to see if there was one on case histories of problems such as Bobbie fancies she's got. There was one by Freud, but hardly the thing to digest in the ten minutes I had. I found a few more copies of *The Prisoner of Zenda* and two stunners entitled *The Nuchal Hump of the Square-Lipped Rhinoceros* and *Reptiles Found within the Mkazi and Ndumu Game Reserves in Northern Zululand*. As profound as this selection was, unless you happened to be crackers, about to impersonate a kidnapped monarch, a rampaging square-lipped rhinoceros, or a reptile en route for northern Zululand, none threw any instant light on Bobbie's phobia.

Even if I were in an English library I wouldn't know where to start. It could all be nothing—just imagination—or it could even be an act, although I doubt it. So if I had access to books about these things, would I look under mental illness or adolescent problems? It doesn't surprise me that sensitive people in these far-flung lands can get like this, and it's how I've always imagined life there to be. I raced in Sweden once, and it's a bit like it there. Weeping schizo-

71

phrenics weren't exactly queuing for admission to lead-lined asylums, nor were suicides falling past the hotel window like autumn leaves. But there was this feeling—at least I sensed it—that the inhabitants couldn't bear other people's "So What?" to the standard of living which was supposed to sweep you off your feet. For me Paris is life, and so is Vienna, and Provence and Greece and Barcelona. Which I think is the way Bobbie feels. I'd rather be poor in one of these places than rich in some outlandish state where you're controlled from womb to tomb. And I understand that where Bobbie comes from they take the controlling even further: erection to resurrection, as the old joke goes.

I keep forcing myself to think about Paula, the marriage and the business, but my mind won't seem to click into the right groove. Although I tell myself that I'm stuck on Bobbie because she's young and attractive, I take a lot of convincing, even from myself.

I grin evilly, because no one's looking, and tell myself how lucky I am and that it can't last, and if it could I wouldn't want it to.

Mostly I've gone in for women who, as long as they didn't exactly revolt me, had circumstances which appealed or fitted in. Some, like Paula, I've really fancied. But Bobbie doesn't fit in at all; in fact, she's nothing but snags. Neither does she "love" me, which, considering the spadework and the usual pattern of things, mildly surprises me. When you consider my ego it's a wonder I'm not too top-heavy to stay on a bike. I've no doubt this phobia is real enough to her, but not to feel anything strikes me as a bit unnatural, although you do get women like that. Wasn't it Cora Pearl, the Grandest of the Grandes Horizontales, who reckoned she never experienced passion or infatuation? (I'm full of gems like this.) And she had more men than I've had hot dinners; a right old boot if ever there was one.

For a second I don't recognize her as she passes the café window. She's got on a leather peaked cap which looks new, and is wearing her checked trousers.

"Why are you looking at me like that?" she says, putting her bag on the table and smiling.

"Like what?"

"You look relieved at something."

"Do I? Perhaps it's because you seem happier than when we last met. Are you? Are you happier?"

"Yes, I think so. I really am dreadfully sorry about those things I said." She looks down ashamedly.

"Aren't they true?"

"Yes. Well, no. Well, yes, really. Oh, I don't know." She squeezes her bag with her right hand, like a cat clawing a ball of wool.

"They were true, but you felt particularly low at the time?"

"Yes. Can we not talk about it now, though?"

"Of course. I'm setting out for Bruges around four o'clock tomorrow. Is that all right?"

"Yes, fine. Will you pick me up at the hotel?"

I've answered yes before I realize that I'll have to find a way to get Romain to the race and back on his own. But I can't think about that now.

"I managed to play my record," she says brightly. "It was lovely. A girl at the hotel has got a little transistor record player. I played it over and over for an hour."

I smile. "Did you? You'll wear it out."

"I always do that with records, then I put them away and never play them again."

I give a little grin to myself. That's how it'll be with me, I reckon. Hammered and slung. "Did you bring any of your poems?" I ask.

Bobbie picks up her corduroy bag and starts to search through it. "I've only got a few with me, ones I wrote coming over. They're not very good. I imagine that technically they're dreadful. The only reason I'm showing you is that, even if you don't understand, you won't laugh. Will you?"

"No, I wouldn't do that." I take them from her. There are four. I read two, and then Cherub brings us our meals. The other two I read while I eat. Poetry is not my line of country and I couldn't honestly say whether they were good or bad, except that to me they seemed all right.

"Can I keep one?" I ask her.

She looks up, surprised. "Why, yes. If you'd really like to."

I select one, fold it, and put it in my wallet.

"Are we going to a hotel afterwards?"

I bite a lump out of my spoon. "Why, do you want to?"

"Only if you do."

I hadn't planned on it, not with the race tomorrow, but she did ask. The trouble is Paula knows nothing of Bobbie or the race, and if she gets demanding when I get home I can offer no excuse for refusing. Oh, I'll chance all that. Anyway, it'll help me sleep. "You bet," I tell her, and I think she smiles.

4

The Man Who Used
This Crutch Is Cured
and Gone Home

THE RACE IS TO START ON THE OUTSKIRTS of Bruges and the
course goes away from the town, out into the surrounding
country. I managed to contact Geyer by phone. Romain did
the talking and for a four hundred dollar bribe Geyer agreed
not to compete. I told Romain that Paula had got wind of
the race and to throw her off the scent it would be better if
he and I traveled separately. He's following us later in the
van, with bikes, scooter and Alphonse. A Bruges man has
been contracted to pace Romain.

It now appears that Bobbie will talk about anything other
than her no-feeling problem. I put it to her that she won't
talk about it any more because it's her intention to move on
as soon as we get back to Ghent, after which she'll never see
me again. She laughed and said she'll stay in Ghent at least
until the weekend.

Time's getting on. I install Bobbie in the rather stark covered grandstand that has been erected at the finishing line,
borrow a bike, and do a slow lap of the eight-and-a-half-
kilometer circuit. It's easy and fast, except for a slight cobble-
stoned hill with a sharp bend in it. This part of the course

75

particularly interests me and I get off and examine it. The weather's not the best, and while it isn't exactly raining it has dampened enough to make the cobbles greasy. The road is not very wide at the bend and spectators won't be allowed at the roadside for about seventy yards either side of it. It's an old part of the district and has obviously been chosen to put some spice into the race. For a while I stare at the bend and think. It's a lefthander, which means the right side will be the approach taken for maximum speed. On both sides is a very narrow high sidewalk, wide enough for only one pedestrian at a time to walk. On the left—the slow side— the high edge of the sidewalk is unbroken, whereas on the right of the curve the sidewalk meets the road at one point in a gentle slope. There's just enough slope to push up a handbarrow or a cycle. I figure that if one could aim at this slope and so get onto the actual sidewalk, one would be on the outside of anyone who, having cornered on the road, believed himself to be on the outside. It would mean riding on the sidewalk for a matter of fifty yards until you came to another slope which would let you back onto the road. For the time being I can see no real value in my discovery, but I carefully note the two slopes which would let you ride onto and off the sidewalk.

While I'm examining the bend Loncke, the danger man, rides up. He nods to me and gets off his cycle. Groups of enthusiasts have seen us and, knowing as we do that this bend is the crucial point of the race, are discussing among themselves the possible outcome.

Our van comes along and I'm joined by Romain and Alphonse. I take them to one side and tell them what I have discovered about the corner. Through Romain I ask Alphonse if he thinks he could drive the scooter up the small slope, onto the sidewalk, and off again at the next slope.

While Alphose walks up and down looking at the road surface, Romain says to me, "It will be impossible! All it will get you is on the extreme outside. A tremendous risk for little tactical advantage. It will be under artificial light, and impossible to carry out should just one official position himself on that narrow sidewalk. If anyone stands there you'd hit him."

I shrug.

Alphonse comes back and tells Romain that he could make the exit pretty fast, but would have to slow to about thirty kilometers an hour to make the entry. I have a long think. "Right. If necessary, then, I'll hold up four fingers like this on the last of the motor-paced laps. I'll make the sign as we pass that car-park notice back there. Both look at me as we pass the notice. If I make the sign, I want you, Alphonse, to get onto the sidewalk, up that slope, as fast as you can. Don't worry about my losing contact; I can keep with you. You, Romain, to corner on the middle of the road, but ride wide so that it's natural for you to drift to the right, more or less into the path of whoever we're trying to beat—probably Loncke. If it's damp, and I think it will be, it'll be dangerous, so be bloody careful. Especially you, Romain. But when you swing wide on the bend, you'll probably lose contact with your pacer, so have a big gear ready to catch him. We can't confide in, or use, your pacer."

Romain scratches his head. "All right; so I've checked the opponents and they're shouting their heads off at me. You've gone by on the outside and are going toward the line to commence the solo lap. Then what?"

The three of us walk back to the van and get inside. I say to Romain, "Once all this has happened the motor-paced bit is virtually over. With or without your pacer you, being prepared and with your great ability at solo riding, will catch me, and when you have you take over the scooter's job and pace me on that last lap. This all may be unnecessary, the race pattern might be different. We could still use my plan if there are two or three opponents closely spaced. Perhaps we'll annihilate them and it will be easy and straightforward."

I drive the van back to the changing rooms and as we go along I run through it all again, with Romain double-checking that Alphonse has understood my instructions.

◆

I never thought this would happen again, me lining up for a race. Romain, myself and both pacers are wearing T.B.H.-Aigle vests. We buckle on our crash helmets and come out of the van. A religious procession is disbanding in the square where we're to start from, and a shower of fire-works lights up the sky on the far side of the town. Like box-ers coming from the dressing rooms, across the arena and into the ring, we edge our way through the crowds.

It's quite like old times. People grip my arm and wish me luck, others pat me on the back and say it's nice to see me back. It gives me a good sort of feeling—a feeling I never knew I'd missed until now. The race will be neutralized until we've picked up our pacing scooters and left the square; we wait at the line while officials hurry about getting everything in order. There are twenty-three competitors, and farther up the road the scooters begin to warm up. I look to where I left Bobbie. She waves her bag and mouths Good Luck, and I wave back.

"Do you know how old I am?" I say to Romain.

He's busy spinning his front wheel and pressing the palm of his track glove against the revolving tire to remove any small pieces of grit. "About thirty-five, aren't you?"

"And do I look thirty-five?"

He scarcely glances up. "I suppose so. A bit less, perhaps."

"I'm thirty-seven."

"Oh."

The rising crescendo of motor exhausts tells me that the start cannot be far off. I look at her again and once more she waves. If she goes on to England, I feel I won't see her any more, ever. Life's like that. If this were a bloody film, we'd meet again. I'd be forty-three, slightly gray, a smart executive suit, a successful business that runs itself. The place: among the deserted parasoled tables on the Champs Elysées. She'd be twenty-five, matured and more beautiful than ever, all her phobias behind her. I'd say, "The last time we met you told me you were unable to feel anything about anybody." And she'd throw back her head and laugh. "Did I? Did I *really*? You should try me now." Then we'd exit, hand in hand, knowing little glints flashing between us like berserk kamikazes.

A tubby man comes up wearing a large rosette and carrying the starting flag. I grin because suddenly I feel a fool. I'm going to get slaughtered, and after going through all this trouble to impress a bird who'll be off forever in a few days. There's no fool like an old one.

I'm using five gears, closely spaced, bottom one of eighty-five inches, which is the one I'll start in. My left foot is already in the toeclip and I give the strap a pull. Romain taps me on the elbow and gives a thumbs-up sign—the British Thumb, as I've taught him to call it. The funny thing is I feel scared, but I don't know why.

Tubby man gets his signal that the pacers are ready and with a pompous flourish he starts the race. We roll forward and I quickly find my right toeclip. As we approach the scooters, their riders, looking back at us over their shoulders, start to pull away. I see Alphonse; he's still wearing his T.B.H. vest, only I see that now it's stretched to bursting

79

point over a thick woolen pullover.

The din from the scooters and the crowds is terrific. Quickly I latch on to Alphonse and Romain picks up his pacer without any trouble. As soon as we've passed the *Départ* banner stretched across the street between two stores, the race is officially on. Engines rev, scooters lurch away with the riders sprinting after them, each duo trying to snatch the lead. Experienced pacers are hard to come by. There doesn't seem to be much in riding a scooter so that a cyclist can follow it, but believe me it's an art. I can see that most of the pacers here are friends of the riders and would, for two pins, turn it into a scooter race. A master pacer like Alphonse knows the cyclist is the artist and that his own job is one of accompanist. Alphonse was himself a pro road man and he knows where and when a motor can accelerate faster and when the cyclist has the edge over the scooter. His job is to supply a smooth liquid power at speeds that you can match and hold, but even more important he has to sense how you feel, when you can't attack and when you're strong enough to go past. Other than a few simple signals, communication between rider and pacer is impossible.

Most of the amateur pacers are throttle happy. Already some of them have shot away and left a gap between them- selves and their cyclists, and are now either slowing too suddenly or forcing the cyclists to fight to close with them. Romain's man seems reasonable, and Loncke's certainly knows what he's about. He's doing what Alphonse is doing: keeping steadily and ominously near the front.

The street lights, and the floodlights which have been put up for the occasion, throw a dull sheen on the damp road. We pound along steadily at about thirty-five miles an hour. The road at this point is straight with a good surface. Two unknown duos begin to pull away and effortlessly

Loncke goes with them, followed by Romain and myself. The trouble with pacing is that you can only take your eyes off the scooter's rear wheel for an occasional glance. At speeds such as these, riding in a close bunch, on a damp surface, with your front wheel separated from the pacer's rear wheel by six or seven inches, the utmost concentration is needed.

I daren't look round, but by the sound of it there's a big pile-up behind. As the road curves away I shoot a quick glance behind and see a mass of tangled men and machines strewn over the road. About three duos seem to have escaped the crash and are coming up fast behind me. An ambulance comes toward us with its lights flashing and sirens blaring. We keep to the right and let it pass on the left, and as it goes by we're joined by the three who missed the pile-up. Together we pass the line and grandstand, but it's impossible to take my eyes off the road and look for Bobbie.

We passed the dicey corner all right, and as we come toward it for a second time one of the young riders gives a signal to his pacer and away they go. Romain, Loncke, the four others and myself chase hard. A light misty rain is now falling and the spray is coming off our wheels and soaking us even more. As we hit the cobbled approach to the hill a scooter skids but the driver, after a short wild struggle, regains control. It seems to unnerve us all. Loncke goes first into the corner and takes it fast and expertly. Like leeches Romain and I follow him and the three of us all signal for more speed to catch the young runaway. We draw level with him just before the grandstand, and the four pairs cross the line together. The corner must have taken its toll of the others. Almost as one our heads click round and we see them about two hundred yards behind.

Loncke begins to act a bit nervy. He keeps giving us

glances and doesn't seem to be able to decide what gear to stay in. I figure that because of the dangerous conditions he might not try any sort of break while we're being paced. I see no reason why I shouldn't use my plan. After all, I'm the one taking the biggest risk. We come to the car-park notice and Romain and Alphonse look to me for the sign, which I give. The other two see it but have no way of knowing what it means.

As we approach the hill I begin to have second thoughts. In fact if Alphonse looks round I'll signal him to forget it. It's really raining now and it's going to mean riding off the cobbles, diagonally, at a gap about three feet wide and in poor light at some thirty miles per hour. I couldn't be any wetter if I'd been slung in the river. As I lift myself from the saddle and stand on the pedals to meet the slight gradient, I feel the water squelch out of the airholes in my racing shoes. Alphonse accelerates and we come up directly behind Loncke, who leads. Loncke's pacer takes the widest and fastest arc through the corner. Alphonse half looks round, not long enough to actually see me, but he seems to sense I'm still with him. He comes out from the curb and then crosses back, heading straight for the gap. I fix my eyes on his number plate, grip my bars and follow him. The scooter hides my view of the road, so I have to trust in Alphonse's judgment. All in the matter of a split second I feel the jarring sensation from the cobbles stop, then a switchback motion as I hit the slope. Thirty miles an hour is very fast in these conditions, and is now made worse by the unpleasant feeling of almost brushing the walls of the houses with my elbow.

We tear past Loncke and I hear him shout to his pacer, who's got his own problems as he sees Romain drifting toward him through the rain. I hear a crash and a succession of thuds but can't look back. Alphonse's hand leaves the bars for a second as he signals the approach of the exit back onto the cobbles. He knows he's blocking my line of vision and that I can't really tell where the slope is. When he comes to it, he crosses gingerly and then opens up a bit suddenly to make up for the pause. It's then that I manage a quick look back up the road. Romain's bike is lying on the ground and I get the impression Romain himself is standing by it. Coming at me at a quick gallop is Loncke tailed by the youngster whose name I don't know.

"*Allez!*" I shout to Alphonse, who responds immediately. God knows what's happened to Romain. I only hope he's not hurt. I wonder if I ought to quit and just call it a day. Romain's futile effort hardly broke Loncke's rhythm and the heavy rain slowed Alphonse's exit to the road. All I've got from it is a thirty-yard lead, and the way Loncke and the youngster are coming at me it's only a matter of time before I'm caught. I'm now faced with the choice which many times faces all bike riders. Do I work like hell and try to keep my lead, or let myself be caught and try to fight it out in a sprint at the finish? If I do try to hang on to my advantage and am still caught, I won't have much strength left to use at the end.

Alphonse takes me to the line and is flagged in by an official encased in oilskins. Under the floodlights the finishing line passes beneath me like a shimmering gray strip. The rain hisses down and makes what my mother used to call "little men dancing in the road." I glance at the covered stands where spectators are crouched under hats and upturned collars, but I can't see her. Away from the stands the only spectators left are huddled in doorways or under umbrellas, peering through the rain trying to identify the riders.

I plod on, the jet from my front tire hitting me in the face, and the one off my rear wheel drenching my back like a farmer hosing out cattle pens. A car full of officials and reporters joins me and some flashbulbs pop. I don't feel shattered, just cold and numb from the wet. When I glance round I see Loncke and the youngster working together and closing on me fast. I keep going at a steady pace, about twenty-two miles an hour, and make no effort to stay away on my own. Two men, taking in turns at the front and with a definite target to catch, have got it far easier than I have, stuck out there alone.

We barely exchange glances as they catch me, and I fall in with the routine of doing my share of the work at the front. It's a funny thing, but the other two are just as soaked as I am, yet are suffering more. You can see it in their faces. If this were heat, and the temperature and conditions the same for us all, it would be me taking the beating. I'm like that. I never did seem as affected by wet and cold as some riders are. The sun's all right for lounging on a beach, but if I've got to do something really hard like climbing the Iseran, then give me cold every time.

Loncke doesn't know what to make of me. I've come across him before, but never in a direct way. As I spent my last few years riding mostly on the track, Loncke probably associates me with sprinting and is planning how to end his ride. To him this is just a bread-and-butter race and he's counting on the winning prize to make up for the unpleasant way he's having to earn it. He's a Flandrien and, although obviously choked by the wet, is well used to hard, cold events like these.

The youngster's arms and legs glisten pinkly and his fair hair is plastered to his forehead. He's a big strong lad, probably Dutch, and when he sees me looking at him he grits his teeth and puts on a determined look. The course is too flat to shake them off, and the finishing straight too wide and exposed to try anything clever. It would be better with a bunch of riders, because then some pattern would emerge and a tactic could be used.

There's nothing I can do. Loncke's a very strong finisher, and the youngster looks as if he is too. I planned it all for nothing. Many dollars down the drain. Ten years ago I would have been certain of taking them, but their combined ages don't amount to much more than mine.

Ahead I can see the stands. I feel mad and confused. If I lead out now they'd let me go and take me at the finish. What would Romain think of me? I don't know what to do except plod along at Loncke's elbow.

Gray shapes shout encouragement at us through the falling wet. It seems to have some effect on the youngster, who tries for a long sprint. He keeps close to the fence, knowing that neither Loncke nor I would dare crowd him into it with all that space and all those witnesses.

I follow the kid and Loncke tails me. There're only fifty yards to go now and we stay in that order: youngster, me and Loncke. I expect Loncke to pip me at the line, but he comes past me on the other side, so the three of us are spread out, neck and neck across the width of the road, like three rank amateurs. All I can do is give it all I've got. I put my head down, quickly drop to a slightly lower gear, and sprint. Shouts from the crowd, hissing wet, flashing bulbs, and it's all over. I apply both brakes but they're so wet nothing happens. At least it was close and I know I'm not disgraced. To stop I have to pull hard on both levers until I've slowed enough to plonk a heel on the ground. As I go to dismount, the local mayor, accompanied by an umbrella-carrying retainer, comes out of the murk and thrusts a bouquet of flowers at me. He smiles, makes a short speech in Flemish, and pumps my hand. I know that sometimes I'm not very bright, but it looks as if I've won, and I feel as excited as I did when I won my first race.

With the rain filling my eyes and dripping off my nose and chin, I remount and ride my "lap of honor" up and down in front of the stands while a grand march is played over the loudspeaker. A minor race in the pouring rain in a little country, but I couldn't feel better if I'd just become champion of the world. A few moments like these and all the hard slog doesn't seem to matter. Lately I've been cynical about the sport and the futility of having had a long but unexceptional career. But as I ride back and accept the check and a kiss from a local beauty queen, I know I would always have become a bike rider, even if I'd left school at twenty-nine with a certificate in flower arranging.

She's standing more or less where I left her, her hands thrust deeply into the pockets of her duffle coat, and smiling. "It was ever so exciting," she says. "I'm glad you won. What a state you're in!"

I kiss her, but the audience makes her feel awkward. Her lips are cold and hard, and scarcely move. "Are you cold?" I ask her.

"Frozen. But what about you?"

"Still hot. Listen, my teammate piled up, so I'd better go and find him. I'll try not to be long. See that café? Wait there for me. Get yourself a hot drink. Have you got any money? I'll be about half an hour. Okay?"

"All right. Don't be long." She pulls up the hood on her duffle coat, ready to run to the café. As she goes to leave I catch her arm. "Say six kids," I ask her.

She puts her head on one side and looks at me as if I'd been touched by the do-dally stick.

"Say what?"

"You heard—six kids."

Her eyes open wider and she says, "Sux kuds."

I roar with laughter and give her a gentle push toward the café, but she keeps looking round at me with the same blank expression.

"Won't be long," I call after her.

◆

"You bloody fool," Mottiat says.

God knows what he's doing here. Mottiat is the bête noire of the T.B.H.-Aigle setup.

His friendly greeting is directed at me, but I ignore him and speak to Romain, who's lying on a bunk in the changing room. I lift the blanket and look at Romain. Through the bandages that encase his right leg and arm I can see blood oozing.

"Did you win?" he asks.

I nod. "I'm sorry about this."

"Oh, I'll be stiff for a couple of weeks, then we'll be back to normal.'

"You might be, Hendrickx," Mottiat pipes up, "but by then it won't be any of Mr. Davenport's concern or business."

"Don't be absurd!" Romain twists himself onto his left side. "How can you blame Terry? It's my own damned fault for not paying more attention to what he tells me." He starts to blink.

Mottiat steps forward and jabs a sausage-shaped finger through an imaginary hole. He learned his English in America, and apart from being a pig is a curious sort of Yonkers-Ypres cocktail. Summer and winter he seems to wear this long black overcoat and gray homburg. He's built like a packing case and has always reminded me of a village idiot impersonating Rod Steiger impersonating Edward G.

87

Robinson. "Davenport's orders—"

"Mr. Davenport was given to understand—" I cut in.

"—were that you should ride in selected events. Safe, selected events. So that your sprinting would improve. What does he do? He sticks you in a motor-paced event in the pouring rain. You, a potential Tour de France winner!"

We all speak at once, but I shout Mottiat down. "Look! Listen! Before you burst your buttons you'd better hear what I've got to say. Right? I know a motor-paced race can be dodgy, but the field was small, the course—apart from the hill—easy, and Romain's had a lot of recent practice behind motors. The last lap was unpaced and offered every chance for a sprint finish. Which is what happened. You want his name brought before the public so that he gets a lot of sympathetic publicity before the Tour? Here was a good opportunity—a chance for him to win before a fairly large crowd. I myself even rode to nurse him along! When the race started it was only damp. I can't help it if it belts down. How would it have looked if he'd quit? He would have done his image a lot of harm. Tour de France winners don't pack in because it rains."

The banana prods at me. "Tour de France winners shouldn't be there in the first place. What is this race? A spectacle! Everyone hoping to see a crash. A carve-up for young hopefuls and has-beens."

"Like me?"

"Like you, Davenport. Nobody cares if you break your neck. Trainers, managers—ten a penny. Tour winners—one in thousands."

"Listen, Fat. Do what you bloody like. You can't sack me; my contract's till September."

He glares into my face and I catch a breath like an Arab's armpit. "True. But *I* decide what you do during that time.

You're finished with Hendrickx. Office work for you—that and sorting out the hopeless hopefuls. I'll make it so hot for you that you'll *want* to quit."

We stare at each other. I toy with the idea of punching his teeth down his hatch, then I look at Romain, whose blinking eyes alternate between us.

"Is Alphonse driving you back?"

"Yes."

"And you'll be all right?"

"Yes, of course."

"I'll be round first thing in the morning, then. It's no good talking with this high-strung fool. See you."

I give the door a shove and stalk out, back into the stands. For a minute I stand there looking at the café opposite, then I walk to a dressing room farther up.

The hot shower feels good. Mottiat of all people, I keep saying to myself. If it had been anyone other than he I could have smoothed it over. It'll be no good telling Bobbie about it, because she thinks I'm a full-time pro. Anyway, I mustn't act depressed tonight if I'm to try and keep her. I put on a clean shirt, shovel on some Old Spice, and try to shut Mottiat out of my mind until tomorrow.

Because of the weather and the festival, the café is fairly crowded. She's having to share a table with a fat Belgian family whose life's mission appears to be to decimate forever the mussel population of the North Sea. The mother, a gross hairy thing, has a plastic pail beside her to drop the empty shells into. If I weren't so hungry and thirsty I'd grab Bobbie's hand and leave. She's furtively writing something on a piece of notepaper and covers it as I sit down.

"Poems?" I ask.

"Not really. Congratulations, Terry. I don't know how you managed to even see through that rain. Wasn't it close?"

"Yes. I thought I'd lost. By the way, how much did I win by?"

She opens her hands to a distance of about two feet.

"An inch is enough," I tell her. "So you enjoyed it, did you?"

"Yes, very much."

It was inevitable that I'd be spotted. People keep nodding and smiling at me. Perhaps they all saw the same film of the same Royal Tour. It occurs to me that somebody might come up and say "I thought you had retired" or "It's good to see you back" or something, so I order a steak each and try to look as small as possible.

She uses this silver lipstick, and when she smiles and her lips stretch they look as metallic as a pair of handlebars—if you'll forgive the comparison. "I'd like to kiss you," I tell her. The smile goes up a kilowatt. Looking at her now, it's hard to visualize her as confused and wretched as she was the other night.

"Do you want to see another race?" I ask. "With or without me in it."

Her hand goes to one side as her smile dies to a half-smile. "I really ought to be going this weekend. I've got to get a job. There wouldn't be as much choice here."

Although I know she's right, I answer, "Oh, I don't know."

To think I was racing as an amateur when she was born. I wonder what I'd have thought if somebody had come up to me then and told me that thousands of miles away a baby had just been born whom I'd one day be crackers about. I shouldn't have started all this, I know. It's all very well to talk about "having things in common" and "getting on well together," but it's always a thousand times harder, and better, when the bird's beautiful.

The steaks arrive and we tuck in, both too hungry to talk. There's a steady clinking sound as the mussel eaters top up their plastic buckets. It's hard to know how Bobbie sees me. I've always thought of myself as being like one of those paneled reflectors where a slight movement makes the light catch another panel. I'm different things to different people, which must be true of us all. To some I'm a bit of a lad, good for a laugh. Others see me as a right bastard. Yet Bobbie can't see me as either of these two panels. Is there physical attraction, or am I a Nice Man like I was to a Swiss bird I picked up with a couple of years back? She was about twenty-two and was really looking for a father, not a lover. Mind you, she'd do it for friends and hadn't an enemy in the world. I got chatting to her in a park. All the talent was there, bursting out of its summer dresses and sweating inside its nylons, yet I picked on her because she looked a bit plain and, I hoped, easy. And it's true she was. See, I'm a realist. I'm not fooled like some blokes are. They think just because a woman's done up and got a tight skirt on, then it's fine. But you've got to have imagination enough to visualize these frumpy birds stripped down. Which, in spite of how a lot of people kid themselves, is what It's All About, really.

"Are we going to stay at a hotel for the night?" She scarcely looks up and could just as well have asked me to pass the salt.

"Do you want to?" As this is the second time the suggestion has come from her, I feel a hot wave of optimism.

"I don't mind, Terry. It's up to you."

I go on eating. "It would be nice if you wanted to."

She shakes her head. Some hair falls forward and she pushes it back. "I've told you. I can't feel anything."

For the first time I feel myself getting a bit annoyed with her. "Don't be daft. You must feel something. I'll spare you the clinical details because it might upset the mussel eaters, but if you didn't feel anything, anything at all, your body wouldn't respond as it does. Neither would you be here with me now, and this is the second time *you've* asked *me* about going to a hotel."

She appears not to notice the edge to my voice. "I'm sorry it's so confusing. I do like you, really."

I sigh. "Then you must feel something, am I right?"

She looks down at her plate. "Something, I suppose. I don't know."

The musselers are beginning to show interest, so I drop the subject.

"What were you writing when I came in? A letter home?"

"No." She pushes a piece of paper toward me across the table, and then sits staring into my face. I turn the sheet round. The handwriting is squarish and slopes backwards. I read:

> For the past year I seem to have lived outside myself. I have been an observer watching some absurd play in which everyone has worn a mask. I cannot even recognize the actors. Things have been going on, happening very quickly, but nothing has touched me. I have watched someone else scheme, tell lies, plan farewells, write poems, cry, make excuses, rattle off learned phrases, but it's all so unreal. I cannot seem to wake up out of a dream, wake up to reality. If I am being selfish and thinking only of myself, as I seem to be, which me is it that is being selfish? Is it the actor who faces all the problems and situations but is only a plastic front? The actor walks away, having provided an answer or asked a question, but somewhere something else asks, What did I say? Was I really there? Is this happening to me? Does it take some enormous shock to jolt these parts together? Once the act is finished the parts break up again and it all seems to have happened to someone else. Where am I? Even now I have written this I don't know if they're things I think or things I think I should think.

I push the sheet back to her. She picks it up without taking her eyes off me. "What do you think?" she asks.

As I answer I take a deep breath. "At nineteen, with new experiences coming along all the time, we all had 'problems' of some kind." I grin. "Don't think I didn't have mine."

"But when do they end?"

I think. "They don't, really. Other things come along thick and fast, and there's only room for so much. Suddenly one day the original problems don't seem as important. They're still there, but you've got new ones to worry about. It's always like this. It never stops. I myself am sitting on a boxful right now; they weren't here last year and next year I hope they'll be gone."

She lowers her voice to throw our audience off the scent. "But you're talking about external problems. I've just had these: leaving home, getting here, et cetera. What about inside, though, the thing that's really you?"

"Yes, I'm talking about that. I used to wonder what I was and all that sort of thing. Then, I think, one day I realized that basically not only myself but everyone is rotten. It's been so long since I even cared what I am that I'm a bit rusty on the subject. I usually take what's going and envy the bloke who's got what I haven't. Sorry to have to tell you this, Bobbie, but I'm not really a very nice person. I'm a sort of nonpracticing criminal."

She takes hold of my hand and the musselers nearly choke. "Only a nice person could admit that."

"That's what you think. Shall we go?" As I stand up I almost knock a plastic bucket for six.

Outside, she says, "The rain's easing. If it helps any, I do want to go to a hotel. I won't worry much if we don't, but I'd rather go than not." She swings her bag and puts on a take-it-or-leave-it expression.

"Okay, but not all night."

"Why not?"

"I've got things to do."

She's never asked me before, but now of course she does.

"Are you married? You are, aren't you?"

"Would you believe me if I said I wasn't?"

"No. A single man wouldn't have to get home."

"As true as I'm standing here, I'm single."

She looks at me sideways, through strands of hair.

"Honestly," I tell her. "Would it make any difference if I were?"

"It might." She thinks for a few seconds. "No, of course it wouldn't. How could it? I'm off shortly."

We arrive at the car park. I can't see the van and assume Romain and Alphonse have gone. As I open the car door for her she looks back at me, smiling. In the neon lights, with her deadpan makeup, she looks very pale and very young.

I get in beside her. "What would you think if I told you that I'm more or less engaged to, and living with, a woman of my own age?" I turn the cab light off, but the street lights are bright enough for her face to search mine.

"And that's why you've got to get back?"

"Yes. I told you I'm not very nice."

I start the motor and drive off, out of the town and toward the highway back to Ghent. She sits looking at the road ahead. At last she asks, "Do you love her?"

I was sure she'd ask me this and I knew I wouldn't have the answer myself until I began to reply. "In a way I do. Certainly I'm very fond of her. I'll tell you this in all honesty: You're the only person who could stop me marrying her. You could stop me almost by lifting your finger."

She turns and stares at me and I glance at her. An oncoming truck lights the cab. "You love me, then?" she says quietly.

94

"I'm not going to use the word, because it'll make everything so much harder. I've said as much as I'm going to; now it's up to you. If what you say about your phobia is true, you could wave me goodbye now and never give me another thought."

Her hand touches me just above the knee. "If I left you right now, I'd never forget you."

"Only because I was the first."

"No, even if you'd never touched me. Tell me about this woman you're engaged to."

"The antique shop, remember? She owns it. It's a very nice business and one I'm interested in. The fact that Paula's an intelligent attractive woman who loves me makes the whole setup very appealing. Outside of cycling I'm nothing. I'm virtually too old for competition and too independent to manage a team to orders. Back in England my name might just as well be Joe Soap. I'm too old to 'train,' got the wrong accent and not enough bits of paper to say I'm 'clever.' In the antique business I could really do something, but to start properly on my own would take more money than I've ever had in my life." I realize I'm belting along, sending water spraying out as if we were in a speedboat. I slow down in case I catch the van, which must be somewhere in front.

"You're really marrying for money, then?" she asks.

"Partly. In a way."

"Oh, I don't blame you. Don't think that. It's probably what I'll end up doing."

"You shouldn't have much trouble finding someone." It hurts me to say this, but you've got to keep up the old cynical front. "Look, I don't want to catch up with my mates in the van and I'm fed up with creeping along. We'll stop at the first shady hotel we see, eh?"

5

If You Can't Fight,
Wear a Big Hat

I HAVE TO WAIT. HERR DOKTOR IS with Romain, dressing the saber cuts. When he's finished I go into the room where Romain lodges and find him lying stiffly in bed. We both go at once to say. "I'm sorry.

"No," I tell him. "It's I who should be sorry."

"No, it's my fault, Terry. You didn't fall off and yet you rode up onto the sidewalk and off again. I wish I could stay on a bike as you can. It was all going well, when suddenly— whoosh—the bike just went from under me. Where the devil did Mottiat come from?"

He's even got a plaster the size of a hand towel across the bridge of his nose, making it look wavier than ever.

I sit on the edge of the bed. "Search me. Went there for the festival, I suppose. What's he going to do? Come round here?"

"He said he'd look in."

"Yes, he's dead worried about you, I don't think. You're a bloody business investment, Romain, that's all."

"I know. Here, I am glad you won. Didn't you feel good? Beating a man like Loncke too. Wasn't he well up the list in Liege-Bastogne-Liege last year? Why don't you make a comeback?"

"No, no, it was just a lucky sprint, something I could never repeat. And how long could I come back for? Three years at the most. As with everything, the body wears out. This isn't football or cricket, where all you've got to be is 'fit.' It's the hardest sport there is. You know, I started cycling so long ago that in England some wrinklies were still wearing black tights for racing. I even wore a pair once—looked like the Sugar Plum Fairy." I laugh at the memory of it as I get up from the bed. "Mind you, if I get the push and then don't marry Paula, I might well be glad to come back."

A car pulls up outside; I move the curtain and look out. "Speaking of getting the push, here they come. Mottiat himself, Isambard Kingdom Brunel, Old Uncle Tom Cobleigh and All. Mottiat's looking at his mill owner's watch and probably telling himself that Time Is Money. Isn't his wife Spanish?"

"Yes, I think so." Romain sounds tense and a little scared.

"She's decided to wait in the car, so God can't be expecting to scatter corn for long. I always imagined her with a pile of hair and a garden fork stuck in it and castanets for earrings. She looks as bloody horrible as her husband. I'll go and let them in."

I wait for the knock, shoot a glance back to Romain and open the door. "Come in, gentlemen."

They push past me. As I close the door Pilar transmits me a withering glare from the sanctuary of her Hispano-Suiza, which by some accident at the factory has a Ford badge on it.

Romain drags himself up in his bed and offers chairs to the Three Wise Men. I call the tall one Isambard Kingdom Brunel because I once saw a photo of him wearing an enormous top hat. His real name's Vignolo and he's not a bad bloke. The trouble is he doesn't know much English and is dominated by Mottiat. Uncle Tom Cobleigh's name is Lemare. He's in charge of the Aigle cycle side of the business, while the other two are publicity managers for T.B.H. Lemare's a crafty peasant, literally. He's like most country people when they imagine they're being artful. They think you're as daft as they are and can't see through them, and that you're blind to the greed or lies or what-have-you that lights up their eyes like Brighton Pier in October.

Mottiat points at Romain and says to his two companions, "The proof, gentlemen. I need say nothing. Our Tour de France winner, swathed in bandages, in bed, unable to move. And why?"

He points at me. "Because this fool enters him in a scooter-paced race of no importance, on cobbles, during a cloudburst!"

Mottiat and I now repeat practically word for word the argument we had had in the dressing room. If I've got an ally at all, it's Vignolo, but he's about as good at English as I am at French, and by the time he's worked out part of what one person has said, the other has replied. I repeat the argument slowly in French and look at Vignolo while I do it. I think he follows it, because suddenly he lets go a mouthful of French at Mottiat, who comes back even harder with a larger mouthful. Lemare chimes in and Romain and I sit and wait. I gather Vignolo is getting the worst of it. Suddenly Romain starts up. I am able to get the gist of some of it, which is that Mottiat and Lemare want me out; but for most of the conversation my imperfects and conditionals fight a lonely battle in the wings.

Still jabbering, they get out of their chairs and make their way toward the door. When they reach it, Mottiat points a finger in our direction. He yells at us, and as the sentence is short I translate it as meaning I'm fired. Then, as if I needed it, he says in English, "You're through!" Lemare walks out without looking back; Vignolo shrugs sympathetically. Outside, and all the way to the car, they keep jabbering and waving their arms. I walk to the door and slam it. "Jesus Christ, to think we won the war."

"Pardon?" Romain calls out.

"Nothing." I know I've just uttered the stock cliché that unpleasant Continentals can always drag from every maligned Englishman. Romain's too young to appreciate its full meaning.

As I walk back to the bed I say, "Well?"

He throws up one arm and half raises the injured one. "Bloody fools, idiots. Mottiat simply won't listen. If you're out, then I'm out with you."

I sit down. "No, don't do that. I know more about riders' contracts than you do. It's too late in the season to join another team, and your contract is such that they'd bleed you white if you walked out on them. As for my contract, they can't break it, only make things unpleasant for me. I expect I'll get a letter telling me I'm being 'given the chance' to resign and that for their part they'll raise no objections. Something like that."

Romain begins a marathon blink and goes on about how he'll ride in the Tour and deliberately finish last and how he'll run down T.B.H. products when interviewed. I let him get on with it.

When he's finished I say, "If you want to do me any favors, you'll win the Tour. Normally I wouldn't put it like this, but as the Bad Times have struck I'm forced to be a bit blunt. You see, if you can get enough money you'll marry Susan and take her away from home. I can then marry Paula. Oh, no need to look so surprised. I know you'd never see it like this, but then you're not the natural schemer I am. Even if Susan is Paula's daughter and they get on quite well, for a thing like marriage to work two people have got

100

to be on their own."

Romain's voice crackles at some unknown pitch. "What! You're all waiting for me?"

I do my best to calm him and give longer and softer versions of my original statement. "You can only do your best," I tell him. "Nobody can plan to win a thing like the Tour. And as you yourself have said, the King of the Mountains prize will be enough for a good start to marriage. Even if you don't win a franc, things will work out. They always do."

He sits there glumly looking at the bottom of his bed while I make some coffee on the electric ring. His voice has got a catch in it. "You see, even if I went mad at these other races and did everything I could, took big risks to try and win, I couldn't. In races where money's to be made, I'm just another good rider. If I'm ever to make any it'll be in the big tours, and only then with an outright win or the Mountain title. All I'm getting is enough to keep myself while they nurse me and pay you to train me. If I married Susan now, how could I bring her here?"

"You couldn't and nobody's asking you to. All we can do is hang on, accept what's coming from Mottiat, and hope you pick up some loot in the Tour. What did Doktor Franz Joseph say to you?"

"He said rest for a week, walk about on the second week, start cycling gradually on the third."

"You'll be all right. Lucky it didn't happen nearer the start of the Tour

◆

So I don't know whether I've got a job or not. There are T.B.H. riders other than Romain, but when I get to headquarters they all seem to be out on a training run. At least I can meet Bobbie this afternoon instead of waiting until tonight, so I phone the hotel and arrange to see her. This time I've pretty well got to settle something one way or another, although I don't know what. Persuade her to stay, I suppose, but if I manage this, I can't imagine what the outcome would be. Each time I've met her I've half expected it to be the last, and I can't visualize anything beyond seeing her just once more. Yet when I think of our parting, stomach butterflies elbow one another with uncertainty.

I go back to the shop and guard it for ten minutes while Paula has a snack. Nobody comes in; a good thing because I don't feel very servile. The earliest I can expect a letter from Mottiat and Co. is tomorrow. It's something like waiting for your call-up notice to come.

Susan comes into the shop and stands there looking at me. She is done up something wicked, and I stare back, not knowing whether I'm supposed to comment favorably on the get-up. There's this short cape thing she's wearing, fastened with a clasp the size of a pair of handcuffs, and a tall hat reminiscent of a section of land drain. Working downward we come to a houndstooth mini-skirt, Robin Hood tights, and black thigh-high flagellants.

"Where's your bow and arrow?" I ask.

"Nasty."

I'd expected a smile but don't get one.

"Lectures finished?"

"Got the last one at four. Thought I'd come home in case you were here."

I lower my voice. "Why? Got a sudden urge?"

She doesn't answer but walks around me stealthily, eyes on mine. "Where's Mother?"

"Upstairs having a bite."

She walks back thoughtfully toward the door. "You know the café round the corner?"

"Of course. Why?"

"I'll wait for you there. Come as soon as Mother gets back."

I go to ask her why, but the sound of her opening and closing the door checks me. All very odd, I think. Why the mystery? I know, she's seen Romain and it's something to do with getting, or not getting, married. Either that, or something which should have happened hasn't.

Both Susan and Paula know about Romain's crash, but of course he didn't tell them I was in the race. I'm glad he had the presence of mind to do this.

Paula comes down the stairs, drags me behind a Chinese screen and kisses me.

"What's all this about?" I ask her.

"Hold me," she says, putting her arms under mine and linking them behind my neck. "You've been very withdrawn lately, Terry. Anything wrong?"

I give her a big hug, the sort all flowers like.

"That's better," she purrs.

"Everything's fine."

"You sure? Have you had second thoughts about parting with your money?"

"No, of course not. It's for us, isn't it? And if it wasn't I'd get it all back." I go to kiss her, but pause to look at her mouth. It really is a lovely mouth, and right now her lips are moist and parted like in a lipstick poster. After a bit of heavy breathing I look at my watch. "Sorry, Paula, must fly. Business before pleasure." I plonk a kiss on her forehead and let her go. "See you later," I call out, and leave her straightening her hair and smiling.

In the café, Susan's sitting in a dark corner with the land drain on a chair beside her.

"How's Romain?" she asks as I sit down.

"Haven't you seen him?"

103

"Not since they brought him back last night. When have I had time? I've been at lectures since eight-thirty this morning."

I order two martinis. "You should be with him now, not yacking to me. What's it all about, then?"

"I don't know how to start."

"Well, think about it." She's a funny girl. If she'd wear her hair like Bobbie's it would suit her better. As it is, it's combed straight back, which, with her rather high forehead, doesn't suit her. It's fair hair but for some reason always looks a bit greasy. For a girl with a spotlessly clean mother, she's a bit extreme in her hygiene. There doesn't seem to be any state for her between being a right heap and being done up to the nines. She has straightish arms and legs and is a bit thin with a big frame. Her eyes are blue—quite nice—and her ears small and white, as if there were no blood at all in them. For a girl she has long feet and very long toes. If she lived in coconut country she'd be a top shinner. "Have you thought yet?" I ask her.

"Perhaps . . ."

"Just start at the beginning."

"All right." She wriggles in her seat and drinks half her martini in one go. "Naturally I left Romain quite late last night. I had to wait and see he was comfortable. As I walked back I saw your car pull up outside the Hotel Albert I. A girl with fair hair got out, kissed you, and went inside."

Being a natural liar, I'm all ready with "You know I was at the race with Romain. I gave her a lift on the outskirts of town. As she got out she said, 'Perhaps I can do something for you one day,' and I said, 'You can; you can give us a kiss,' and she did. Is this why you dragged me down here? To tell me this?"

I don't like the look of it. She's got a bitter grin and is shaking her head. "No, Terry, I know you. You've been very odd these last few days, and you've been elsewhere for your fixes. You've not touched me, and I'm pretty sure you've bypassed Mother as well."

"How would you know that?" Cheeky cow.

She looks a little embarrassed, possibly because it's her mother we're talking about. "I usually know. The walls in that flat are so thin."

"There's the daytime. What about when you're out?"

She fights to hold the smile, but her bottom lip's beginning to quiver. "You know as well as I do Mother's too busy to do anything like that other than *au lit*. But even if I'm wrong on that score, there's this faraway withdrawn sort of attitude you've had. Give up, Terry. You can say what you like. I *know*."

"Good for you!" I knock back the martini. Oh, I don't care what she knows. It's nothing to do with her, anyway. She's getting her share.

Susan slides her elbow along the table and rests her chin in her cupped hand. "My God, don't you ever give up? Three women, to my knowledge."

I poke her arm with my forefinger. "Of which you're one, remember?"

Her head moves in a shaking motion. "As if I could ever forget. To me personally it doesn't matter whether I'm one of fifty. What about Mother, though? Are you going to keep this up when you're married? I don't want her hurt. I've always imagined that you cared for her quite a bit, but that being Terry Davenport you had to have someone like me on the side. Silly, I know, but it was a temporary yet cozy setup. And now there's a third~possibly a fourth or a fifth. Really, Terry, I'm forced to conclude that you don't care a damn about Mother and are marrying her because of the business."

The waiter happens to be passing, so I order a couple more drinks before turning my attention back to Susan. "God knows why I'm sitting here explaining things to you," I say.

"Don't. Get up and walk out."

"I could, I know. But as Paula's your mother I suppose it's reasonable for you to be concerned. I shan't attempt to 'explain' my actions; women can never understand things like this. But I will give you my assurance that I do care very much for Paula. Beyond this, any explanations or assurances would be pointless, and besides it's nothing to do with you. What I think is bloody amusing is that you should find my 'three women' so upsetting. The fact that two of the merry trio are mother and daughter strikes you as all right, 'cozy' even. Right and wrong doesn't mean a thing to me. There's nothing left to shock; I've heard and seen it all. But you, who have got to have yardsticks and a line to draw, your standards seem so cockeyed to me."

Her thumb springs from her cupped hand and she begins to nibble the nail. She takes her eyes off me, studies the nail, and then looks at me again. After a few seconds she lets go a ladylike snort. "Huh. What a setup, isn't it? Does number three love you?"

"No, I don't think so. In fact I'm sure she doesn't."

She smiles. "Oh, dear, and you're one of these men who can never make out why all women you fancy don't immediately fall in love with you. Aren't you? You behave irresponsibly and think it gives you a boyish charm. Oh, I know I've behaved badly as well, but I was seduced into it. You leap about, womanize, keep riding when you don't have to. Soon you'll *have* to give up some of these things. What happens to people like you, Terry, when they are old?"

I wish she wouldn't talk like this. I don't know whether to bash her, walk away, or both. "I don't know, Susan, I don't know. They say you never see a wild elephant die of old age. Of course they do die, but nobody ever sees it. That's how I am. I'm a Young Man, the same as you're English and a female."

She touches my hand and looks really upset. "I'm sorry." We both take a drink and she goes on: "I suppose I'm 'the other woman,' that most damned of characters. In old films they always have mean mouths and black hats. Yet I'm sure they're misunderstood characters. I'm sure that if all 'other women' met the 'woman' they'd get on well and would probably be friends. My mother has been so good to me that I think I'd go mad if she found out about us. I love her, and in different ways I love Romain and you. I'm sorry to mention the word because I know we agreed not to. I tried to do what you wanted and regarded you only as an occasional sleeping partner. A man can easily adopt this attitude, but for a woman love *must* come into it somewhere down the line, no matter how hard she tries to keep it out."

I've never known her to rabbit on like this before. It's what education does for you, I suppose. "You're very wise today," I tell her.

"Am I?"

"Yes. Well, what does it all lead up to?"

She sits back, slumps, and picks up this bloody great hat. After turning it several times through her fingers, she says, "What you do is your business, but for my part our little liaison is over. It had to end shortly, in any case. We've been playing with fire and have been very foolish." She grins. "I won't say I haven't enjoyed it, though. I'd like to think you'd give up number three, especially after you and Mother get married. But I don't suppose you will. I remember you saying to me once that when your time came you wanted two things nailed down with you: a bike wheel and a pair of frilly drawers. Do you remember that conversation?"

I nod.

"You told me that you're positive you could have done so much more with your life if you'd had the right chances. I don't suppose many people would believe you, but I do. Really, Terry, you're a great big act, an act that life forced on you and which has stuck and become so much a part of you that you believe it yourself. Physically you're a strong man; it's the way you were born and something an unfair world can't take from you. I never knew you when you raced, but I can see from your scrapbook that you're a very courageous person. If you feel at ease with people, you can make them laugh. Your type, as far as the younger generation goes, is somewhat passé. Fifteen years ago when it was In to be tall dark and handsome, I imagine you cut quite a figure. Fortunately I'm a bit old-fashioned myself. So as your mistress I hereby hand in my resignation. I would have left things be had I been the only one; but as I'm not, I find the whole thing too explosive. From now on you'll always be Big Terry Davenport. I'll never know you as a boy again."

I seize at a lighthearted way out. "A boy! At thirty-seven! Twelve stone four pound! What do you mean?"

She stands up and plonks on the land drain. I think the martinis have made her a bit giddy, because the hat finally settles on the front of her head. She looks like a guardsman peering out from the ground floor of the Leaning Tower of Pisa. I can hardly see her eyes beneath the little brim, but I think she's close to tears. "When we were together, and you were finishing, you'd cling to me tightly, like a child would to its mother, like a boy. As if you really needed me." She walks away slowly, looking round once when she reaches the door. I don't try to follow her, because there's nothing I could say.

◆

"Another drink, monsieur?" the waiter asks me. His outline is quite fuzzy and I must stare at him a full thirty seconds before shaking my head.

I walk gingerly from the café. Luckily my car isn't right outside the shop, and I manage to get in it without Paula seeing me. It's not that I want to avoid her, it's that she'd want to know why I'm a bit tipsy and not with Romain. The way I feel I couldn't face a lot of questions. The Ravens must have left the Tower, or something, because I feel this sensation of impending doom. So number two's quit, and if number three's going, then today's as good a day as any. I've noticed this before. Suddenly everything goes right and then, equally as sudden, it all goes wrong. There doesn't seem to be anything you can do. Big things, little things, they all blow up in your face. There's Romain covered in bandages, Susan doesn't want to know, Bobbie's probably packing her bag right now, Mottiat will be drafting my notice, Paula will find out everything. It's the sort of day you'd duck down an alley to have a quiet scratch and look up to see a crowd of people watching.

I tell myself that the worst thing that could happen would be Paula finding out about both Susan and Bobbie. This would be so bad that, in my present state, my mind can't visualize it, but somehow none of it seems as disastrous as Bobbie leaving. If only I could swap all this trouble for physical pain. I sit in the car, hazily blinking as Romain does, trying to think of the ultimate physical pain which I'd endure in exchange for everything being as I'd want it. I run through all the usual tortures—the iron boot, thumbscrews, and the rack—but they don't seem even plausible. Then my horrible mind sends pictures on to my mental screen of myself hanging up by my arms and long steel hatpins being driven right into my taut armpits. Yes, I can imagine this and think it would be a fair swap.

The old mind feels sluggish, but I try to fathom why I should want Bobbie so much. At the root of it is probably the fact that she doesn't love me. If she was all over me I'd no doubt withdraw to my usual slightly guarded position, the victor with the whip hand. It's funny how you can do this by unconsciously juggling with your attitudes and image. I play it one way with Paula and she dotes on me; to Susan I'm somebody different again and she's not as keen. Modesty almost stops me from saying that if I'd played Susan differently I could have her dancing my tune. But of course I've never wanted her to get too interested in me. Yet I've tried hard with Bobbie and it doesn't seem to have worked. You can't win all the time, there's no infallible way. Perhaps if I only knew it, things are going my way after all. If Bobbie did want me I'd be forced to choose between her and Paula. Life with Paula is so predictable, I know it would work out all right. I'd have a cushy, interesting existence and be comfortable and well off. With Bobbie it would be into the economic wasteland. When I think about it, I haven't even got much in common with her, not as much as I have with Paula. And Bobbie would only be Paula's age by the time I have to queue up with my pension book clasped in my shaking emaciated hand. That is if I could even keep her that long, which is doubtful. Oh, I was a bloody twit to start it; it's all my own fault. You don't miss what you've never had. All I can do is my best to keep her, then if she goes (which is likely) I can at least say I tried. Should a miracle happen and I can somehow keep hold, only then will I think about breaking with Paula. I haven't forgotten the phobia, but I'm sure this is just adolescence and will pass.

I look at my watch. Time to pick her up.

◆

"Would you like to come up to my room?" she says. "I don't think they'd mind."

I look around. If nothing else, I'm an expert on the attitudes of hotel management. They look safe enough, the sort who don't care what you do as long as you pay and go about your sins with discretion. We smile at the desk clerk as we pass, and he smiles back. We're in.

She walks up the stairs in front of me and has on this short dolly dress. I can see up the backs of her legs. If an old dear hadn't that moment come toward us I think I'd have taken a bite out of Bobbie. She's that type of girl. You know it's all hopeless and wrong, but you can't help it. At least I can't. It's one of the twists of life that girls such as Bobbie who physically have got everything to offer never want anything from you. Unless they're on the game, that is. A pop record delighted her. At the other end of the scale you get those for whom you're doing a favor, always on the cadge.

A couple of years ago there was this bird, fiftyish but preserved, you know. Not too bad at all, especially at a distance. Well, I thought, give it a treat. "I shall pass through this life but once," et cetera. It had actually crossed my mind that I might be in line for a few "presents," especially as it was well heeled. Blow me down, no sooner had I finished—it wasn't much, as it turned out: corsets and things—than it started to hint it was open to receive gifts. That's right, dear, I thought. You've just had the only gift you're getting.

"This is my room." Bobbie unlocks the door and we go in. "I've still got use of the girl's record player, so I'll play you the record. Sit there, Terry."

"Still playing the tune, then? Aren't you tired of it?"

She spins round coquettishly and both hair and dress

whirl out. "No, it's lovely."

"You know," I say as I sit on a sort of recumbent chair, "I rather fancy that that record and I will fall from favor about the same time."

"Don't be silly," she says, looking round as she switches it on. It starts to play and she adjusts the volume.

"How's your phobia?" I ask.

She looks awkward. "Haven't thought about it lately."

"Since that first time," I remind her, "you've been very reluctant to talk about it. Why's that?"

She smooths her hair down, using both hands. "Oh, I don't know. There's nothing new to add. It's all just the same as it was."

I grab her hand and pull her toward me. As we kiss she sits on my lap and nestles in, expecting the usual.

It's no good beating about the bush. "When are you leaving?"

She looks at me quickly, and then at the record. "Tomorrow. I'll have to go."

We're both willing to kiss so as to break the short awkward silence that follows her words. For her it's an excuse to close her eyes and not look at me. Her eyes still won't meet mine when we've stopped kissing. "Don't look at me like that," she says. "You're making me feel all silly."

I lick my lips and can taste her silver lipstick. It has a tacky, sightly bitter taste. "Can't you stay?"

"No."

"Don't you even love me a little bit?"

"A little."

"How much?"

"As much as I ever have anyone."

"That's not saying a lot."

She clenches her fists. "I can't help it. I tried. Perhaps I could in time."

I take hold of her clenched hands. "Then stay here and give yourself time!"

"No, no! Listen, Terry, I didn't want to tell you this, but it's the only way. From the short time you've known me, would you say I was out to get what I can—materially, that is?"

"No, of course not."

"And that really, by going to bed with you, I've given more than I've taken?"

"Yes, but why the buildup?"

"And although I'm traveling very light, would you say I was a dressy sort of person?"

"No, I wouldn't say you were."

"My little old scooter is my dearest possession. I'd rather have it than a Rolls. Do you believe that?"

"Yes, and I repeat: Why the buildup?"

"I'm getting to that. In short, then, you'd say I'm not a grabber?"

I close my eyes and say, "No, you're not a grabber."

She takes her hands away from mine and sits up straighter. "The next thing I'm going to tell you will contradict our mutual conclusion that I'm not on the make. You see, I'm a lazy, unambitious person, and the only thought in life that really touches me is where I see myself leading a comfortable, worry-free existence, lounging in the sun and traveling leisurely to interesting places. This is the only positive thing I know I want. Now, ask yourself, who could give me this sort of life?"

I look at her sideways and ping my fingernail against my teeth. "And I wouldn't have enough?"

"Well, would you?"

"No."

I look into her eyes and she turns her head guiltily. "Do you blame me?" she says quietly.

113

"Of course I don't. If I were an attractive girl it's just what I'd do."

She looks toward me eagerly. "I don't want to lead an ordinary dreary life. Just because I can't feel strongly about people doesn't mean I don't like to be with amusing ones. I'm not antisocial or anything. And if people—men—leave me pretty unmoved, then I might as well get a rich one as a poor one. Where's the difference? I think I could love children if I had them. If I could get a rich man, have two children, and get him to keep us in the south of France or somewhere while his business kept him elsewhere, that would be ideal."

"Lovely."

"But you've just said you'd do a similar sort of thing."

I rest my head on the back of the chair. "Yes, I suppose I would. In a way it's what I'm doing, isn't it? With Paula, I mean. Only I am fond of her. But for my part I'd chuck it all in for you. Do you believe that?"

"Maybe," she says sadly, "but you'd be a fool if you did. I'm not a grabber, Terry, am I? I only want money to buy time with, time to sit in the sun or by the sea, to play with my children, to write poetry. If I had a fortune I wouldn't buy any more clothes or things than I do now. Is it so wrong to want to escape drudgery? Isn't what I want everybody's secret wish? Oh, I know I probably shan't get it, but I must try while I've got something to offer and a clear ten years ahead to use it. I don't imagine I'll get very far at first, because it will take time to build up acquaintances and introductions. Anyway, in London I might stand out as being a bit of a raw colonial. I shan't change at all within myself, nor shall I develop into one of these extrovert English social women. Can you imagine me like that! What I shall develop is timing and what *not* to say, otherwise I'm offering myself much as I am. I don't want to return to New

Zealand, not ever. It's been written of as the Great Mediocrity and the land of the Long White Shroud. Apt titles. I want to live surrounded by at least some vestige of civilization; I don't want to become a vegetable." She cocks her head to one side. "Well?"

I take a big breath, hold it, then let it go with a whistle.

"No comments?"

One side of her hair has fallen into her face. I push it back into place and sit stroking it. "I don't know. Where you come from attractive designing girls might be rare and have a chance of success, but the nearer you approach money the harder competition gets. In the south in the summer they're lined up like prostitutes. It's a buyer's market. No doubt you could get something like an architect or a dentist, but could they give you what you want? Most men want their wives with them, not miles away sitting on a balcony writing poetry. Why don't you sell your talents for ten years to rich clients, then get out and invest the proceeds?"

She shakes her head. "No, I wouldn't like to do that, not for ten years. A week or two at the right time, maybe, but not as a way of life."

"And if this plan doesn't work?"

She shrugs. "I'm not afraid to die."

"Don't be crazy. Anyway, the very best suicides never talk about it."

She shrugs again.

"What about me?" I ask.

"I'm sorry, terribly sorry. I'm not a 'designing woman,' as you put it. It would be hard to imagine anyone simpler than myself. Do you know, I could sit in a bare room and stare at the wall and be quite happy, but to do even that costs money. It's not much to ask to be free to sit quietly on my own, is it?"

"But you could live with me and sit quietly on your own."

"What, in a bed-sitter? In Belgium? And what happens when I want a change of scenery? Besides, I can't cook or sew or anything. If you were able to give me the necessary time and freedom, I'd be only too pleased to have you. I'm really very fond of you, and you have done me one favor which I hadn't expected yet."

"And what's that?"

She smiles and looks coy.

"That!"

"Now I'm ready: my first lesson. I thank you for gentle and expert tuition."

"Yes, while some other bastard reaps the fruits."

It's rare for her to laugh, but when she does it's a funny deep sound.

"So I'm just the first affair in a long line of affairs? And you'll go on until you click with someone who's got the right size bank account. Why don't you save yourself a lot of trouble and settle for me? We'd get by."

Bobbie gets off my lap and goes over to the record player, which has switched itself off. She starts the record again. It's a slow tune, the sort that makes you want to sit still and sway from the waist upward. She leans against the table and rocks her head in time with the rhythm. "I don't suppose, by some miracle, you're in line for an inheritance?"

"No," I tell her above the noise of the music. "Out of interest, how much would you need?"

"Oh, I don't know anything about amounts. Enough not to have to worry, to up and go when I felt like it, not to be beholden to anybody. How much would that take?"

I run my hand round my face. "God knows. A bloody fortune, even though it sounds little enough to ask."

"Yes, isn't it sad that it costs money to do nothing? Don't think I'm taking the first rich man who offers. He'll be no use if he wants me to join the social whirl, or live in England, or be a doting wife. If I ever get enough, especially if through divorce and its allowance, I'll get you to join me."

"Oh, ta. So what you're after is a gullible idiot who's worth a bomb. If you want my opinion you might as well blow your brains out now. You're a very attractive girl whom a bloke like myself is glad to know, but money can buy birds like you by the hundredweight, and with no strings attached. I've been a damned good cyclist in my day, but in a full professional field I'm just another rider, the same as you're just another pretty girl. Honestly, Bobbie, if you marry your rich man I can't see all the rest of the plan working. Just to marry for money is plausible, but not to escape afterwards to some idyllic freedom. Even if this sitting-in-the-sun bit also worked, I can't see you doing it without your husband. You haven't got some darker notion in mind, such as murder, have you?"

The music stops and she comes and sits by me. "No, I couldn't hurt a fly. I shouldn't have told you all this. You're putting doubts into my mind."

"Theory and practice are very different things," I tell her. "Theoretically I should have won the Tour de France six times on the trot. But in practice I never got near to winning. When I tried last year to get a reasonable job in England, theoretically I should have got one. In practice I didn't, which is why I'm still cycling past my time and marrying for money."

She shakes her head and looks thoughtful. "It's tough in England, is it? Hope I'll get a job all right."

"Birds are always all right, because it's mostly women who do the employing. For me it was impossible to get a job there. Have you read the want ads lately? I've noticed how the wording has changed over, say, the past ten years. They now push such things as 'hard work' and 'frenzied atmosphere' et cetera in the same way they used to push holidays with pay and luncheon vouchers. It all seemed to get much worse after Iron Knickers' coup. The sort of thing you get now is 'Wanted, man to sweep up, must be bilingual brain surgeon.' Yet it's funny the ideas people get about the place. Not long ago I got roped into a social do with Paula's friends, and some expatriate English were there. When the job topic came up I gave them much as I've just given you. There was some redbrick flat-chest there with letters as long as an English winter behind his name. He said I painted an 'Orwellian' picture of England, as if I, straight from the labor exchange, was the one out of touch. It was all right for him, with his weekly hamper arriving from Fortnum and Mason's. Bobbie, will you do me one favor?"

"If I can."

"Keep in touch, even if it's only a card now and then. If things don't work out, or if you ever need help, I'll be there. Will you?"

"All right."

"I don't disapprove of your plan, it's just that I have a natural bias toward thinking it should be me you ought to try it with. I'm game, but could only offer a tin hut and Marmite sandwiches. Tomorrow you'll be gone. Life's for living, not buggering about." I take her by the elbows and pull her gently into a standing position. She looks wistful as I kiss her. After a few minutes I unzip her dress. It falls round her ankles and she steps out of it.

6

Give Flowers to the Rebels Failed

I AM STILL CARRYING MOTTIAT'S LETTER in my wallet, next to Bobbie's poem. It had arrived the following morning, just about the time Bobbie left. Talk about the Night of the Long Knives. Mottiat's letter boiled down, in the expected formal jargon, to "In view of the recent disagreement over policy it is felt you might wish to take this opportunity to tender your resignation." As opportunities are things which don't come my way very often, I seized it and sent a four-line reply addressed impersonally to the company. If I stayed on and that bastard put pressure on me, there'd be a killing, that's for sure.

I felt like a great big rubber lemon when I said goodbye to Bobbie. I'm sure she was genuinely cut up. She said she would write and gave me the address in London of some friends she would be staying with for a while. I felt terrible. It was awkward and sad and it rained as it always seems to on these sort of occasions.

Now I'm in a real quandary. I'm not so keen to hustle Susan out of the flat, yet without a job I'm forced more than ever to be in or around the shop. If Susan did go, the way would be clear to marry Paula. I'm white and over twenty-one, so there would be no reason not to marry. It's daft, I know, but I'm sure I'll see Bobbie again, and I'd like to stall things with Paula in case I do. I know it's only a slim hope, but perhaps Bobbie will soon realize the size of the task she's set herself and get discouraged. Don't think I haven't walked around this shop telling myself over and over again that I must be mad, that Paula's a beautiful intelligent woman and that my future with her is assured. Yet when I think of Bobbie I get this feeling like you have when you haven't eaten all day.

Romain's out and about again. He's still a bit stiff and not back to his old form. They've employed the same bloke to train him as is going to manage the international team in the Tour de France. He's a beak-faced German-speaking Swiss who had some successes in six-day races back in the old days. I think he's a toffee-nosed nit, but he's the sort who jumps when men like Mottiat bark, so he should go down well. Romain doesn't go on him at all. He does what he's told and then comes round in the evening to ask my opinion. The Swiss geezer—Harich—seems to me to like lolling back in a car and giving instructions through a microphone. Also, his training method appears to be to give Romain little else but fast roadwork. Romain doesn't need much of this, it's not one of his weaknesses. He needs prac-tice at it, of course, to keep in shape, just the same as he needs to have a go at the hills now and again. But Harich thinks he's learned from my mistake and keeps Romain well away from any rough and tumble.

Paula was upset over my losing the job. I thought it best to tell her the truth about the race and having ridden in it. Naturally I didn't give the real reason for taking part; the excuse I offered was that I had the old urge to have another go. Paula's a great comfort to anyone in trouble. It seems to bring out something in her. I got kisses and cuddles and assurances that I "need never worry about money," all of which helped. When Susan heard that I'd raced again, she showed the customary surprise before going on to giving me queer little looks.

I suppose it's too early yet to hear from Bobbie. As much time as possible I spend in the outbuilding behind the shop, sorting out and cleaning suitable Collectors' Corner items. I sit in this old chair, armed with a tin of Brasso, wire wool, rags, linseed oil and wax polish, working my way through cabinets, swords, pewter, brass, bits of armor, coins, lamps and a thousand and one things. I even find a box full of those miniature china pots in countless shapes, each one with the crest and name of some British seaside town on it. Grandmother used to have a glass-fronted cabinet full of these until a flying bomb fell a few blocks away and plastered them all over the opposite wall. I was told how she cried as she picked the pieces out of the wallpaper. A lot of the stuff's broken, which is why it's out here. It wouldn't be worth Paula's paying someone to mend it, but there's not much that I can't fix with a fourteen-pound coal hammer and a couple of tubes of Araldite.

Paula brings me in a cup of coffee and a plate of biscuits. "How's it going, darling?"

"Okay. My hands are covered in goo. Stick a couple of biscuits in my mouth, will you?"

She laughs as I stretch my mouth to get the whole biscuit in. "You're like a baby bird," she says.

"Hang on," I say, spraying her with crumbs, "I'd better wash or I'll never be able to let go of the cup." I go over to the big galvanized sink and stick my hands into hot water and detergent. As I wash she comes up behind me and puts her arms round my waist. "You big hunk." I feel her rest her head on my back. "Try not to be too despondent. I know you feel a bit useless without a job." As she speaks I can feel her jaw moving against my spine. I wipe my hands and turn round.

"I'll be all right. There's a fifty-kilometer kermesse here next week. Thought I might have a go."

She gives a big smile so that I'll think she's wild about the idea. I'm sure, really, that she worries a bit. "That's good. Yes, you enter."

"Right. I'll have to do some training."

"Of course. Oh, Terry, don't explain things. Do what you want. I know you feel dependent on me, but what's mine is yours. Lie in bed all day if you like. You don't have to do all this out here to justify your keep."

I kiss her and say, "I know."

"Let's just get this Tour de France thing over so that Romain knows where he stands. It won't be long now. For my part I'll marry you tomorrow; today if it's possible. We're married now in everything but name."

I drink the coffee. "A double wedding and Romain with a few quid under his belt will be much better for all of us."

She bends down, looks in an old mirror, and adjusts the chiffon scarf she's wearing tied cowboy fashion outside the jacket of her gray costume. "Did you know I offered Romain some money as a sort of dowry?"

I'm surprised. "No, I didn't. I bet he refused."

"Yes, he did. I admire him for it. I think Susan is lucky to have him. Romain's got enough principles for the two of them. Oh, dear, I think there's someone in the shop." She hurries off, smoothing her costume jacket as she goes. Poor Paula, dear Paula. A person loves someone and thinks that because of this they should be loved in return. But their loving you doesn't really mean much if the feeling's not fully repaid. It's cruel, I know, but "I love you" from someone you don't love means about as much as "I collect stamps" or "I think it will rain later." It seems to me that in all love there must be one who loves more than the other, one whose price is lower. I've never found it yet to be dead mutual.

After a while Romain comes into the shed and flops down in an old armchair.

"What's up?" I ask him. "You look shattered."

He undoes the zip neck on his track suit. "So would you be after a hundred kilometers, as fast as you know how."

I pour some Brasso over the lid of this warming pan that's nearly black with age. "Harich is still pushing sheer speed, is he?"

Romain sighs and nods. "He tells me to be like Coppi and be so fast that there's nobody left at the finish to sprint against me."

It's going to take wire wool on the Brasso to shift this muck.

"Coppi was exceptional. You've got as much chance of developing a powerful sprint as you have acquiring Coppi's killing speed—in both cases nil."

He looks hurt. I go on: "In actual fact you've *got* a reasonable sprint, it's just that you're too timid to use it. Coppi would have won twice what he did had he had a sprint. It was the only thing he couldn't do well. Ask mate Harich what happened to Coppi in the '49 world championships when he did everything he could to drop Kubler and van Steenbergen. He towed 'em for miles and they both out-sprinted him at the finish. Ask him why a superman like Coppi was only World Champion once, why Bartali never was, nor Anquetil. All for the same reason: no great sprint. Also ask him why a lot of undeserving bums have been

World Champion, and if Harich is at all honest he'll tell you it's because they *did* have a sprint. This coming Tour won't even start until it's through the Pyrenees. Just look at a map of this year's course, and look at the riders. You'll all be watching one another so closely that it'll be one bunch finish after another. The Pyrenean stages aren't much this time; they've been played down in favor of the big Alpine cols. Once you're through the Pyrenees, the rest of the race is divided into three sections, each section favoring a specialist rider. For you and the climbers there are the Alps. There's a long hard time trial for the *contre la montre* boys, and some good hard fast stages for the sprinters and rouleurs like van Faignaert. Somebody's got to be race leader, I know, but I think it will be suicide for any of the potential overall winners to lead before the Pyrenees."

Romain picks up a brass New South Wales fireman's helmet and plonks it on his head. "How's that?"

"Gorgeous."

"And if I don't win, who will?"

"Luck—don't forget luck."

"With luck, then, who'll win if I don't?"

"Van Faignaert."

"You think so?"

I nod. I think van Faignaert will win anyway, but I don't want to discourage Romain. "If all the stages up to the Pyrenees have bunch finishes, and if you finish in them as you usually do, you're going to start the important part of the race with a pretty big time handicap, aren't you? Oh, I know you won't be dropped and that you'll be in the bunch, but I want to see you at the front end of the bunch, not the rear. If you lose a minute per stage it will mean making your mountain bid with about a twelve-minute deficit, and that will want a lot of getting back. And don't forget the couple of fast flat stages back to Paris which come after the Alps."

He takes the helmet off and studies it. "Harich wants me to try for the Hour Record."

For a second I think I've heard wrong. "He *what?*"

Romain jumps so much that he drops the helmet. "The Hour Record," he says blandly.

"Good God!" I slump backwards in the chair, clasp my brow with Brasso-stained hand, and close my eyes. "Go on. Let's hear it."

"Harich want me to try at Milan, just before the Tour of Italy starts there."

"In May! You know—everybody knows—September is the ideal month. This is when all the Greats have attacked the record. But you—with no chance at all—you've got to do it in windy May." This has really annoyed me. I stand up and fling the cleaning gear to the ground. "You don't honestly think you've got a chance, do you? Do you?"

He's blinking and looking sheepish. "Well, I might have. Luck, don't forget."

"Luck! It doesn't come into the Hour. Only two things really count: phenomenal class and ability to ride against the clock. Also a lot of meticulous preparation's necessary, and how long have you got? A few weeks!"

Romain gives the helmet a kick. "I suppose you're right. Harich said that if I could ride at Milan as I rode today, I'd get it. He said that if I broke the record, it would give me tremendous prestige to start the Tour with."

I'm so mad that I don't know where to start. For a while I seem to splutter and wave my hands. "Look, Romain, get this. *You* can't break it. Not now, not in May, never. I can tell you what you'd do: about twenty-seven and a half miles, which is a great many of miles short of what's needed to put you in the running. Coppi did nearly twenty-nine

125

miles in 1942, and we both know how many times it's been broken since. And while we're on Coppi, do you know what he said about the Hour? He said it was the longest, hardest hour of his life. I saw Rivière's first breaking of it. The organization's fantastic. Harich couldn't run a fairground stall. I'd hate to organize it myself; in fact I couldn't.

"You talk of pre-Tour prestige. What about the harm it can do if—and when—you fail. And if you smashed the record wide open, how's it going to help you win the Tour? You want to get out there in the kermesses, get the old elbows out, learn how to carve people up. You're a bloody climber, mate, and a good one. Now, suddenly, at the wrong time, with little preparation, controlled by a gibbering idiot, you fancy you can break the record that's the blue ribbon of cycling. You, a climber, on the track. The money and the glory are in road racing, especially the big tours. It's possible for you to win these tours on your climbing ability if only you don't lose too much time on the flat. How many times do I have to tell you this? Are you deaf or something? You fancy you're going to soar in those Alps and everything's going to be fine. Perhaps van Faignaert can't climb, but there are all the other stages, and he's captain of a strong Belgian national team. They'll slice you up something wicked. You're going to have to fight every inch of three thousand miles just to finish respectably."

"All right, all right," Romain says and sighs loudly. "I'm no good and I can't win anything."

"I'm not saying that."

"Well, it sounds like it. Anyway, Mottiat thinks the publicity will be good whether I break the record or not, so they're going ahead to make arrangements. I shall start track training here tomorrow and will go down to Milan in about ten days' time. I'll do all the real training there for two weeks and will try for the record sometime during the week before the Tour of Italy starts."

I know it's not his fault, but I've got to take it out on someone. "Well, pick a nice windy day and make a real fool of yourself." I give the brass helmet a hefty kick and it lands clattering at the other end of the shed.

◆

I sit up in bed, my bowels knotted in anticipation as I reach the end of chapter one, then I close the book and toss it on the floor.

"Book no good?" Paula asks, looking up from her reading.

"Not really."

"What's it called?"

"*Pedaling the Modern Pianoforte.*"

"You're joking."

"No I'm not. I can't seem to concentrate on anything, so I might as well read something that's completely meaningless to me."

She tuts and goes back to her book. The bee next door has been buzzing for hours. Perhaps it's not a person at all; perhaps it's the plumbing. Nobody could have that much to say.

I'm more than choked. Why the hell doesn't Bobbie write? A card with one word on it would do. Something, anything would be better than nothing. Twice I've written to the address she gave me, and twice I've torn up the letters. I know that the minute I post something, a letter from her will arrive. Tomorrow I'll write another and this time I'll post it.

Ever since our chat in the shed Romain has been acting all hurt. I imagine that more than anything he wants to prove me wrong. Good luck to him if he can. It's a subject I'd be glad to be wrong on. He thinks that all there is to the

Hour Record is to ride as fast as you can round the track for exactly sixty minutes. The breaking or otherwise of the record lies in the actual distance covered during the sixty minutes. Now that it's well over the thirty-mile mark it's getting very hard to break. I've seen it broken; there's nothing very spectacular about it. Just one man on his own going round and round, yet it's an unbelievably hard record to crack. To attempt it properly it all has to be worked out to a schedule, with signals given to the rider on each lap. It's so fine now that to fall behind your schedule for a couple of laps can be fatal. Romain is daydreaming to think he'll get far in Italy. There are mountain records to attack, such as Mont Faron. He could have a go at that one if it's prestige he wants.

Surprisingly, I haven't seen much lately of Susan. She keeps to her room quite a lot and seems to be digging into her studies. A queer bird, but not as daft as I once thought. It's not often you get big feet and brains going together.

About two weeks pass before she decides to give more than polite conversation. She chooses one afternoon around four o'clock, when Paula's likely to be tied up in the shop. I've been getting on well with all the stuff and have got a lot of it cleaned, repaired, priced, and stacked in groups. Whereas Paula doesn't believe in cramming the goods and prefers the floodlit egg cup on a velvet cushion filling one window approach, I myself like a bit of organized chaos. People prefer to think they're going to find a bargain tucked away, even if they're not.

"My!" Susan says. "You are getting organized. You've really taken to this, haven't you?"

The Friendly Approach. All right, I'll go along. "I've been enjoying myself, although I'll have to knock it off a bit as I'm racing next week."

"So Mother was telling me. I hope you win."

"Thanks." She's in one of her rare medium states of dress and is wearing a reasonable-looking skirt and sweater. The hair's scragged back as usual, exposing an acre and a half of white forehead and those small bloodless ears. I notice her squarish jaw is well set and that whatever she's going to say is drawn up in a moral square around a brigade of questions. She adopts an awkward stance against a chest of drawers. Five, four, three, two, one—

"How's number three getting on? You don't seem to have been out much lately."

Slowly I start to wipe my hands, just in case I have to clobber her. "I could tell you to mind your own business."

She folds her arms. "Go on, then."

"Mind your own business."

Like Bobbie, she seldom laughs, and I'm given a treat. "No, I'm not being nosy. Silly man. It's just that I care about both you and Mother, and number three does have some bearing on matters. I don't care about *her*, not as a person."

I walk over to her and she looks a bit scared until I take her gently by the arm and lead her away from the door. "Would you really like to know about number three? You would, wouldn't you? You're going to wonder for the rest of your life, aren't you, unless I confess.

I sit her down on a chair and pull up a tea chest for myself. She has a pleased look on her face. "Would you trust me with such information?"

"Why not? You know the one important fact that number three exists. The who-what-why I could always deny if I wanted."

She bites her lip thoughtfully. "I suppose you could. All right, I'm listening."

I give a stretch and a yawn, and start: "She's nineteen,

129

just landed in Europe and is in transit from the colonies to the Mother Country to lay a wreath on the statue of Queen Vic and fire a cannon. You know, the Grand Tour. She came into the shop to buy something and in the conversation the opportunity popped up for me to ask her to dinner. I asked, and she came. We haven't a lot in common, although considering our vastly different backgrounds she's quite easy to chat to. I usually find that with Antipodeans the English language is useful only for small talk and giving directions, and that real communication is impossible. Number three is, thank God, an exception. She appeals to me physically and I find her oddly interesting and attractive."

The questions are lining up as if outside the Gents after closing time. "Why does she appeal to you physically? She must be built like a goddess for you to enthuse."

"No, she's only of average build."

"She appeals to you much more than, say, I do?"

"More than anybody ever has. The appeal is in her face."

She didn't like that answer. "And why is she interesting? Is she clever?"

"No, pretty useless, I'd say. She's got a lot of problems which she thinks are 'her,' but I believe it's just her age. Her main ambition seems to be to lie in the sun and do nothing, and the only way she can get to do this is by marrying a rich man. Which is what she plans to do."

One eyebrow goes up and sends a ripple across the wasteland of forehead. "Then you're out?"

I decide at this point to stop being completely truthful. If people went around telling nothing but the truth the world would go mad. "Yes, I'm out. She's gone on to Ring-a-ding-ding Town to find The Man."

I won't mention the expected letter.

"I see."

130

"Why, looking for reinstatement? Miss being cozy?"

"Perhaps. And is that all there is to number three?"

"Pretty well; she was just a girl who passed through Ghent."

"But you'll never forget her?"

I laugh. "No, why should I? I remember all the women I've known. I shall remember you. Memories give you something to think about in later years. All most of us will get is a plastic cover for our pension book. I remember everything, everybody, even Beryl Franks."

Susan grins impishly. "You've told me about her, but I can't remember what was so special."

I move forward confidentially. "She was the one with the artificial leg who wouldn't lie on the grass in case she went rusty."

Susan snaps her fingers. "That's it! And whom did she marry in the end?"

"A wall-eyed corn chandler from Stowmarket."

"Of course!"

I sigh. "Lovely couple. They deserved each other. I hadn't laughed so much since my operation."

She goes solemn again. "If you could have had number three, would you have turned Mother down? Perhaps it's expecting too much to get an answer to that one."

"I don't know, Susan, I really don't. There are times when I think no and times when I think yes. That's all I can say."

She stands up and gives my shoulder an aunty-ish grip. "Poor Terry. I think a lot of your love is self-love. You always seem to be proving things to yourself. I'd better be getting back. While you're serious for once and in a mood for confession, tell me, yes or no, will Romain win the Tour?"

I put my hand on top of hers and squeeze it. "No."

7

I Shall Return

SUSAN PUTS DOWN THE RECEIVER and turns to Paula and myself. I gathered from the conversation, and can now see it in her face, that Romain's Hour Record attempt has failed.

"He sounded awful," she says. "The line was bad, but it sounded as if he was crying."

Paula puts her arm around her, which is not a thing I've seen her do to Susan before. "If you want to fly down to Milan I'll give you the fare. Terry would drive you to the airport. You could be with Romain in a matter of hours."

Susan shakes her head. "He said he was leaving straight away, but that he was breaking his journey in Paris."

"In Paris?" I ask. "Did he say why?"

She shrugs. "No. He sounded very definite and determined, not at all like Romain."

"Terry, do you know why he should go to Paris?" Paula asks.

"Haven't a clue," I tell them. "It's what I'd do, though, after being made to look a charlie. I'd have a right spree."

"That," Paula says emphatically, "does not sound like Romain.

I go upstairs and leave them to speculate. I not only don't

know why he should go to Paris, but I don't much care. My problem is that I haven't heard from Bobbie. I wrote about a month ago, but still haven't had a reply. London couldn't have swung her so much that she couldn't scrawl a message and stagger to a postbox. To tell the truth it's put me in one of those moods where everyone gets on my nerves, and the only relief I've had has been in the few races I've tried. Not that I've actually won anything, but I have had the satisfaction of seeing off a lot of younger men. Every time I've crossed the line I've thought of Susan's words telling me that I shall soon have to start slowing down a bit, and every time I've pushed myself hard I've half expected to blow up and come freewheeling in looking like death. I suppose I should stop poncing about and try to find a new decision-maker image. In my own sweet way I reckon I'm as daft as Romain. But somehow I can't see myself as a young trendy dad with a model-like wife and two kids named Apollonie and Peregrine.

◆

I hear a car draw up, doors slam, the sound of Paula opening the shop door, then voices. Romain and Susan I can hear chatting away, but at the same time I hear Paula talking and other voices I don't recognize.

"Terry!" Paula calls out. "Could you come down."

I drag myself off the bed and bob down to look in the mirror on Paula's dressing table. After straightening my tie I give my hair a comb, switch off the light, and go down into the shop.

Romain's at the bottom of the stairs with Susan clinging my-poor-darling fashion to his arm. He has on a navy nylon trench mac, undone, and is carrying a special pair of wheels he had made for the record attempt. His face is flushed and he looks cut up about something.

Behind Romain is Mottiat, who has with him a man I recognize as Arthur Downes, an official in the British Federation. I haven't seen Downes for years simply because I've had nothing to do with British cycling.

Romain puts his wheels down and shakes off Susan. "Terry," he says loudly, "have you read the reports yet of my attempt?"

"No," I tell him, coming into the shop and looking Mottiat up and down. "The only paper I read is an English Sunday one. Why?"

Romain strides uncharacteristically between Mottiat and myself. "Then you don't know what I did?"

"I haven't a clue."

He points at me, like an American D.A. about to put the hard word on a bestial blonde in the dock. "This is important, Terry. Tell us what you *think* I did."

I stick my hands into my pockets and my tongue in my cheek. "Forty-five kilometers?"

For the first time Romain smiles and turns to face Mottiat, who leaves the African tom-tom he's supporting and comes over to me. His fat belly looks inviting for a right jab as it protrudes obscenely through the front of his unbuttoned black overcoat. "Hendrickx did forty-five kilometers fifteen. You are very astute, Davenport. How did you know Hendrickx wouldn't get near the record?"

"Because I know him and what he can do."

He takes off his homburg and wipes the inside band with his handkerchief. His jaw sags as he thinks. At last he says, "I won't pretend I like you, Davenport, but the long and the short of it is that Hendrickx here refuses—and I do mean refuses—to ride the Tour without you."

"As manager, I hope you mean!"

"As a rider," Mottiat says slowly, putting his homburg back on and wiping his fat white hands on the handkerchief.

I turn away from him and lean against the staircase. "You must be daft. By the time the Tour got to the tough bit, my In Memoriam notices would be in the papers." I look over to where Arthur Downes is lurking. "Hello, Arthur. Long time no see. I hope you're not involved in this."

He comes over and shakes my hand. "Hello, Terry. You're looking well."

"Not *that* well," I tell him. Downes is a thin upright man with a clipped ginger mustache. Every time he makes a statement he squares his shoulders, clenches his fists, forces his arms straight down his sides, and sucks in air through his teeth. No wonder he never got fat. He had this habit when I last saw him some ten years ago, and it looks even more permanent now. I don't know how he keeps it up; you'd think the endless squaring-clenching-forcing-sucking would drive him barmy.

Romain says, "I've told them, Terry, I'm not riding without you. They can do what they like. Send me to prison for breaking my contract—I don't care. Do you know what they did to me in Italy? The spectators booed and laughed. I've never felt so bad in my whole life. Apparently it's too late now to substitute you for Harich as team manager, so the only way to get you with me is for you to ride."

Mottiat interrupts: "And with you actually in the race, you'd be in the perfect position to get Hendrickx up near the front."

Downes goes through his routine and says, "This is where I come in, Terry. I was in Paris seeing about the British entries when Hendrickx came to see me. We simply haven't got enough home-based pros of Tour quality to make up a full team, and there's little to choose between the ones who are eligible. Our old friend Bert is, perhaps, the one obvious choice, and we've more or less decided on a young Australian rider named Kimber. With your experience it would suit me fine if you'd make up our consignment of three. None of you has, I know, a chance of winning, but if only you could keep the flag flying with some honor until another Simpson or Kelly comes along. British interests won't suffer, either, if you contribute toward a Luxembourger's victory." He's still on the fist-clenching bit as I say to Mottiat, "No. Count me out."

"Please, Terry, for Romain," Susan says.

"Why not, Terry?" I hear Paula ask.

"You've been doing well lately from what I've heard," Downes finally gets out.

But I'm watching Mottiat, who has produced a checkbook as big as a London telephone directory. "If you'll at least start the race and give me your word you'll ride as far in it as you're able, I'll write you a check now for two thousand dollars. This is my personal check and has nothing to do with fees or prizes."

I throw up my hands and sit on the bottom of the stairs. "But you're all talking as if I were some great deciding factor in the race. At my best I was never more than a good reliable team man. I'm thirty-seven and out of training. What can I do? I'd be sucked along in the wake. It takes a team of first-class men to have any sort of control over the pattern of the race. What influence could an isolated veteran have?"

Mottiat loses his calmness and starts to prod fat fingers and checkbook in all directions. "Give the boy advice and encouragement, work him to the front of the bunch, protect him from rough stuff. Nobody expects you to finish the race. Just help him over as many of the flat stages as possible.

Hendrickx has told me you don't think the race will really start until the Pyrenees are passed, and I agree. In fact, it is the general opinion in knowledgeable circles. If only you could get him to the Pyrenees highly placed, how can he lose?" He beams at everyone, dazzled by his own logic, and opens his checkbook again.

"Put it away," I say to him. "I'll have to think about it."

"I'm very sorry," Downes says, "but I'm due in London tomorrow with the names of the three riders whom I recommend. I must know tonight. I've come up into Belgium as it is to see you."

"I don't know." I scratch the back of my head. "Paula, could you give these gentlemen a drink while I have a few minutes with Romain?"

Without another word they fall in behind Paula and shuffle into the small living room behind the shop. Mottiat, who is last, stops at the door and looks round before going in. I take Romain's arm and lead him away from the door.

"Listen," I say, "even if I didn't get dropped all I could do is keep telling you to get up near the front and not to be elbowed out. It'd be easier if I had a record made which you played every night. I might appear to you to be a maestro when we have little carveups down at the track, but put me in a bunch of a hundred top pros all jostling for position, and it's every man for himself."

He grabs the lapels of his open mac and wraps the coat tightly round his chest, then throws the coat open in despair. "But Terry, I *need* you. I need your moral support. You know how fed up I can get when things go against me. I can't get this feel for a race that you have; you always seem to know what's going to happen. And don't try to make out you're so old and useless. No one could ever block you or push you around—and you know it. All right, so I'm timid. I can't change. But as you've said, if I don't lose too much time before the mountains I can, given luck, win the Tour. Knowing that and knowing how you could stop others pushing me around, how can you hesitate? Whatever I make—whether you finish or not—I'll split fifty-fifty with you. There could be several thousand dollars in it for you—"

"Stop it, Romain, you're dreaming again. Riding the Tour isn't just a matter of beating other riders. You've got to overcome the distance, the terrain, the weather, Lady Luck, and your own—everybody's—natural desire to quit. It's over three thousand miles. The international team and Harich won't help you much, so you've got to ride a defensive race against the big combines."

Although he tries to keep his voice down, his natural excitement gives him a breathless high-pitched tone. "Exactly! I'll be alone! I thought you were my friend! Not only do I need your help, but I could make us both a lot of money. One *can* win without a strong team—look what Gaul did in a mixed team. What have you got to lose? Surely it's in your own interest that I should win? Assume I can pull it off. I'd get married and leave the way clear for you and Paula. I thought you would have jumped at the chance. You'll be getting good money, to say nothing of Mottiat's check. Why won't you?"

I don't really know why myself. For several seconds I think. "Mostly, I suppose, because my body wouldn't let me do everything I wanted to help you. Also I'm frightened of the humiliation of being dropped. Pride's a funny thing and I've got more than my share of it. Also it's one bloody hell of a long way. I was thirty-three when I last rode the Tour. When I got off that bike at Paris I said never again, and that was four years ago. But I suppose if you're set on having me, then I'd better ride."

"Terry!" He grips my arm and I feel embarrassed.

"One thing, though. As long as I'm in the race, we play it my way."

Now he shakes my hand. "It'll be a pleasure!"

"Huh. In my life I've hired out many of my talents—most of which are unmentionable. But I've never been paid before for the use of my elbows."

◆

Later, when I ponder over it, and all the Good-old-Terrys have died down, I think what a fool I am. I suppose I said yes to please everybody, but of all those at the shop that night, only I really know the score. The Tour's a monster Goliath that eats men; it's a big hammer. I keep a scrapbook of professional cycling, and at the back I've been pasting certain pictures. Not photographs showing victory and success. They're easy to find. No, my pictures are of beaten men, of great riders who bit off more than they could chew, once too often. I've a picture of Robic taken in the 1959 Tour, riding desperately slow and dropped by the field. He'd won the race in 1947. There's one of van Looy, snapped in 1967, his tongue hanging out, his face covered in sweat, and unable to close with the others. Van Looy! At the back of the bunch! Five years earlier the thought would have sent people groping for their Bibles. I've a very sad one of Bobet, the great triple winner, abandoning the Tour on the Iseran pass in 1959, when he was thirty-five. Of Bartali, super champion, still in the Tour at thirty-nine, pushed down into eleventh place by men he wouldn't have had in his team a few years before. Also I've one of the incomparable Coppi, in tears, beaten in the Lombardia and realizing his number was up. Still, they were all immortals of the sport. I don't imagine many will notice if

I do take a hiding. I suppose, to balance things, you do develop something extra when you're old. You lose your speed, you get tired quicker, but when you get like me and realize you're out of time and second chances you seem to find something else. It could be seen in a lot of old riders who weren't *mentally* finished with racing, old men who still had "the fire of victory" in their bellies. Riders such as van Steenbergen, van Looy, Albert Hendrickx, Bartali, Schotte, van Est. They seemed to develop an extra ability to suffer as a sort of new talent to replace their lack of speed.

Naturally I shall be training hard from now on. The whole Collectors' Corner idea will have to wait awhile because Romain and I will be out on the road every day, whatever the weather. There's this eight-day classic in France: no great mountains, but a tough race just the same. Many big names will be in it. A lot of Tour riders use this race as a training warm-up. It's hilly and tough with a fast pace whipped up by men not riding in the Tour or by riders after selection in the big race. Ten of the T.B.H. team will be entered, although neither Romain nor I has any intention of trying too hard. We'll push things only to help one of our team members. Otherwise we'll sit in, with the accent (as usual) on trying to get Romain near the front at the stage finishes.

In a way I'm glad to be doing something hard again. As we get the kilometers into our legs, hour after hour, I have plenty of opportunity to think of Bobbie, but am usually too shattered at the end to actually get around to doing anything about her. Paula and I had arranged that I go to England to attend an auction sale in London. The date of the sale is about a week before the Tour starts. A two-day break about that time would be a good thing, but I'm keeping quiet about it in case it's suggested that Romain should go with me. If I hear nothing before, I shall do my best while in

London to see Bobbie. Training also has other advantages. It lets me out of the social do's which Paula sometimes gives for her Ghent-domiciled English friends. They're all very "nice" people and easy to small-talk to, but if I met them too often I'd end up in one of those places where they take away your shoelaces and use a plastic tube to feed you. It's all right for Paula, of course, she's such a good chatter and it gives her a chance to be more extrovert than she is with me. If there's anything positive I've got against Paula's friends, it's that they won't acknowledge me. There's some saying to the effect that to recognize a man is to make him your friend. I was not an outstandingly successful professional cyclist, not an all-time great. Had I been, then everything would be dandy. If the gods in News Media had selected me to be In and in their infinite wisdom had said I was brilliant—or if I'd made a packet from the sport—then I might have satisfied the values of Paula's chums. It's not so much that I'm a Cyclist with an Accent, it's that I wasn't a Top Person at my profession. Also they don't go on me because I have wide interests and know a few things and can dress smartly. I'm not In My Place. People like to pigeonhole you. Perhaps what really irks them is that I know them, but they're a bit baffled by me. Possibly these people have nothing, can't do anything, and know nothing much. Yet if somebody else sets himself up in a job or hobby or profession where he's judged by such a talentless mob, then he had better be well acclaimed. You could drag me off my deathbed, put me on a bike, and I guarantee I could beat each and every friend Paula's got. But this isn't enough. The fact that I've thrown away countless chances of winning just so that a better-placed teammate could consolidate his position— things such as this mean nothing to them. It means nothing that to even be a professional cyclist you've got to be athletically head and shoulders above other men. The really annoying thing with all this is that they refuse to talk about cycling or to acknowledge what I've been. They'll talk to me endlessly about certain "safe" subjects, but have a polished yet predictable system of turning any lead which might arrive at My Cycling Career. They just don't want to know. It's a curious English mixture of snobbery, hypocrisy and jealousy, in proportions that are unknown to me.

Paula does not know I see her friends in this light. Without giving a reason, I have made her and Susan agree to keep my Tour ride a secret. Unless Paula or Susan tells them, they'll never know. I mean it's hardly likely I'll be mentioned by the news organs; you have to be winning or In for that to happen. Anyway, they live like typical British expatriates: B.B.C. Overseas News, *Illustrated London News*, and Oxford Marmalade. If and when I get caned in the Tour, I don't want to feed further conviction into their gloat boxes. It would be nice to take such people aside and say, "All right, what do you really *know*? What can you do that I can't?" They're safe because they don't expose themselves, and I don't think there's much there to expose.

8

Crime, Banditry, and Distress

LONDON. WOWEEE! DO-WHACK-A-DO. Hemlines and prices different from last time, everywhere speculation, site cranes, olde worlde greed. Much fyllynge of ye pockettis byfore the Sun Finally Sets. I think I'll nip up to Negretti & Zambra's for a new pair of bifocal pebbles, get my hair cut at Topper's, sell some shares, settle my account at Liberty's and get Purdey to knock me up a quick gun.

This place always has an odd effect on me. I suppose it's home, and yet I've always been so unlucky here. There's this feeling I get each time I come back, as if I were an imbecilic child driven out of the nest because I wasn't "quite right," yet who persists in hanging around hoping he'll be reinstated and forgiven. I was last here back when all that had been reasonably fair and decent was being destroyed for the benefit of a rising rapacious new-rich, to the poor's detriment. I've still got an English twelve-sided threepenny piece on my key ring. It was the last coin I had in my change when I first left England and went to France all those years ago.

Still, I'm feeling very fit. Romain and I rode the eight-day event. It wasn't easy; a couple of times I thought of chucking in the whole Tour de France idea. Worse than those eight days was the training leading up to it, but then training always is worse than the actual race. When the race comes it's almost a relief to get going. I've covered a few miles these last few weeks, I'll tell you. The weather was mercilessly hot. I finished well down on the leader, in thirty-sixth position. Romain came seventeenth, twenty-three minutes down. Neither of us tried particularly hard and Romain didn't play up his climbing ability, in case it made him too marked a man in the Tour.

In my pocket I have a blank check signed by Paula. This is to pay for the purchases in the sale. I won't pretend it hasn't crossed my mind that if I find Bobbie, and she goes with me this time, to use the check to get back my money and to shove off out. Mind you, I can't see it happening, and it would mess up Romain and the international team something wicked. As I stroll up toward Green Park, it's easy to convince myself that I could never do such a thing, but I wonder what I'd really do if things went my way?

The sale starts in an hour. Knowing as I do the sort of people I'm about to mix with, I've dressed for the part so as to blend as inconspicuously as possible. It'll be slow authoritative movements, mouth shut, bidding to be done with slight waves of the catalogue. The last time I jostled with chinless wonders they were reading my best forged references and deciding I Wasn't Suitable. I find it amusing that in a week's time I'll be sweat-soaked, grimy and shattered, pounding along over the French *pavé* for all I'm worth.

Paula's marked the catalogue for the pieces she wants, and by each lot she has written the limit of her bid. Mostly they're china items at several hundred quid a time, which is why she wanted me to attend the sale and bring back any delicate buys. Although she's insured against accidents, there's not a packer born who can safely say he's able to do up a box and guarantee the contents won't be smashed. It always seems that people who handle delicate goods have a personal vendetta against the world, and if they can't actually break the contents of a package then they'll expose it, immerse it, lose it or nick it. The things that Paula wants don't mean much to me, and as far as I'm concerned I'm just doing a job.

There are a couple of lots which I want for myself—not to resell but to keep. One is a collection of early lead soldiers. If I get them—and I'm reckoning on paying eighty pounds —I can in my murky moments, when I feel my mortal coil has finally fused and dragged itself crumbling to the edge of the abyss, take out the soldiers and play with them. These sort of childish games would probably make most people worse, but they always have a soothing effect on me. I know I could buy a modern set of soldiers for a few bucks—but they're not the same. Quality went out with the Lamps of Europe. The other lot, for which I'll go to about four hundred quid, is a cased percussion Unwin and Rogers knife pistol, the sort "grandfather carried in his waistcoat pocket when he walked abroad." I've never seen or heard of a cased one before, so the bidding might be high. Even in my low financial state, I reckon several hundred pounds on a bit of good gear is money well spent and money in the bank.

I won't pretend it wasn't an ordeal, because it was. Even the lackeys, green-baized and on about ninety quid a week, have a way of looking through your armor and into your soul. I got my two lots all right, and most of Paula's. All the small stuff I get into a large suitcase. It doesn't weigh much, as most of the contents are wood shavings pushed in tightly so as to protect the china. A cowed emancipated serf finds me a plywood box the right size for the two big vases. While I wait he puts a carrying handle on the box and packs the vases with loving care. I give him a few pounds and for a second I think he's going to fling himself at my feet and ask me to take him along. I feel like telling him that if things go badly for me I'll be back after his job.

It doesn't take long to get the stuff into a taxi and return to the hotel in Knightsbridge. A wash, a cognac, and I hop on a bus that will take me near to the address Bobbie gave. It turns out to be the top half of an oldish house converted into flats. The woman who opens the door is a housewife, fifty-ish, with short gray hair and a sore-looking clippered neck, and round knees. Lines, into which the lipstick has run, radiate out from her mouth like a rising sun. But in spite of all this she smiles and seems quite pleasant. Bobbie had stayed with her and her husband for about two weeks and then moved into Kangaroo Valley with an Australian girl she'd met, but whom she had since left. Apparently the woman and her husband had emigrated to New Zealand and the husband had worked for Bobbie's father. Bobbie showed up from time to time to see if there were any letters but hadn't been there lately. Yes, she remembered my letter because of the Belgian stamp and Bobbie had definitely collected it. I decide to level with the woman and I tell her that Bobbie and I had had an affair, and that I was anxious to know how she was getting on. She seems sympathetic and agrees to drop me a line as soon as she knows where Bobbie is. I give her Paula's address and my name. We have a cup of tea together and she writes down the address of the Australian girl whom Bobbie had lived with for a while. "Bobbie's such a funny girl," she says. "One minute she's up—quite normal—then she's down and wingeing and moaning and being mysterious, and talking about being fed up with life. Perhaps I shouldn't say this, but between you and me she gets on my nerves a bit."

I should feel angry, but I don't; I know what the woman means. "Love's blind," I tell her.

The Earls Court address takes a while to find, and when I do there's no reply. I have a coffee nearby, then try again. Still no luck. A news theater seems to be the thing and I sit through something to do with a nudist camp, followed by an out-of-date newsreel and a Tom and Jerry.

When I try the room again I hear stirrings within. A chubby blond bird with a boomerang accent asks me what the devil I want. She looks choked and I see why when I spot a bloke behind her in the shadows struggling into his trousers. "I haven't seen Bobbie for ages. Haven't a bloody clue where she is. Gone home for all I know. Wait on; she was going round with some bloke. He was a bit like yourself and looked well off, but you can never tell with you Poms. She said he was an Honorable Something and a company director. It wouldn't surprise me if she was bloody pregnant. Sometimes she used to be sick in the mornings and I think she sent off for one of those pregnancy tests. I remember she wanted a little glass bottle and wouldn't say why. Moody sort of person, not easy to live with. Sometimes she'd babble away, all earnest, and then she'd be quiet. And if you asked her what was wrong she'd say she didn't know what she was. Whatever that meant. No, haven't seen her in ages. Can't help you."

I thank the wench and decide not to leave my address. My first contact seemed more reliable, and one to which Bobbie was more likely to return.

It's dark now, night and neon. The pregnancy bit sticks in my throat, and as I walk along I try to work out months

149

and weeks on my fingers. It couldn't be me—how could it? I have no way of knowing how long it was after me that she bedded with another man, or if at all. I was careful, as usual. All these years and I've never made a mistake. No new-fangled pills with me. Not often, anyway, and not with Bobbie. Instant proof is what I like and instant proof is what I usually get. I must have spent a fortune with that firm. They ought to make me a director, or at least strike a medal for their best customer. I've often thought how ironical it would be if I discovered I was sterile. I think I'd sue 'em and buy myself a Japanese inflatable woman.

Perhaps the blond bird was wrong. Even I've been sick in the mornings, and often looked for a little bottle for some reason or other. Who hasn't?

On this trip I feel there's nothing more I can do. Tomorrow I must be back in Belgium. I could walk these streets forever more and never see her, and as the girl said, perhaps she's not even here. The ridiculous part is that she could be a hundred yards away, in one of these umpteen endless buildings. I walk slower, looking at the faces of passersby, and stand with a group of people looking in a shop window. That supermarket over there used to be a cinema. My mother took me there when I was a kid to see *What's New Pussycat?* We crossed London to see it because it wasn't due our way for a long time.

It's minutes before I realize that I'm looking into the window of a record shop, and that right in front of me is a large chart listing the Top Fifty. I remember her saying that Our Tune was Number One and my eyes begin to search aimlessly among the weird titles. At last I see it: Number Forty-nine. I walk away feeling oddly comforted, back toward the hotel, and think to myself, One to go and I'm out of luck.

♦

"Good trip?" Romain asks me.

"Not bad; got most of what I wanted."

"I wish I could have come."

"Two days at Blankenberghe with your feet up and Susan for company would have done you more good."

Mottiat is acting as genial host to the international team and is giving this all-male cocktail party in his office. Just because the competition this year isn't between trade-sponsored teams doesn't mean there's no trade interest. And Mottiat has his potential winner in Romain and the possibility of a year's glorious advertising. At the moment he's got on his impartial interest-of-the-sport-at-heart face and is playing the big man to Harich, a team masseur, and a Danish rider.

I'm expecting my two Great Britain and Commonwealth compatriots in whose company I am to ride into the Valley of the Shadow. Downes has come to Ghent and is here, stretching and sucking, and making it a Great Day for Us All. Almost certainly the three of us will disappear without trace, unmentioned, unphotographed and unsuccessful. Yet to hear Downes talking between acts you'd think it was a foregone conclusion we'd be finishing one-two-three. Except on the odd occasion, such as when Gaul rode and perhaps this time with Romain, the international team is only there as cannon fodder. It does give the lesser countries a chance to be represented, which boosts the grandeur of the Tour. But it also puts up ten or twelve more men to finish (if at all) way down the list and so make the big guns look even bigger. In lesser teams they usually give it a few days to see if a team leader emerges, and if he does then the others are directed to help him. But I see Romain has been nominated team leader from the word go. Another example of a bit of string pulling and pressure by Mottiat.

Only one of my new compatriots in this corner of a foreign field is known to me. You'll find this hard to swallow, but he really does have the Dickensian surname of Throbnostle—Bert Throbnostle. It's almost too incredible to believe. He's a small bloke, very flat-footed, and has a mouth which usually hangs open as if his nose were blocked. The remarkable thing is that he's not a bad cyclist. His age must be around thirty. He came out here some seven years ago and entered for a minor classic, which he won. This win immediately gave him prestige and he's basked in the glory every since, and although often well placed he's never managed to repeat the success of his very first baptism under fire. Although I like him, he's one of the most ignorant blokes I've ever known. He doesn't seem to know anything about anything. I've seen him ride with unbelievable doggedness, often for no purpose, and when it's all over to get off his bike and shuffle away as if he'd just come home from work. He has an interest in the opposite sex—which is about our only link—but even here he acts oddly. All the talent seems to be in his blind spot; he never appears to notice it. Then suddenly some whore will come along and he'll be in raptures. Perhaps he's conditioned himself to the probable fact that he hasn't got a chance anyway with something startling, so he might as well forget about it. I met him in Paris once with this thing hanging on to his arm. She was about a hundred and twelve and had mauve hair and a big hooter, and close up her face was almost indistinguishable from a coconut.

This is Mottiat's big chance to show off his knowledge of languages. I feel sorry for the solitary Portuguese entrant, as nobody seems to know any Portuguese. He grins at me and I grin back. Harich, who will direct the team, speaks only German, which means the only five riders he can communicate with are the two Germans, one of the Swiss, the Austrian, and Romain.

Downes comes back leading Bert Throbnostle and the Australian rider. As soon as they are in the room, Mottiat holds up his hands for silence. For a while he rabbits on in German, then does a short bit in French. He tries his hand at Danish and it comes as a relief to us all when the Dane pipes up in pretty good English. Then we get the English version, which more or less boils down to a welcome and I'm-sure-you'll-all-pull-together. On Harich's behalf he tells us that there will be no official toleration of drugs and that Harich will give his fullest support to the organizers in discouraging the use of drugs and stimulants. Mottiat then adds—probably off his own bat—that what we take on the quiet is our business and our risk. When he's sat down and cocktails start coming round, Bert and the Australian come over.

"Hello, Bert," I say as I look down at his small brown face and shake his hand.

"Whatto. Right do, innit? Fort you'd slung it in?"

"I did. They'll have to drain my blood before I stop."

"Huh. Vis is Len Kimber from Darn Under."

Kimber looks bronzed, handsome, fit and conceited; he's no more than about twenty-three. He squeezes my hand much harder than is necessary, but I smile back and give as good as I get. To myself I christen him Beach Boy.

"What have you been up to lately, then, Bert?" I say.

"Nuffink much. Up and darn, in and aht, you know."

"How're the birds treating you?"

He shrugs and pulls a face, which I take to mean his luck's out. "Here," I tell him, "watch it with those cocktails. We all ought to be at home in bed eating poached plaice and slippery elm."

They start talking about drugs and give Romain their

assurances that they'll do their best to help him win. So far Romain's kept clear of taking anything, but the temptation is always there and it must be stronger for a potential winner. "Drug" is an ominous word and as far as cycling goes it would be more correct to call it "stimulant." Strictly speaking, a bird who pops an aspirin into her gate is taking drugs, so where do you start and where do you end? I've never bothered with them myself. They weren't too advanced back in the days when I was winning races, and in later years I figured the thing to do was to keep racing as long as possible and to do nothing which might cause me to stop. Personally I'm not against queers, alcoholics, real drug addicts, or anyone, just so long as they don't interfere with me. Probably if I were Romain's age and with his chance of winning, I'd be taking something. Bert does, I know that much. To my knowledge he's been dabbling, yet he looks pretty fit. The reason I'd be tempted to take something would be to help me recover quickly from a bad patch. On the debit side there have been a few riders die through taking things, but it's usually been extreme heat plus the stimulant that's done it. And it's only my personal observation that stimulant takers have shorter careers than those who leave things alone, but I wonder if it's not better to be brilliant (and remembered) for a few years than to drag on virtually unknown as I have.

I suddenly find that the background voices have faded into a sort of rhubarb-rhubarb and that I'm thinking once more of Bobbie. Romain, Bert and Beach Boy are talking about tactics, the height of mountains, wind direction and the strength of van Faignaert and the Belgian team. I wonder if she's all right? I get moments—even waves—of optimism, when I say to myself, Ridiculous, how could it be me? She's probably not pregnant at all, not by me or anyone.

Then something will take my mind off it, and when I think of it again there are murky doubts and I dig up long-forgotten tales of blokes who'd been careful and still come unstuck. I sit there staring at my foot, with a picture in my mind of Bobbie sitting up in bed looking very motherly and nursing a baby, and my face looking sheepishly over her shoulder. "After a time of wonder, born to Terence and Bobbie Davenport . . ."

Beach Boy comes and sits next to me. He's putting on a cool calculating tough act that he's picked up from the cinema or TV. I've noticed he gives wry little twitches to the corners of his mouth before replying to a question. He acts as if he had some Great Inner Knowledge that's denied the rest of us. It's twitching; it's going to speak. He and Downes ought to get up and act together. "What-a-yer going to do? Try for a stage win early on and then quit?" He swills his drink round in his glass, downs it, and sits there pulling a lot of tough faces.

"I'll keep going for as long as I can. Might even make the Pyrenees, with luck. I think the days are past when unknowns were allowed to win the early stages. What about you? What are your plans?"

He smacks his lips and looks directly at me for the first time. "It's my first Tour. I know we're supposed to help Beanstalk here, but if looks are anything to go by I don't give much for his chances. Me, I'll take my opportunities when I see them, try to get noticed—that sort of thing. I don't think there'll be any more national tours after this one. They've only tossed this one in to appease. Yeah, that's what I want: to get noticed and be taken on by one of the big teams. Then, in a couple of years . . . who knows?"

"Kimber wins the Tour de France!"

He doesn't like me grinning at him and tries to outsmile

me. He gets out of his chair and says, "Why not?"

I can see Robert Mitchum and Charlton Heston in his walk as he goes over and helps himself to another drink. If I had to choose anything from Today, I'd have preferred one of the longhaired, spotty, arseless variety.

◆

In the morning we are going to drive to Brussels. Here we'll get everything together, check our equipment, and probably take a short ride and get to bed early ready for the start on the following day.

Paula's been wonderful the way she's stuck to my diet instructions. I know it hasn't been easy getting meals for Susan and herself and then something entirely different for me. Susan is going to follow the race in my car. It's not likely we'll see much of her. The roads are closed to traffic while the race passes, so all she can do is drive to a vantage point before the roads are closed, wait until we've passed and the roads are opened, then follow on to the town where the stage ends. She'll see a lot of France and bits of other countries, but will have to do a great deal of waiting around. But there, that's love for you. The university's closed for the summer holiday and she reckons on bringing her studies with her in the car. One reason I don't mind her being around is that my car will be on hand ready for when I quit, so that I too can then follow the race and perhaps help Romain.

I'm reclining on the settee like a Roman emperor when Susan comes into the room. She has on a gay summer dress and looks quite appetizing.

"Did you see anything of number three in London? I take it she was one of the main reasons you went there." She sits demurely opposite me on a hard chair and tugs the hem of her skirt as birds do on the Underground when forced to sit opposite an ogler.

I put down my paper and look at her. "No. To tell you the truth I couldn't find her."

"How frustrating for you."

"Not at all. I simply wanted to know how she was making out. I saw a woman whom she stayed with, and she promised to drop me a line if she saw or heard from her. As your mother will be forwarding mail to you, perhaps you'd look out specially for one for me from London."

"Will do. And it's all over is it?"

"About as certain as anything could be. She got a note which I sent her, but has never replied."

"In that case I don't mind conspiring. Terry, I know this is going to sound awfully dim of me, but if I'm going to follow the Tour you'd better give me some clues as to what it's all about."

I'll say this much for Susan, she's the one academic I've ever met who, because she knows a few subjects well, doesn't automatically assume she knows every bloody thing. Yes, she looks quite nice today; but having made the break, I suppose we'd better stick to it. If only she'd have a fringe instead of that scraped-back look.

"Clues are all I'll have time to give you. It's easy enough to follow. The race is broken up into daily stages, one stage per day, from one town to another. The overall winner is the man who rides the entire race in the least time. During the race you get the race leader wearing the yellow jersey. He's the man who, at that particular stage of the race, has ridden the race so far in the least time. A man can wear the *maillot jaune* for the whole race and still lose on the last stage. Likewise a rider can move up into first place on the very last stage and so win the Tour but never actually wear the *maillot jaune*.

"I think you've heard Romain and I talking about team fiddles, so I'll spare you all that. A big trade team will pay its big stars many leaves of negotiable lettuce, plus bonuses, that's apart from what they can win. The stars might have twenty supporting riders who cost the sponsors. Then there's all the equipment to pay for. The stars don't neces-sarily win; it's what they can pull in the way of publicity that counts. The star can be an ex-champion, over the hump, or a 'character.' Officially, in this year's Tour, publicity is sup-posed to play second fiddle to flag waving, but don't you believe it. Although Romain is a likely winner, he's only get-ting a fraction of what some other riders earn who haven't a chance of even finishing. They're established and are crowd pullers, Romain's not. He'll probably earn more when he's past winning, in about ten years' time. The winner will divide his earnings among his team and finish up with very little cash to show for his efforts. It's in the months that fol-low the Tour that the winner makes his money—very many more mega-bucks—because he'll enter for any and every-thing. He'll ask for—and get—a high starting fee in all races. It's in these post-Tour races that he must be careful not to crash, because it could rob him of his one big chance to make money.

"In the Tour there are all sorts of prizes. Many of them are silly—such as one for the last finisher. But the important ones are the King of the Mountains (for the best climber), one for the team whose riders' times total the least (the Team Prize), and the Points Prize given to the rider who amasses most points by winning stages, et cetera.

"As I said, the race is run by daily stages, from one select-ed town to another, say from Rennes to Lisieux, then Lisieux to Amiens, and so on. The man who wins the Rennes-

Lisieux stage by two minutes could lose the Lisieux-Amiens stage by one minute, but as overall time is what counts he would still be leading the race by one minute. Compared with shorter races, the Tour isn't all that fast, usually the overall average speed being about twenty-five miles per hour. But for three thousand miles over the highest and roughest roads in Europe, over Belgian cobbles and into head winds, twenty-five miles an hour ain't hay. Okay?"

She selects one of her long butts from a case as big as a cutlery box. "Yes, I think so. It all sounds very hard to me. I feel more sympathy for you, Terry, than I do for Romain. At least he kind of belongs. You're a different generation, out of fashion, and among a lot of, well, 'foreigners.'"

"That's right," I say, standing up. "Give us a kiss for luck, then, and I'll be on my way."

She colors a little and looks wary as I bend down to kiss her, but gradually her mouth opens and her arms come around me. If I didn't break off suddenly and hurry from the room, I know what would have happened; and that wouldn't do me any good just before a forty-kilometer burn-up with Romain.

He's waiting for me downstairs. "I'll be glad when it starts," he says. "I hate this waiting about and the training."

"This time next week you'll be crying for a rest," I tell him. We wheel our cycles down the narrow alley at the side of the shop and onto the road. Tour fever's here all right. As we ride through the town people applaud and call out.

I think about what Susan said. Certainly I'm of a different generation. There's one rider in the race who's thirty-five, a couple at thirty-three, and a few around thirty. For what it's worth, this makes me the senior rider of the Tour. I don't know what she meant about my being out of fashion. I still use Gloria brakes and have twin bottle cages on my handlebars, but she wouldn't know about such things unless Romain told her. Fashion is something I've given up. I can remember being accused of wearing "drain pipes" when the rest were in bellbottoms. Nowadays my accusers wear them much narrower and think nothing of it, and if they wanted to go back to the 1950 style they'd have to have a pair of trousers specially made. Just think of the years it took to get the squares wearing narrow ties, lapels, and trousers. Yet when they do—wham—the tearaways immediately go back to wide lapels and trouser bottoms, and ties like a Dover sole. You just can't win. And she said I'm among foreigners. To me a Frenchman is less of a foreigner than a Scotsman, but I know what she means. We're not highly thought of any more. It wasn't so long ago, before the Square broke, that I could have strutted around here with a brace of leashed Irish wolf hounds, when the mere mention of Light Horse, saber and Gatling would have made them touch their caps and sent them scurrying to wave their Union Jacks.

◆

The Belgian capital might seem a funny place to start the Tour de France. Until recent times the race traditionally started and finished at Paris, but now it only finishes there. Beginning the Tour at various points does give other regions a chance to play their part in the event, but I think the real reason is that Paris is now too choked and sprawling. To close roads leading out of the French capital for a period of several hours does bring an enormous amount of chaos.

With all the paper-shufflers, Brussells itself has big traffic problems. The authorities have therefore closed off an area in the city center that has a wide dual carriageway.

We have signed in, put on our new international team vests, and are waiting our turn on the dais where we are officially presented and photographed. After this we ride a slow lap on the dual carriageway to the ovation of the sporting Belgian crowds, packed umpteen deep both sides of the road. Being smaller fry, we're second off, after the Dutch team. We get a good hand, especially Romain and myself. Me because of the years I've lived here and Romain because of Luxembourg's ties with Belgium. It's like old times again, although I feel a bit sad because I know I'm going to disappoint any genuine supporters I have out there.

The French ace, Audaire, gets a tremendous welcome, but the Belgian team, last off on the lap of honor, has its path blocked by enthusiasts who break through the cordon of gendarmes. The undisputed Belgian captain is World Champion Hendrik van Faignaert. Belgium is the most consistently strong among the cycling countries despite its small size, but has never had many Tour winners. The other two big cycle-racing countries, France and Italy, have periods of brilliance and patches in the doldrums; and the Belgians feel that their own consistency is long overdue for a reward. Van Faignaert is twenty-nine and has ridden in the Tour on two occasions. Once he crashed and had to retire while leading the race, and once he finished third when, if things had gone better for him, he should have won. He's won pretty well every race on the calendar and has been World Champion two years running and is, as they say, *l'homme a battre*. Climbing is his weak point, but unfortunately he can do everything else very well indeed. Even the eleven team men who back him could be, with a bit of luck and support, possible winners. The French hope, Audaire, is a good all-rounder but has just won the Tour of Italy.

It's an extremely difficult thing to do—win both the

Italian and French tours in the same year. It wears me out to even think about it.

It's evening by the time all the hoo-haing is over. As about two thousand people are involved in the running of the race—that's technicians, riders, officials, the press, and the performers and drivers tied up with the publicity caravan—something like a small town is needed to house them. Arrangements will vary from town to town, but generally I expect to share a room with Romain. The race starts at ten in the morning. After we've eaten at a jolly-jolly communal table where I'm sandwiched between Beach Boy and Harich, we go to have a final check on our equipment. Tonight is the only night when the mechanics have an easy time. Most of the cycles are as the riders want them, but from tomorrow onward they'll be too weary to attend to them themselves.

Outside, the city is alive with activity. Stars like van Faignaert are being pestered by journalists, and the hotel where he is staying is surrounded by supporters. Noise at night is one of the big snags I've found with the Tour. It's always holiday time, Tour time, and places that have paid for the privilege of being stage towns want to squeeze as much tourism as possible from their investment. Such things as sleeping pills would affect a rider's performance, and so the only thing he can do if he's a light sleeper is to use ear plugs.

I've got my pajamas on and am thinking about bed when the door opens and Harich shows a man into our room.

"Terry!"

"Jeff!"

"Terry, how the hell did you get in the Tour?"

"I lied about my age."

We shake hands. I haven't seen Jeff for ages. He's a Walloon Belgian ex-roadman who retired a couple of years after I started, but in those two years he helped me and taught me a lot of things about the game. He bought a café but had some trouble with his wife, so they parted and the last I heard of him he had a bar in Corsica. He had spent many years in England, which is why his English is so good.

"How's the bar in Corsica?" I ask him.

"Fine. I married again and my wife's running it."

"What are you doing here?"

He smiles and takes a card from his pocket. "Press."

"What? You?"

He nods. "It's a sort of holiday. I hadn't seen a real race in so long, and the local paper wanted somebody with 'experience' to cover it. I've only got to phone them every night with a little story; they'll fix the grammar and everything!"

"Well, good luck. Sit down, Jeff." I grab him a chair. Quite chubby now, in his mid-fifties, Jeff has gray balding hair, chunky hairy hands, and thick square fingernails. He has a nose like a small new potato, and although his face shines and smiles there's an intent sort of sadness in his eyes. We talk of the old days and bring each other up to date with news.

Romain comes in and I introduce him to Jeff, then he lies on his bed while the masseur works him over.

"Are you going to win?" Jeff calls over to him.

Romain lifts his head a few inches from the pillow. "Ask Terry."

"Yes," I say. "With luck."

Jeff screws up his eyes shrewdly. "With enough luck I could win. What about without luck?" I shrug, but for a second my eyes meet Jeff's and I think he gets my message.

"And so, my friend," Jeff says, "it's your job to get Romain to the mountains as unscathed as possible? This is my very first assignment as a reporter, so I had better look the part and write a few of these facts down." He takes out a note-book and sits sucking the tip of a ball pen. After a minute he begins to write laboriously, his lips moving as he spells out the words to himself. "It's tomorrow, at Arras, when this job really starts. That will do for now." He closes the book and puts it in his pocket. Poor old Jeff; I just can't see him as a reporter. He was a good roadman too, one of the best. I remember someone telling me he was once active during 'events in Paris' in 1968, but Jeff himself has never spoken of it to me.

"You will quit the race when your part is over?" he asks.

"I expect so. Of course I might be out tomorrow, but my intention is to get as far as Bordeaux, Dax, or Luchon. I'll be content to get just over halfway—the easier half, that is. Should everything go well and I don't feel too shagged, I might stay in through the Pyrenees and pull out at Nîmes or Carpentras. When I last crossed the Alps I swore the next time would be in a car."

Jeff puts his big hand on my shoulder. "You should not fear the Alps. Even if you have to go up slowly, you won't be the slowest. And as for coming down—zut!" He makes a swooping motion with his other hand. "You are the fastest descender in the race!"

"I know," I say skeptically. "I'm all right on steep climbs, but it's those endless drags that beat me. Mile after mile after mile—you think it's never going to end. I'm the oldest man in the race, Jeff, do you know that? I shouldn't be here at all. I've lived long enough to know what it's like on the other side of the hill."

"And what is it like?" He laughs heartily and I watch his fat throat move up and down.

I stand up and yawn. "It's the same as this side. Exactly the bloody same."

◆

The teams are drawn up like old-time troops waiting to do battle. Romain, blinking away behind sunglasses and looking very fit, grins at me. I've been trying to act the old cynic and shrug it all aside, but secretly I never fail to feel tense and excited at the start of the Tour. They make such a historic thing of it, with speeches and television and celebrities. There is even a special wavelength put aside for Radio Tour so that people can follow the race throughout.

The Belgian team is getting a lot of fuss. Telegrams are still arriving by the sackload for van Faignaert. The Great Man Himself in the rainbow jersey of World Champion rides slowly past us to his position. A voice he recognizes calls, "Hendrik," and he looks our way, smiling, showing gold teeth and a heavy handsome face.

The commercial caravan has been entertaining the crowds. Large gaily colored vehicles are parked around the sealed-off dual carriageway, ready to move out in the wake of the race. An advertiser has been giving out paper hats bearing the name of his products, and most people are wearing one to protect themselves from the sun. It gives a uniformed air to the crowds lined up in their thousands. A group made up of a politician, a well-known pop group, an important-looking bloke with an anchor chain round his neck, and an old whore with a floppy hat and a poodle walk among our ranks like a party down from War Office. They pause, god-like, and talk self-consciously to some of the riders.

Groups of Belgian fans carry large placards and banners singing the praises of, and giving encouragement to, van Faignaert. Soon it will be French fans, then Spanish, and possibly Italians who have crossed into France to egg on their team. For the whole length of the race you get the

placard and banner bearers, and also the fans who paint riders' names on the road and on walls. When the heat strikes,
locals wait by the roadside with hoses to drench and cool
you as you pass.

The first stage is Brussels to Arras, and it's at Arras that
Susan will be waiting in my car to follow the race.

It's going to be fast and hard; there'll be no hanging
about. Van Faignaert can follow only one course. His team
will push the race to its limit by attacking the whole time
and making riders like Romain suffer. This will ensure that
both van Faignaert and his team stay high in the placings,
never far from the *maillot jaune*. If the pace is a cracking
one, then van Faignaert himself suffers, but being as strong
as he is he probably suffers less. Also a fast pace makes a
break harder. A man on a cycle can only ride so fast, and if
he's riding near to flat out all the time, he's not going to feel
much like trying it even faster out there on his own. I don't
think van Faignaert wants the *maillot jaune* until the Alps
are past. That yellow jersey, once got, is a very hard thing to
keep. He'll want to stay within striking distance of it all the
time. Not being a climber, he must lose time in the mountains, but if he can dish out the punishment before the
mountains so that the climbers are shattered, then he won't
lose too much time to them on the climbs. If all goes to plan
he'll use his team to move him up on the last Alpine stage.
This is followed by a long time trial where each competitor
rides alone against the watch, and it's here that van
Faignaert takes, or comes near, the yellow jersey. Following
the time trial are two long flat stages back to Paris and the
end, and they're just made to measure for van Faignaert.

We're told to mount our cycles. A thousand cameras click.

"Scared?" I ask Romain.

"Yes. Good luck."

"Ta. Keep near the front, always."

The race is neutralized until we reach the city's outskirts, and we ride in a steady procession as thousands of spectators line the route to applaud and cheer. Crawling behind comes the armada of vehicles. We stop at a silk tape stretched across the road and get another short speech while photographers fight one another for vantage points.

The director of the Tour ceremoniously raises his chrome-plated scissors and with a flourish and a smile cuts the ribbon.

Hundreds of throats yell "*Allez!*", timing devices are started, and we move forward giving friends last-minute waves, and slipping into higher gears. The pace quickens and already the regimented lines of one hundred and twenty colorful jerseys are beginning to mix. The first stage is the only one where the Tour touches Belgian soil. And with the adulation van Faignaert has had he'll want to be leading as we cross into France. Already at the front I can see the yellow, black and red colors of Belgium grouping round one man in the World Champion's jersey. The crowds are enormous and are giving van Faignaert the equivalent of a hero's welcome, as if he'd already won. It puts a lot of responsibility on his shoulders and I'm almost glad I'm a has-been with no chance at all. I'll be lucky, dead lucky, to get as far as Toulouse.

Part Two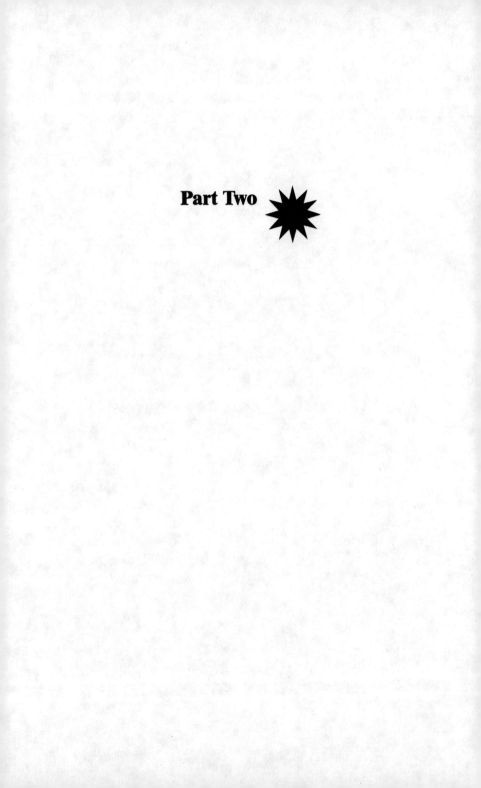

9

We Shall Not Flag or Fail

THE ROAD SIGN SAYS TOULOUSE thirty-five kilometers and there's nobody more pleased and surprised than I am. What a pace! So far it's gone pretty well as I anticipated. I felt so fagged out when we got to Bordeaux that I had definitely decided to quit, but two things changed my mind. On the run-in to Bordeaux some of the hard men had ganged up on Romain, and the next day it was raining, which made a merciful change from the heat of the past week. So I stayed.

Romain, and in fact most of us, took a beating as far as the Pyrenees. He has fought back gamely and made, for him, real attempts to get near the front. A couple of Italians seemed to have it in for him, but I could never catch them in the act. At the end of a stage I took them quietly to one side and in my limited Italian told them that if they didn't lay off I'd fill them in, one at a time or both together. No more trouble.

Through the Pyrenees Romain rode a masterful race that made me really proud of him. Mottiat actually took his overcoat off and strutted around like a peacock with a glandular disease. Before the Pyrenees came, Romain was beginning to show signs of wear from van Faignaert's pace. Once in the mountains, it was Romain who called the tune, and although he took every mountain prime but one (our little Portuguese mate surprisingly took the other), he was never extended. He'd ride at his own pace to within a couple of hundred yards of the summits, taking along anyone who could stay with him, and then tear away to take the prime, collecting points toward the King of the Mountains title and a minute bonus. Yet in spite of this, he has actually used the Pyrenees as a period of recuperation from the hammering he took on the flat. He's looking a lot better now and if he can survive the next flat portion between the Pyrenees and Alps, and can really fly in the Alps, then I think he might make it.

A Spaniard is wearing the yellow jersey of race leadership, and an Italian is second. Both are blessed with grotesque names that have lots of accents sloping in all directions, and I'm tired enough now without trying to get my tongue round that lot. Going solely by facial appearances, I have christened the Spaniard "Butch Cassidy" and the Italian "The Sundance Kid." Third is the French star, Audaire, and van Faignaert is fourth. All these four are close together on time with a matter of seconds separating them. Although Romain pulled back a lot of time in the mountains with his minute bonuses, he is still twelve minutes down on Butch Cassidy and is in eighth position. And me? Well, I'm twenty minutes down in thirty-eighth position, which might sound bad but is better than I'd hoped for.

Not long now to Toulouse; I know these roads pretty well. See that wall over there? In one Tour—I forget which one—I crashed on this spot. There were half a dozen birds sitting up on that wall showing all they'd got. I rode into the bloke in front and broke my collarbone.

Speaking of birds, Susan's still with us, and the thought of that car back there beckons me almost as much as a bed. When she picked up the Tour at Arras I hardly recognized her. She'd had her hair done in a fringe, which, to my eyes at least, is a vast improvement. If I had the time and strength I'd still quite fancy her. She's promised me she'd break her purity pledge—just once—either when I pull out, or on the rest day at Nîmes, whichever is the sooner.

So far they've had no dope tests. I'm quite surprised at this and had expected one early in the race so as to scare off riders from using stimulants. With the race getting harder and the riders more tired, I shouldn't be surprised if those who use stimulants aren't back on them.

I had this funny dream about Bobbie the night the Tour stopped at Dax. You know how sometimes you have a dream that's so real you can't stop thinking about it all day? This was one of them, only worse, because I've thought about it constantly ever since. In this dream Susan brought us our mail, and in it was an envelope addressed to me from London. I opened it and inside was a newspaper cutting, nothing else, no letter. It was from a North London paper, and I don't know why this should happen in my dream, because I've never read any North London newspapers. The cutting was only small and, after the usual blah-blah about Bobbie being on a working holiday and friends stating that lately she had seemed depressed, said that the coroner had declared a verdict of suicide while the balance of the mind was disturbed. In short, Bobbie had put her head in the gas oven and was pregnant.

This really worried me, and all next day on the stage to Pau I hardly knew what I was doing. What with Romain making his breaks, I've had to be on my toes in case he needed help; and while this has pushed the dream to the back of my thoughts, I haven't really been able to forget it for a minute. I thought it would keep me awake more at nights than it has, but I'm so physically exhausted that I stick a ream of cotton wool into each ear and I'm gone. The race doesn't actually touch Marseilles, but if I haven't quit by the time we get near there then I'll confide in Susan and get her to call at the British Consulate. I know the surname of the woman whom I called on, so if there's a London directory at the consulate, and if she's on the phone, then either I or Susan could telephone her. At least it would put my mind at rest. All I needed in the middle of this ding-dong is some big worry on my mind.

Clouds have temporarily hidden the sun, but now it comes out, bouncing off the white road and making me screw up my eyes. I drag my shatterproof sunglasses from my jersey pocket and slip them on. Anywhere in this part of the world one rides in an endless lather of sweat. It starts by soaking you, then blinding you, and by the time you finish you're nearly drowning in it. I honestly believe this is the reason I always did better in countries like Belgium or on the track, where races don't last long. There can't be anything much harder than cycling at competition speeds over the highest mountain roads in Europe in midsummer. There's no way to stop or ease the sweating; my pores seem literally to open like flood gates. All you can do is try to keep it out of your eyes and forget the rest. At the end of a stage I always spend at least an hour in the bath and then stand under a shower until I nearly fall asleep.

I take my feeding bottle containing cold water from its cage and pour the last of the contents over my head. Bert Throbnostle comes alongside and offers me the remainder of his water. " 'Ere are," he says, but of course I won't take it. He takes a swig and pours the rest down the neck of his vest. "Lovely."

"Not long now, Bert."

"Bloody roll on Nîmes, vat's wot I say. A day wiv me plates up, vat's wot I want."

Van Faignaert's squad is controlling the race at the front, but I expect the stages today and tomorrow to be the quietest of the Tour. The riders are tired after the Pyrenees and they're thinking of that rest day in Nîmes the day after tomorrow. After that the dreaded Alps, the time trial, and the drag back to Paris.

Susan has a record of that Götterdämmerung thing by Wagner, and I used to take off the hoi-ho! bit where somebody or other summons the clansmen to celebrate a wedding. When I get the chance, I've taken to riding up to the Austrian member of our team, letting go the handlebars, making an operatic gesture, and lustily singing hoi-ho! in his earhole. Mind you, with the pace being what it is, I haven't had many chances. After Bert asked what it was all about and I had told him, he now rides up when I've finished hoi-hoing and sings into the Austrian's other ear, "Come 'ome Yer bleeder." I haven't a clue what the Austrian thinks of all this, but he always smiles back and nods and seems to take it in good part. I don't think he knows a word of English. Harich has looked after the needs of the German-speaking team members better than he has the rest of us. But I've never been one to covet my neighbor's ox, and so have quite openly adopted the attitude that Harich can go run and jump.

A short but steep hill rises in front of us. There's no prime prize, so Romain won't bother with it, but the descent on the other side might offer a good opportunity for somebody to take a flier and steam into Toulouse alone. Quite a bit of shuffling is going on, so Bert and I pile it on and regroup with Romain nearer the front of the peloton. Beach Boy noses his way past us and tries to get up on his own and join van Faignaert, but in the jostling he gets pushed back and, scowling, falls in with us.

It's The Sundance Kid, second in overall position, who tries his luck. There are only about fifteen kilometers to Toulouse and if he took the stage he would collect a minute bonus plus whatever margin he won by, and take the yellow jersey from Butch Cassidy. A change between these two in overall leadership would not affect van Faignaert's position very much, and so he halfheartedly joins in the chase with the rest of us. The main bunch, tightly grouped, descends at about fifty miles per hour, but the road surface is good, so there's little chance of a crash. It's Audaire who comes out alone from the group and gets very near to joining the lone escapee. In vain two other members of the French team try to join Audaire. Van Faignaert isn't going to let a break like this develop, and he sends half his team to group round Audaire's two teammates. With two other Belgians van Faignaert sets off in pursuit of Audaire and The Sundance Kid, and after about five kilometers' hard work he joins them, hotly pursued by the main bunch. With eight kilometers to go, the whole field regroups and settles down to dispute yet another sprint finish.

Having got Romain fairly near the front, I don't want him to slip back with so short a distance to go to the finish. I shout to him to get behind me, which he does, and Bert falls in behind him to protect our rear. Other riders start to edge their way in, but the three of us stay close and manage to hold our position.

I'm tired and hot, so unbelievably hot. To comfort myself I think of the waiting bath, shower, bed and food; the trouble is I've used this thought every day to cheer myself up and it's wearing a bit thin. I start to think what it was like to sleep with Bobbie, but I never did it enough times to have retained any sharp impressions. She was a marvelous grind, although it'd be no good telling her that. Tell a bloke he's a stallion and he takes it as a compliment, but this sort of talk always seems to make birds feel ashamed. I don't think I've ever realized it as much before, but what a difference it makes when you really fancy a girl or woman. Apart from the odd one here and there, such as Paula and Susan, I've been out with such a load of old rough that I never cared one way or another if they even showed up. And now I'm so tired that I honestly believe I'd turn down the most glamorous bird you could drag out of the Miss World competition. But of course I'll get over it, and here's to that day when I do.

I don't know what to do about Bobbie, really I don't. I realize I'm not in a position to do anything very much, but even a sick man can lash out with his medicine bottle. It would have been all right if she hadn't been so damn young. The Young are always so tied up in themselves, so selfish. They seem obsessed with "What am I going to do with my life?" They want the best from it (we all did), but so many of them act as if they were the only ones who've ever been faced with any choice. And even if at this late date I could have her, I don't know what sort of life we could lead. It'd be a day's work just trying to keep her contented. Financially it would be back to the Bad Times. At least with Paula the Sits Vac page is just something to light the fire with. And those flats they're building in Ghent are really nice. I've always wanted to live in a place with a pond in front of it. I always used to reckon I'd wind up marrying one of the birds in this part of the world—something fiery who bathed in olive oil and carried an infected dagger in her garter. But here, if they're not rich escapees who don't want to know, they seem to be unfriendly peasants whom the old church has got bobbing and hopping.

Now, with the Pyrenees behind us, we are in a greener and more fertile part of France which reminds me a bit of England. For me it will always be too hot a place for cycle racing, but with momentary glances I manage to see some trees and greenery. Scenery is something you can't take in. It's always there but you never see it, and neither do you notice the countless thousands of spectators whom you must pass in the course of the race. You can never be at ease and never let your mind wander for long from the race. Always you're too tired, too hot, too demoralized, too thirsty. The limit of your world is between the leading and tailing riders, and always there's the road in front, winding, ascending, dropping away.

I start to think of Bobbie again, but a rider at the front manages to get clear and again the chase is on. I think he's a rider whose home is in Toulouse and no doubt he's out to impress. Probably his wife and kids, or his girl friend and parents, are waiting at the track side. I reckon the others ought to let him win. But of course they won't; there's no mercy in the Tour.

Buildings start to appear more often as we get near Toulouse. I glance round to see if Romain is still with me. A quick grin flicks across his sweat-covered face as I turn away and try to take him up nearer the front. We press on into the town. The break has strung the field out and it snakes like a giant centipede through the streets of Toulouse and up to the track where the stage finishes. I keep seeing gaps which we could get through, but the pace is so fast that by the time I've built up enough steam to get past, the gap has closed. Literally inch by inch I fight my way to the front, but by then we have entered the track, where I'm just in time to see the local breakaway get screwed at the line by a Dutchman. I drop back and let Romain go through. He rides flat out toward the line and just manages to catch two riders in front and they cross the line together. Bert, myself. and a whole lot more finish next, followed by small and large groups of riders, and finally the stragglers. Not a stage where the positions will have changed much, especially among the leaders. And now for that bath.

◆

Stage 16. Toulouse-Béziers.

"A nice flat stage, compared with what you've come through and what's to come." Jeff lifts his straw hat and dabs his forehead with a green handkerchief.

There're only a few minutes to go before the start. I take the folded newspaper he's carrying and fan myself with it. "Yes, and a bloody hot one. I wish it were Nîmes today instead of tomorrow, then I'd pull out."

Jeff lifts his hands and shrugs, and I see the circles of sweat under his arms. "Why not keep going? You're doing better than a lot of them."

I shake my head. "There's no reason to stay now. Romain will either win, alone, in the Alps, or it'll prove too much and he won't. Either way I couldn't help him. I've done all I can. He could be better placed, but when you consider the opposition, I suppose I have managed to get him higher on the list than he would have got on his own. I can't make any more money by staying; there's nothing ahead for me but a lot of suffering. If I finish the race, all I'll be able to do in years to come is boast to the other old fogies like yourself that at thirty-seven I finished the Tour de France. And I ask you, who'll care?"

He shrugs again and fans himself with his hat.

179

As we ride out of Toulouse I can sense that the heat and the coming rest day have made the stirrers a bit sluggish. For the first time since leaving Brussels the edge has gone out of the race, and I for one am glad. I wasn't going to mention this, but one of the hazards of long-distance racing in the heat is to get a boil right on the bit where you sit down. Now I know a racing saddle might appear to be only a long strip of leather, but actually it's quite comfortable and what's more it supports the weight of your whole body and keeps it off legs that are tired enough as it is. Not that I've actually got a boil, but I keep getting that prickling sensation that makes me think a little private mountain of my own might be imminent. If it comes to anything it'll be just right for Susan to pop in Nîmes. Boils can, of course, be serious. Bobet won the Tour three times in succession but couldn't try again for three years because of this trouble. Van Steenbergen won a world title with one for company; he simply cut a hole in his saddle right in the spot where the boil came. If mine comes up quickly this is what I shall do, but if I wanted a decider to tip the scales over to quitting, then this would be it.

This stage might be flat by Tour standards, but for my money there are still enough hills. I've not tried any of my old desperate descending such as I was once famous for. Either I've had to go down in Romain's company in case he's needed me, or it's been tactical to stay behind him on the road so that I can be coming along should he puncture or crash. On the next stage, Béziers-Nîmes, there are a couple of cols I could have a go on just for old times' sake. I could sort of go out of the Tour with a bang, boil and all.

We come to a feeding station where bidons of cold tea are being handed to the riders as they pass. I seize mine from one of the helpers, toast Romain with it and gulp some back. It's as my head tilts backwards that I notice one of the

French national team ignore the drink and wind it up on his own down the road. By the time the others have tumbled it he's got quite a way. He's a rider low on general classification and the effort, in this heat, of pulling him back would be considerable. I see van Faignaert shrug to one of his team as if to say, The Frenchman presents no danger and it's a long way to Béziers.

It's only after I've drunk my tea and, like everyone else, tossed the bottle, that I notice something about Audaire. I happen to ride near him and see his bidon of tea stuffed in his down-tube bottle cage. Big think. A man only keeps a drink if he's going to need it later on, also Audaire is at his strongest on long flat stages. Then he's got one of his mates already up the road well placed to help him. I look round for Romain, but he's riding quite a way back next to Bert and Beach Boy. If I drop behind and warn him, then Audaire will be sure to go and I'll have lost contact. I try to beckon to Romain to join me but I can't catch his eye and my actions are making the others suspicious.

We come to a dodgy patch of road. There are a series of tight bends and the tar is melting on the road's surface. Ahead I can see the French team car cruising as near to the front of the peloton as it dare. Suddenly I see the team director remove his cap and wave it, and as one Audaire and two of his team sprint from the bunch and ride for all they're worth. I sit right on Audaire's wheel and go with him, taking with me a member of the Spanish team.

The three Frenchmen pile it on, so much so that I daren't even look back to see what's happening behind. Any moment I expect to see van Faignaert and his gang come up and join us. At last we hit a straight stretch of road and I glance back hoping to see the bunch bearing down hard, but all I can see is the solitary Spaniard, his mouth open and his head lolling from the effort. I know we've been moving, but I can't believe Audaire could put that much daylight between himself and van Faignaert in so short a time. Audaire's two assistants get ahead and take turns at pacing him, riding in staggered formation so as to protect their leader as much as possible from the cross wind.

Audaire looks round at the Spaniard and myself and gasps to us in French that the break will work much better if we all do our share of work. What he says is true, but the correct thing for both myself and the Spaniard to do is to be good team men and try our best to slow the break by doing no work: the Spaniard so that Butch Cassidy can catch up and me so that Romain can bridge the gap. The Spaniard has a moment of indecision and then decides to double-cross Butch Cassidy. He comes out of his saddle and stamps his way to the front to help the two Frenchmen. Audaire looks at me and I shake my head. My job is to stay fresh so that when I see Romain fighting his way up I can drop back and pace him to Audaire. It hasn't escaped my notice that the Spaniard who's leading us at the moment is normally in the same trade team as Audaire. When he gets home they'll probably stand the bleeder outside Barcelona jail and shoot him, and the money Audaire will give him for his help (especially if the break works) will buy him one first-class funeral, with castanets.

I feel fairly confident of being able to hold on to the others, but the way they're going I wouldn't last long if I did my ration of work. If only I knew what had happened to the bunch. Again I look back but can't see a thing. Suddenly several team cars, my own included, come toward us going like the clappers in the direction from which we've come. I try to shout to Harich but he either doesn't see me or doesn't want to. Someone in the French team car says something to

Audaire, who looks back quickly before gasping the news to his mates. All I can gather is that there's been a crash.

Ahead is the lone Frenchman who had been the first part of this well-planned break. He's riding slowly, but quickly joins in with the task of sheltering Audaire. Now that all the interest is centered somewhere back down the road, I notice the French team car switch to the opposite side and drive at a speed slightly faster than the breakaways. This has the effect of not only sheltering them from the wind but also of pacing them. It's not often a team car gets a chance to do this, because it's highly illegal, but I think many of the cars would do the same given the opportunity.

The other five riders ignore me; they ride and relay as if I didn't exist. The stakes are high for all of them, and whether or not they tow an old rider who's a member of a mongrel team does not matter one way or the other to them. They work with such frenzy that I wouldn't care to get under their feet.

We thrash on toward Béziers. I'm nearly out of water and so take only an occasional sip to keep my mouth moist. Then, to make matters worse, I drop the bottle as I pull it from its cage on the handlebars. My hands are slippery with sweat and the bottle shoots from my grip like a wet piece of soap and clatters away into the gutter. The dormant boil seems to hear the clattering and takes it as a cue to start throbbing. By observing the road signs and my watch I estimate Audaire's group is averaging around thirty miles per hour, which is good considering the sharp cross wind. Audaire takes the flask of cold tea, which he's kept since before he made the break, and passes it to one of his team. The man drinks and hands it to the next man, and so on; but I get nothing.

More jabbering passes between Audaire and the team car,

and whatever news they get seems to buck them, because they pile it on even more, if such a thing were possible. At last a motorcycle comes through with a ciné cameraman seated on the pillion. As they pass I ask in French what has happened to the bunch, but they ignore me and go up to Audaire and start filming him. He acts suitably grim and determined, and the motorcycle does a little bit of crafty pacing before an official car comes into view. Finally, at long last, a press car comes along and I search desperately for Jeff's face. He leans across the man next to him and waves from the window. "Terry!"

I have to gasp above the noise of the motor. "What the hell's happened?"

Jeff cups his hands. Fortunately he doesn't try to give me a blow-by-blow account, and has the good sense to shout only the bare facts. "Panic to chase Audaire. Wet tar. Skids, big crash, nearly whole bunch involved. Dutch team car skids, piles into riders sprawled in road. Many hurt, one badly. Faignaert concussion, delayed but still in race. Romain's cycle smashed and long delay getting another. Other highly placed riders held up by injuries. Mostly together in bunch about thirty minutes behind. They're finding their pace again, but Audaire actually gaining on them. This is the Big Break, Terry. Like in 1960."

It's all too much to digest and it will take me some time to work out the implications. "Got a drink?" I croak.

Jeff disappears behind the man nearest the window and pops up some seconds later with a bottle. "Only Coke. Don't swallow it."

It's advice I don't need. I rinse my mouth and spit, then repeat the operation until the bottle's half empty.

"I'll try to get you something," he calls as the driver gets fed up with cruising by me and puts on a spurt so that the reporters can observe Audaire at closer range. Where, I wonder, are all those sporting spectators you always see in photos passing out water to riders as they pass. They're like bloody coppers—never there when you need them. I curse Harich even though I know he's right to stay back there with Romain and the rest of the team. All I wish is that he'd shoot forward long enough to give me a drink and some grub. I had only a few glucose tablets with me and have eaten them. It's getting so hard now to hang on to Audaire's group that my mind will only cope dimly with the news Jeff gave me.

I don't know for sure the positions held by Audaire's supporters before the break, but if we're a half-hour up it must be Audaire leading the race by a tremendous margin. His mates will fill the next four positions and I must be sixth. It's very nice to be so high on the list (actually I have been higher a couple of times in the past), but a fat lot of good it'll do me. A miss is as good as a mile and I might just as well be two hours down. I can't, at this moment, see anything to stop Audaire from winning the Tour.

Audaire's a queer sort of bloke. He's aloof and strikes me as being a bit better educated than the usual run of pro. For about two years he's been out of favor with the French public because of the way he's lorded it over French cycling as a whole. He did all he could to get trade teams for this year's Tour but lost out in the end. When you're a very rich megastar you can carry a lot of weight on how things are run. His recent win in the Tour of Italy has done a lot to restore his image, but I think quite a few behind-the-scenes boys have got it in for him.

At last I get a bottle of water from a spectator. Although I'd like to, I don't drink it all and pour half of it over my head. News of the break has brought out spectators in their thousands, all there to cheer Audaire to an almost certain victory. When I hear the news that the main bunch is still in one piece, thirty-two minutes behind, I think that all Romain can hope for now is the Mountain prize.

Tablets which look like glucose are passed to the four Frenchmen and the Spaniard, although for all I know they could be some super boost to make them go even faster while van Faignaert is too low to hit back. Perhaps it's because we're getting near to Béziers, or perhaps it's my imagination through being very tired, but the pace does seem to go up. The crowds are thick and press so far forward into the road that they shelter us from any wind. If Romain's going to show, he'd better show quickly. I look back down the long straight road and can see nothing but team and press cars, motorcycle escorts and row after row of shouting faces turned in our direction.

Audaire's four helpers look all in from the pace they've held. As they gasp and glisten, Audaire himself finally goes to the front to make his supreme effort. He looks round, glances at his watch, selects a gear, and goes. This lad's not a star for nothing. He doesn't even look back to see if his men can stay with him. One of the Frenchmen cracks and falls behind, his legs and jaw shaking like a birthday jelly. It's not that I'm stronger than he is, it's because he's done a lot more work.

Audaire is about fifty yards ahead and the crowd has gone crazy. I'm down on the bars as low as I can get, in my highest gear, with a knot the size of a cannonball in my stomach. The blinding sweat forces me to keep closing my eyes, and when I open them again I expect to see I've lost contact with the wheel in front. I daren't even relax long enough to wipe my forehead. By blowing upward I try to keep the sweat from my eyes, but my jaw seems to have taken out a mortgage on a sagging position and the effort's wasted.

The sweat that runs into the corners of my mouth has a bitter tang and reminds me of the taste Bobbie's silver lipstick had. I suppose if I hadn't wanted to show off to her, I wouldn't be here now. That was the first link in the chain of events. If I could, I'd laugh. I try not to think about her, but I suppose I might as well. In a small way it helps me forget what is now an acute physical agony. Really, it's like when you have a dog which grows old and dies. You're upset, but probably it's more because that dog represents a chunk of your life that's past and ended. It could be like this with Bobbie. It's not so much she as a person but more because, in all probability, she's the last really young, truly attractive girl I'll ever have. And I couldn't have held on to her for long. Bobbie: what a silly name. I don't even like it very much.

I come to as the Spaniard slumps over his bars and veers across the road like a metho trying to ride a bike for the first time. All I manage to see as I sneak a glance round is him riding slowly in the gutter. I know what happened; he came near to blowing up but just stopped in time.

There're no sprints or anything as myself and two Frenchmen freewheel across the line together at Béziers. Audaire is already surrounded by press men and well-wishers. I almost fall off my cycle and lie there in the road gulping in air, pressing to my head a cold towel which someone's given me. Now that the slight cooling you get from cutting through the air has ceased, the heat hits me in waves as if I am being pushed slowly toward a furnace. I watch the other Frenchman and the Spaniard come in, looking like two ghosts in search of somebody to haunt.

A couple of reporters ask me what I think about it all and I tell them the truth, that it was hard and fast and until I've heard the official times I don't know what to conclude. I wait until Jeff's done his duty at the Audaire shrine, then he comes over and helps me to my feet. He knows from his own hard experience that at times like this you don't want to talk, so he wheels my cycle with one hand and guides me toward the hotel with the other. As we get near, two Tour officials come up and ask me if they can accompany us to my room, where they would like me to give a sample of urine. Me, I don't care what they do. They can pop my boil while they're at it. It's starting to come up, anyway. They insist on watching me in case I'm doped to the eyeballs and slip the bottle to Jeff for him to fill up.

Our hotel overlooks the street where the stage finishes. I'm just easing my aching carcass into the bath when I hear the crowd cheering and applauding below. In the room outside I see Jeff walk to the window and open it.

"They're finishing," he calls out.

I grunt and slide down into the bath so that my chin rests on the water.

Jeff comes in, writing away for all he's worth. When he stops I ask him, "How far down were they?"

"Give or take half a minute—thirty-five minutes down."

I study the tips of my toes, which look like a row of peas floating at the far end of the bath. "Which means if I was twenty minutes down when we set out at Toulouse, I'm now fifteen minutes up on whoever's the highest-placed rider in the bunch that's just finished, and that's probably van Faignaert."

Jeff nods briskly and mops his forehead. "You must keep going, Terry. You could finish in the first ten."

"After what I've just been through I don't think I'd keep going to finish third. Say I could finish in the first ten—or the first five. There would be no money in it for me, not a bloody penny. And come this time next year, who's going to remember or care? It'd be important if I were riding my first Tour; it'd put me among the possible favorites for next year's Tour. But me, I'm finished." I stick a big toe into the mouth of the cold-water tap and give it a wiggle.

Jeff sighs loudly. "I'll go and see how they've all fared. Romain should be here in a minute."

He goes out. I know I should have waited at the finish, or had a quick shower and gone back, but I'm so creased up that all I want to do is lie still.

Something like half an hour passes and nobody comes to the room. The water's getting chilly, so I get out and stand under the warm shower. When I'm dried and have put on a pair of shorts and an aertex shirt, I glance out of the window. Below me the crowds are standing about expectantly and there are even riders still talking to press men. I assume the sprint must have been a close one and they're still waiting for the result. It can't be the badly injured rider they're waiting for; he would have gone back to Toulouse. I collapse onto the bed and close my eyes. The sheer bliss of it. Cycle racing certainly makes you appreciate simple pleasures.

I feel myself jump as the door suddenly flies open and Jeff comes in leading Romain. Even now I don't get up. "How are you?" I ask Romain as he sinks wearily onto the bed next to me. He has a bandage round his head and another on one knee, and is still wearing his racing outfit.

"Temporary dressings," he says, "until I've had a bath. God, what a mess. You should have seen it, Terry. Vliani was really hurt—a cracked skull, I think. You didn't know him, did you? Poor devil. It certainly shook me up. When I tried to ride, my legs wouldn't stop shaking. After the crash it was like a battlefield. There's no chance of my winning, not now. Still, you made out. Good old Terry—quarter of an hour up on van Faignaert."

Jeff goes into the bathroom and turns the water on for Romain.

"Are the cuts bad?" I say to Romain.

He frowns. "No, not too bad. It was the gravel that did it. I expect my leg will be a bit stiff tomorrow. Actually I got off lightly. Van Faignaert was out cold for several minutes, and groggy for a long while afterward. You've got to hand it to him, though, he's as hard as nails. Once we got going it was he who did most of the leading, but even after the shock had worn off a little, we still couldn't catch Audaire. He must have ridden the race of his life. I'm pretty sure it was all part of a plan. Impossible to prove, I know, but I saw how it started. One of Audaire's men—Leseur—rode into the back of van Faignaert and sent him flying. It could have been an accident, but I doubt it. I'm sure it was a suicide attempt to stop the Belgian. The coincidence of Audaire attacking at the same time is too much."

I go to answer, but my eye catches Jeff standing in the bathroom doorway drying his hands on a towel. He has a strange, excited look on his face. He comes toward us and says, "I've just been letting you two put each other in the picture before I tell you something."

"Like what?" I say.

Still wiping his hands, he comes and sits on my bed. "They're taking dope tests on the first ten riders to finish. Audaire refuses to give a sample and he's got"—Jeff looks at his watch—"another quarter of an hour to make up his mind. The other four riders in the Audaire break gave samples which have been proved positive." He looks at me craftily, grinning, his round face shining with perspiration.

I'm half off the bed in semi-standing position. Romain is next to me, already standing, his blinking eyes making the bandage move on his forehead.

"You mean—" I start to say.

Jeff slaps his hands together. "As yet I don't mean anything. We'll soon know. I'll leave you to think about it." He takes Romain and leads him, dazed, toward the bathroom. "At the moment the most important thing is to get this lad bathed so he can get some proper dressings on. All this should be Harich's job, but I don't suppose he can drag himself away from the grand conference they're holding downstairs."

◆

It must easily be the longest half-hour I've ever known. Romain, scrubbed, still blinking, and wearing the temporary dressings, sits opposite me in silence. Jeff stands by the window looking at the street below. Occasionally I swallow, which inside my waiting poised mind sounds like a rock being dropped into a deep well.

Harich comes in first. I'm sure he's visibly aged since I last clapped eyes on him this morning. Behind him are the director of the Tour and two senior officials. Harich goes to speak to me, but realizing I don't know any German, addresses Romain. When he's finished, Romain looks slowly at me and in a voice that is little more than a movement of his lips, says, "They've disqualified Audaire and the other four. They're giving you the *maillot jaune*."

I'm not really conscious of what they do. I think they shake my hand and mumble platitudes. They go out of the room and leave me with a neatly folded and pressed yellow jersey in my hands. It must be the quietest presentation in the history of the race. The only reporter present is Jeff; all the rest are still busily interviewing Audaire. When I've seen this sort of thing before there have been laps of honor, photographs and speeches. It's almost as if they were having me on—playing some sort of huge joke. I can see that neither Harich nor Romain has coped with it. They both sit stunned, their minds working their private thoughts. I turn the jersey over slowly in my hands. That damned sorry symbol, Christophe once called it. Jeff grips my shoulder and whispers so that Romain can't hear. "Terry, you can win!"

◆

The reporters have gone and Susan has arrived. At least their coming made everyone snap out of it. Romain picks up a couple of used flashbulbs and tosses them into the rubbish basket. The French reporters weren't very happy. "How long do you think you'll keep the jersey?" "How does it feel to have stolen the race from under Audaire's nose?" These were the sort of questions they asked.

Harich doesn't like it at all. He makes out to be glad and shakes my hand, then slips away to phone Mottiat. Every phone in the town is occupied or booked, but Susan has reserved a call to Paula in Ghent for ten o'clock tonight.

I think that Romain has finally thrashed out at least some of it. He sits on the bed and says, "Terry, could you win?"

I throw up my hands and sink back onto my pillow with a sigh. Jeff appears between us and says to Romain, "Of course he can."

"You forget," I say, "that I'm only in the race to help Romain."

"But Romain's twenty-eight minutes down on you!" Jeff bangs his big fist into the palm of his hand.

"I know, I know, Jeff. But there's only one way I can go— backwards. All Romain can do is gain."

Jeff bangs his fist again. "But he's twenty-eight minutes down. It's he who should help you!"

192

"Jeff, you and I are both old men; naturally you'd see it my way. In reality it's van Faignaert who's got the best chance."

"No!" He cuts the air emphatically with the edge of his hand. "Romain has more chance than van Faignaert because from now on it's mostly big mountains."

I prop myself up on my elbows. "But van Faignaert's a bloody good descender and Romain is not; and he's got a full team behind him—Romain hasn't."

"Will you two experts shut up for just one minute and give Romain a chance to speak?" Already Susan's fringe wants trimming and she brushes it with the back of her hand the way Bobbie used to.

Jeff sits heavily on Romain's bed and grunts.

"I'm sorry," I say. "I got carried away. Let's hear from you, Romain."

He gets off the bed, cupping his head wound in his right hand. After a few winces he draws himself up straight. As if he were addressing a meeting, he says, "Terry is my best friend. If I'd been as alert as he was, I too would have caught the break. He has the yellow jersey and a half-hour lead on me. We are in the same team. Terry will never have another chance; I'll have many. Do I really have to tell you that I'll do everything in my power to help him?" He sits down quickly and holds his bandage again.

I look at Susan. I don't think she herself knows what to think. Jeff shakes his head and looks pleased.

At last I say to Romain, "If you attack hard from tomorrow onwards you could make up your loss on van Faignaert. On the other hand, if you hang around helping me to fall back, there won't be enough race, or mountains, left for you to gain any time in. As I see it, if you help me, we both lose. Oh, I know you'll get the Mountain title and I'll have been *maillot jaune* for a few days, but if you attack now and forget me you can win the race. Susan, nag him, will you? Nag some sense into him."

She stamps one of her long feet on the floor. "Oh, don't ask me! I want you both to win."

Romain says as he stands up again, "There's nothing more to discuss. It's Terry who must win. He owes it to himself, for all the good luck he never had as a young man. I'm off now to get these dressings changed, ready for going to bed."

"I'll come, darling," Susan says, and they go out together.

As Jeff and I look at each other, one of his eyebrows goes up and stays fixed in that position. "Well, what are you looking at?" I say to him.

"At the winner. Who else?"

"The winner!" I say contemptuously.

"You remember Cerami? Giuseppino Cerami?"

"Of course. And I know what you're going to say."

"Let me remind you, in case you've forgotten. He turned professional in 1948, and it wasn't until 1957 that he won anything important. Then, in '58, '59, nothing. But in 1960—how old was he then? thirty-eight?—he started winning: Paris-Roubaix, Flèche Wallonne, I forget the others. And of all the tours he rode in he never won a stage—until . . . until he was forty-one. Bordeaux-Pau it was, in 1963."

"Yes, I know all that, and if I remember rightly he didn't finish the '63 Tour."

"Ah, but you're going to be different; you can pull it off. Cerami won a stage. You have a fifteen-minute lead. Think also of van Steenbergen and van Est, both going well at thirty-seven."

"Not on the road, they weren't. Leastways, not in the Tour. God, when I think about it! Why the hell didn't this happen to me ten years ago? Why? Why? Ten years ago and a fifteen-minute lead, there wouldn't have been a man in the world who could have stopped me. It has to happen now. It took today's ride to show me how old I'm getting. I know I kept up, but when you get to my age it takes you so much longer to recover afterwards. I won't pretend to you, Jeff. I've known you too long. Of course I have a spark of hope that I might pull it off. I know, as you say, that it is just possible. But you must agree that in the long run Romain is a safer bet than I am. And for my money, van Faignaert is still the man to beat."

His chubby face is dead serious. For a second I think back to when it was lean and he had hair. "Like me, Terry, you were never lucky. This is life's last chance. Take it. Romain can win next year, and you can direct his victory from the comfort of a car. Take your chance, Terry."

◆

I hardly slept a wink. My mind raced on, with my thoughts a knotted mess of minutes, kilometers, gradients, heat and sweat. Twice I dozed off and for a while I dreamed the Bobbie dream again. Not all of it—just the part where I open the envelope and take out the newspaper cutting. It was really a repeat dream, in exactly the same detail and just as disturbing. When I get to Nîmes—that town a million miles away—I think I'll see the Tour doctor and get some sort of mild sedative that won't affect my riding.

The boil's coming up worse, so as soon as it was light I got out of bed and bathed the damned thing. Then, when I could get to my cycle, Jeff and I cut a hole out of the left side of my saddle for the boil to poke through. One of my thoughts during the night was that Paula's friends must now know about my riding. Dainty-tea eyebrows will be raised to the regulation watermark this morning over several breakfast tables I could name. And if I fail, what will they say? "I don't believe he ever was actually *much* good." When I phoned Paula last night she didn't sound as pleased as I had expected. You know how the Right Sort always put it on and go a bit gushing? Although, as I say, I'm very fond of Paula, she does have this way with her like they've all got. Only last night she didn't seem to have it. Still, perhaps the news stunned her.

Harich has kept himself to himself and isn't behaving at all like a man with two potential winners on his hands. I gather Mottiat is going to be waiting for us at Nîmes, where I'll bet you anything you like he'll try to persuade Romain not to help me.

Bert, Romain and myself talked about cooking up some plan, but other than sticking together there seems little we can do. It will be impossible for me to actually gain any more time, so all that the three of us can do is try and stop me losing too much of my lead. The nearest riders to me on overall classification are van Faignaert fifteen minutes three seconds down, Butch Cassidy a further minute behind the Belgian, and The Sundance Kid another thirty-seven seconds down. So our course is simple: Where these three go, we go too. I've only (I say only—it's a word I've got hold of) to stay with them to keep my fifteen minutes intact.

We ride out of Béziers with 189 kilometers of uncertainty before us until we reach Nîmes. Many of the riders, and in particular van Faignaert, look a bit stiff after yesterday's pile-up. In my prime, or with a full team, I should have attacked now before they can get into their stride. But to be stuck out there alone or with little help for five hours isn't exactly a happy thought. The crowds are big for several miles, but then suddenly peter out. I think the mob that descended to see Audaire make his kill stayed around out of curiosity to see what the new *maillot jaune* looked like.

The yellow jersey after all these years. To tell the truth the one they've given me is rather tight, no doubt part of some dirty French trick to restrict my breathing. I feel a bit like when I first had winkle-pickers and started to shave.

The country now is getting harsher, more barren and dusty. It's not long before the Belgian team starts a break. Away go two of them in an attempt to get themselves a few kilometers ahead, ready for when God breaks and joins them. I make no attempt to follow; I'm not going to kill myself chasing two blokes who are probably about an hour down on me. After half an hour two more Belgians get away, but take an assortment of other riders in their wake. Quickly I assess who, and how low on classification, they are. One of them's a bit near, but I chance it and let them go. It won't be long now. I glance round to see that Romain and Bert are close, and a panic seizes me when I see that they are not. Two Belgians have edged their way in between us, not so much to separate me from my "team," but more to block Romain's path so that he'll miss the break. And I can't drop back or I'll lose contact with van Faignaert on whose rear wheel I'm sitting like a broody hen.

"Romain! Get up here!" I shout over my shoulder. I look round again and see his worried face and blinking eyes bobbing up and down between and behind the two Belgians.

Fortunately it's Bert who does it. He rides up behind one of the Belgians and grabs hold of his jersey, and Romain nips into the space that the Belgian rider was occupying a few seconds before. And he's just in time. I'm watching van Faignaert very carefully and can sense he's getting ready. He goes and I go with him. Behind us the whole bunch gives chase, and although I stay directly behind the Belgian leader, I'm powerless to stop the rest of his team riding up on all sides of me. After a while van Faignaert eases, and part of his team goes to the front to do the pacing. Romain isn't behind me but has got himself placed to one side, out on my right. I'm literally surrounded by Belgian riders, completely boxed in, but still holding my trump card by sticking like glue to van Faignaert.

It must be for about twenty kilometers that they keep the pace going, during which time the field gets broken up into several groups. I've lost sight of Butch Cassidy and The Sundance Kid; all I know is that they're behind me, and that's all I care about. Somewhere down the line Bert got dropped, but Romain is still to my right.

After sixty-five kilometers we come to the Col du Vent, one of the lesser, third-category climbs, and here we catch the four Belgians and the others who had earlier broken away. Although our leading group now consists of some thirty riders, the whole Belgian National team of twelve is there, plus three from the Belgian "B" team, whose loyalties lie you-know-where.

Effortlessly Romain goes to the front on the climb, but try as I may I haven't the strength to join him. Fortunately, neither has anyone else and so we plod up the long rocky mountain road, sheltered in places by pines. Van Faignaert turns on the heat during the descent on the other side and here our group splits into two, the descenders in the front lot and the more timid in the second. It's not long before the two lots regroup, and again the Belgians turn the gas up. I begin to get very weary, which I attribute more to the lack of sleep than to the racing. Ahead now is another lesser ascent, the Col de Rogues, and the pattern of the last climb is repeated.

Not long after we're down the col, Romain punctures. By a miracle Harich isn't far behind in the team car, but by the time they've done a fast change with Romain's rear wheel there's a quarter-mile gap between Romain and myself. Anyway, I can see that van Faignaert is getting fed up with not being able to shake me off, and he takes Romain's puncture as a cue to start getting tough. The road's still hilly and broken, and when we are out of sight of officialdom and cameras, the old jersey pulling starts. Two of them grab me, one from each side, while van Faignaert draws away. I lash out backwards and catch one of them on the side of the face. He lets go. Before I can get my right hand back on the bars ready to let go my left and clobber the other puller, he releases me and sprints ahead, blocking my path. Five riders spaced across the road can effectively block it, and this is what now happens.

We top a rise and for a few seconds are in full view of the following vehicles, so my five friends thrash about as if they're really going, trying to make it look as if I've just that second arrived behind them. The road drops down, and ahead I see a winding tricky descent. I'll have to act quickly, because if I'm to catch van Faignaert this is the place I'll do it. Behind is a string of riders from various teams. I can see no vehicles yet, nor any sign of Romain. From its retaining clips I take my pump and ride hard until I'm a couple of feet from one of the Belgians. Using the pump as a saber, I bring it down plonk in the middle of the bloke's back. He lets out a groan with a timbre midway between a smoker's cough and the sort you give on receiving an envelope marked Your Tax Return. He loses control. I'd hoped he'd crash into one of the others, but he rides into the bank and goes sprawling. The others try to block me, but I ride straight at them with the bent pump held low, ready to thrust into anyone's spokes. When they see the position of the pump and the look on my face, they melt away like virgins before a roaring rapist waving his trousers.

I toss the pump, go straight into top, and start winding. It's not a long hill so I'll really have to move. What I've just done could bring me a load of trouble, but if it does then all I can hope is that there'll he some unbiased witnesses among the riders who saw it. It's been a few years since I've tried one of these suicide descents, but I'm on home ground and fling the bike into the first bend like a Surrey crone let loose at an Oxford Street sale. On the dangerous side of the bend are trees. Usually it's a rock wall or a drop. I feel the ends of branches sting my face and legs as I lay the bike right down, my right foot loose and poised and ready to dig into the road should I feel the bike sliding.

I'm round. Straight away I fling the machine to the left. It's not possible to ride right to the edge of the road as there seem to be a few small rocks dotted there. So far I haven't used my brakes, but now I have to as I come to a real snorter. I apply them alternately so that they won't fade. Ahead I catch a glimpse of van Faignaert. He's one of these descenders who tucks everything in and goes all streamlined, which is fine on a long run down but not on a short one like this. Also it's not a fast descent, being at the most around fifty miles per hour. There seems to be only one more bend—a tight one—before the road straightens out. We both have to slow to about thirty miles per hour and I whip my foot out and dig the heel in as I chuck the bike round and almost draw level. My foot sends up a cloud of dust that startles him. I don't think he knew I was there.

He says something which I can only describe as "an oath" and looks around wildly for signs of his team. I go back to my former broody hen position, my front wheel nearly touching his rear one. He knows it won't be any good his steaming away, because if he does he takes me with him, me and my fifteen minutes. And if I take off he'll tail me, which is what he'd like me to do, but I'm defending my lead, not trying to increase it. After a few more wild looks he eases up. The road still slopes downward, so he stops pedaling and we freewheel together, waiting for the others to catch us. Press motorcycles, dropped on the descent, reach us first and use up a few miles of film before the chasing group of Romain, the Belgians and other assorted riders make contact with us.

Van Faignaert and his team hold a conference. They ride quite slowly and we're all glad of the rest. They know they're safe and that no one will have the nerve to attack such a strong team. Because the Flandriens and the Walloons don't get on too well, the Belgian "A" team has the Flandriens and the B" team the Walloons. The "A" team groups together and mutters while we others strain our ears. The Belgian team car comes up and God rides alongside talking to the manager. Romain, still gasping from his chase after the puncture, tells me he understands Flemish and that the Belgians aren't going to protest over the clobbering I gave one of them. He says he thinks they've got orders to ride to their limit as the manager doesn't believe I can last the Tour, and that the harder they push the sooner I'll crack. Well, my legs are like iron poles, my head fuzzy and my boil standing in for a rhythm section, but anywhere these bastards go between here and Nîmes, yours truly can go too.

◆

I don't even have time to wipe my face or comb my hair before the television cameras are turned on me. Jeff's holding my cycle and I don't know what to do with my hands. Now I can see the benefit of a pipe or a hand microphone. The interviewer, judging by his attitude, must have had his life's savings on Audaire, and he fires questions at me, leaving me no time to finish what I'm saying. I remember Susan's advice to speak in short sentences, keep to the present tense and avoid pronouns. I know the pink-handed types who get jobs like this interviewer's got, and I know what he's trying to do to me. He's trying to present me as being incoherent in French and, by the raising of an eyebrow at the right time, to hint that I'm pretty dumb even in English. I answer slowly and give out platitudes like "I hope to win" and "One can only do one's best." By the time I escape and push my way with Jeff's help to the hotel, I'm pretty mad. Reporters follow me, trying on their English.

"What do you think of van Faignaert?" one asks.

"We're just good friends." He writes it down.

"What made you come to France in the first place?"

"I'm part of the Brain Drain."

"*Quoi?*"

"You heard.

"What do you think of that?"

I look to where the reporter who spoke is pointing.

Outside the hotel where I am to stay is a large framed sheet of paper about six feet square. On it is drawn a very good likeness of me, in a yellow jersey. I'm zipping along in a wheelchair and holding my back as if I had arthritis. Behind me Audaire sprawls in the road, a big knife in his back.

"What do you think?" the man repeats.

They'd love me to be annoyed and would make a big thing of it. I feel the caked dust crack on my face as I stretch it to a big smile. "A very good likeness," I say and continue toward the hotel.

After the bath, shower and massage I put on a clean shirt and shorts and complete the ritual by sprawling full length on the bed. Romain finishes about the same time and we run through the day's events. By the time we'd got to Nîmes

I was near to cracking and had, in fact, dropped right to the back of van Faignaert's bunch. I'd hung on desperately, thinking any minute that I would die, and although the Belgian team rode themselves into the ground to drop me, I just scraped home. Van Faignaert won the stage, for which he collected a minute bonus, and finished a minute ahead of me anyway. So I lost two minutes to him, leaving me with thirteen now in hand, and the only consolation I got from it was that both he and his men also finished in a state of near collapse. I made him earn his two minutes.

"What fools we are to suffer like this for other people's entertainment," Romain says more to himself than to me. "Why do we do it?"

"I've thought about it, but I don't know why. Perhaps it's because we want to be famous and we choose a way which to us seems most likely."

"Perhaps." He lets go a long sigh and I see his long body sag as he tries to relax it.

"What made you take it up, anyway?" I ask him.

He opens and closes his eyes twice before answering. "I used to be a butcher's boy. The local banker lived in a house on the top of a hill and I had to cycle up to it every day. About five times out of seven the banker's wife would send me back to fetch something else. She had a telephone, and so did the butcher's shop. I could never make out why people should do things like that. I would never walk up this hill, even though I was skinny and kids called me telegraph pole. I always rode, and a loaded tradesman's cycle is no light weight. As I turned the pedals I used to pretend I was stamping on her head. I still pray, but in those days I was given to what I now call striking-a-bargain prayers. You know, when you ask God for something you want, and you say that if you get this thing you'll be good and will do so-

and-so. In my prayers I would ask forgiveness for having figuratively stamped on the head of the banker's wife, and I would beg that her attitude would change. But it never did. I suppose I got a little bitter about it all and reasoned that if I was going to suffer on a *vélo* I might as well do it for money. And so I took up racing."

"It was much the same with me," I tell him. Perhaps Romain does so well when he's out on his own because he relives the sensation of stamping on the woman's head, whereas in a tight bunch his thoughts get too distracted. I've known riders like this before. They have a habitual "picture story" which runs through their head and acts as a sort of fuel. Although I've never mentioned it to him, I've thought for a long time now that Romain is religious, which probably accounts for why he's been a good boy with Susan.

"Do you think I'm mature, Terry? In your opinion, have I grown up?"

"Sure," I tell him, and he looks pleased.

"How old were you when you felt you had matured?"

I laugh. "Now that's asking! God knows, it was so long ago. Yet sometimes, even now, I feel Maturity's still to come. Perhaps it never comes. All my life I've felt that the Present is just a stamping ground for Tomorrow, when Life really begins. I've often thought that one day I'll fall into a long sleep and wake up happy and rich, and from that moment Life would begin. But it never does. All I'll wake up with tomorrow is legs like jelly and a boil on my bum. I suppose, though, if I had to give a time when I first felt I'd grown up, it would be when I realized that fences were round army camps to keep the soldiers in, not the enemy out; and that coppers weren't really there to protect you, but to clobber you at the first opportunity. Things like that. I don't know. It's different for all of us."

We both look to the door as it opens and Susan comes in. "Yesterday's English newspapers," she announces and throws a roll of papers onto my bed. "I took the car in for servicing and should be able to collect it around nine-thirty in the morning. What shall we do tomorrow? Drive out to see the Pont du Gard?"

I blow a raspberry. "—to the Pont du Gard."

"Charming," she says.

"I don't think I'll stir from this bed."

Maybe I look rough, I don't know. She says quietly. "No, perhaps you'd better not."

"Let's see what the dear old English press has got to say, then. Ah, my favorite: that'll be full of Rough Games for Chaps. I'll be lucky to be billed above Budleigh Salterton croquet. . . . What's this? 'Twenty of the world's leading bridge players lead breakaway group'. . . . I wonder if it was as hard as the break I was in today? Probably not. Here it is! 'Veteran British rider leads Tour de France'—so-and-so, so-and-so—'it is not thought, however, that Davenport constitutes a serious challenge to overall victory in the race.'" I throw the papers on the floor. "Get rid of 'em; they'll all be the same. They all get their opinions from the same source. Some 'expert' probably wrote that over a muffin tea in Cheam."

Susan picks up the papers and sticks them behind a chair.

I've started to sweat again. "Why do all these hotel rooms look the same? Perhaps I will go out tomorrow."

She smiles and touches her fringe. "That's more like it. By the way, Mottiat's hovering downstairs."

I close my eyes and blow out my cheeks. "It tolls for thee, Terence Davenport."

"I'm sorry about the papers, Terry. I should have read them first."

"That's all right. You see, Susan, in this world there's only room for a certain number of heroes. If they let too many in, the whole system loses its point. So you're either In—or you're Out. Me, I've always been Out."

"Terry's going to win," Romain pipes up, "if I have to push him all the way to Paris."

"You might have to." As I finish speaking there's a knock on the door. It opens, and in comes Mottiat. I hardly recognize him at first; he's actually wearing a sporty-looking shirt and a pair of cotton trousers. I know the temperature's down to about seventy-five degrees, but it is evening and it might drop even further. I feel like leaping up and throwing a blanket round the poor bleeder's shoulders. "I would like a few words with you gentlemen," he says.

I point to an armchair. "Take a seat." He can't be a lot older than I am, but he drops into that chair so hard I seriously doubt if we'll ever get him out again.

"Now then," he says, putting his fingertips together and studying them. "Stop me if I am wrong, but as I understand it Hendrickx has abandoned all ideas of winning and is going to help you?"

I go to answer but Romain gets there first with a yes.

He starts pulling reasonable faces and I can tell he's going to try his own brand of logic. "But don't you think, Davenport, that Hendrickx has a better chance than you? Oh, I know you have this big lead and wear the yellow jersey, but . . ." He opens his hands, puts on his lovable-cuddly-character look, and chuckles. "I don't wish to sound disrespectful . . ." He chuckles again.

"Go on," I say.

"Well, surely you are too old to nurse hopes of actually winning? You have done well and have been lucky, but to win you'll need luck like that every day. Hendrickx here is only twenty-three minutes behind you, and"—he gets excited—"and only ten behind van Faignaert! With the Alps to come, with his youth, I ask you, Davenport, if Hendrickx hangs around helping you he'll ruin his own excellent chances for the sake of your impossible ones. Now won't he?" He beams benevolently between Romain and myself. Romain goes to speak, but I hold my hand up to him to let me talk first.

"In the first place it was Romain's own idea. My own opinion is that Romain and I are on opposite ends of a seesaw, each the same distance from the center and with about an equal chance of winning. It's van Faignaert who's sitting in the middle and if I was given to worrying, he'd be the one I'd worry about. Perhaps Romain's youth and climbing ability do more than make up for the twenty-three minutes I have over him, in which case I suggest we both ride our own race, and if Romain beats me, then Good Luck.

"Terry, I'm not going over all that again," Romain says. "You've got a good chance and a last chance. Perhaps I could still win, and perhaps I couldn't, but I've more or less written off this Tour. The Mountain title will give me enough to get married on and the experience I've gained will make it all that much easier when I win next year. Terry, I've seen your scrapbooks. Only I, another pro, can fully appreciate all the kilometers you've ridden, the sufferings, the disappointments. This race will make up for everything."

Even before Romain has finished I can see the change in Mottiat. He's almost back to normal with one fat finger poised ready to waggle. "Now you listen to me! Maybe I can't make you win, Hendrickx, but I can certainly stop Davenport. Harich works for me, and he's the man in the car, the man who sees you're passed drinks, that your food is okay. To have him working against you would be very unpleasant. A little something in your drinks—you know—nothing dangerous, just something to make you sick halfway through a stage. And the bikes: a faulty tubular, loose spokes, a frayed cable. Need I say more? You're both in my hands and I'm telling you, Hendrickx, to win, and you, Davenport, to forget about winning. Hang on to the lead as long as you can. I'm a reasonable man; just don't expect Hendrickx to act as your *domestique*."

Surprisingly it's Susan who speaks first. "But if you're only worried about the advertising, surely you could get as much from Terry's win as you could from Romain's?"

"It's not quite as simple as that," I tell her. "But let me first answer Farouk here. You two are my witnesses that Mottiat has tried to use commercial interests to sway the result of an international race. The Tour director will be very interested to hear about it. In his black book it rates only next to doping." I snap my fingers. "They'd replace Harich like that!"

Mottiat leaps up and waves his arms. "They won't replace every mechanic, or every cook and waiter in the hotels to come."

I ignore him and look at Susan. "You see, he's got Romain signed up for three years, which means two more tours, two more commercial ones with trade teams. And two likely wins. Romain was a gullible fool, and if I'd known him at the time I'd never have let him sign. He can earn big money if he wins, but the actual retaining wage he's on for the next two years is a pittance. Also Romain is better advertising material than I am; he's more local, boyish, someone whose career the fans can follow. And if he wins this Tour it'll be from the front. Can't you just see it? 'Twenty-three minutes down, a storming ride through the Alps, pulling back minutes on every stage, a duel to the finish with van Faignaert.' Young men, popular men, winning in a popular way. Who really cares if I win? A few supporters back in Belgium perhaps. It's not as if I even earned the yellow jersey. Fat wants me out quickly so that Romain can forget about me and concentrate on winning."

"My God!" Susan says, lifting her hair and holding it up in the air. "What a business! You'd both be better out of it."

"Can I just say something?" Romain's voice is very quiet. "I suppose at first I was disappointed at the thought of helping Terry, and of riding a defensive race through the very country I'd been waiting for." He looks at Mottiat. "But you . . . you come in here with your threats and insults and use them on a man whose boots you're not fit to lick. All right, so I signed a contract. I've got no money, so they can't fine me. All they can do is send me to prison, and I doubt if they'd do that after they've heard what I'd tell them. And if they did send me, I'd go rather than bow down to you. I'll tell you now, Mottiat, as soon as this is over I'm going to shout all this through every news organ I can. I'm taking this story to the League and the Union."

Mottiat is trembling. He stabs one of his banana fingers at Romain and shouts, "Right!" Then he strides over to me and sticks his face so close I can count the blackheads on his hooter. "Right!" he shouts again.

"Fat," I say, standing up, "I've had a hard day, but I'm not so tired that if you're not out of here in two ticks I won't kick you down those bloody stairs."

"Right!" he yells once more and bounces out of the room, pausing at the door to wave a final finger.

I slump back on the bed, Susan sits down heavily with a "Wow," and Romain wipes his forehead with the back of his hand. One thing I'll say for Romain: When he does come out of his shell he doesn't hang about. "Thanks," I say to him, but he doesn't look up. Even though I tell myself once more that my affair with Susan has in no way I'm aware of taken her away from him, I still manage to feel rotten about it. I sigh. "He's right, you know, Romain. You ought to forget about me and still try to win. It's thousands of dollars you're chucking away."

His head is resting on his pillow, and he turns it away as he replies. I think he's crying. "Terry, please, I'm going to help you. That's all . . ."

Susan catches my eye as she lifts her hand and signals me to say no more. She says to me in a loud voice, as if nothing were wrong, "Did you see Mottiat change when Romain stayed firm on helping you? I was watching his eyes. They changed like a dealer's when one suddenly stops talking about buying and mentions selling. Can he sabotage your bike or slip you something in a drink?"

"I suppose he can have a good try. If he's going to, then it'll be soon. His whole aim is to get me out pronto so that Romain will take off. If he doesn't try within the next two stages then I don't think it will be worth his while."

I feel Romain turn his head our way, and I try not to notice his watering eyes. "What can we do about him?"

"I'm going to have a little chat with Jeff, then go and see the Tour director. But first the doctor and this boil, then something mild to make me drop off quickly, then—I hope—a good night's sleep."

10

Pancho's Villa

NÎMES IS HOT AND CROWDED, so we decide to drive down to the coast. We're almost in the Picasso Belt and it might be hard to find somewhere quiet that isn't private. Susan elected to drive, and she speeds along with Romain next to her, while Bert and I loll like lords in the back seat. Sitting as I am on one cheek, I'm forced to stretch a leg across Bert in order to brace myself on corners.

I'm grateful for two things. First I slept well, and second I'm not riding a bike. It seems almost too good to be true that my legs aren't thrashing round and my heart pounding. All the windows are down in the car and a glorious breeze, smelling of sea, tears at my hair.

"Drat," says Susan, stopping the car. "I should have taken that other road back there. It looks as if this one peters away into nothing."

Romain gets out. "Well, you'll never turn round here." He clambers up the bank and Susan leans across the front seat and sticks her head out of the window on the far side. "It's all right," he calls down. "The road simply goes along this hillside and rejoins the other road farther up."

We get going again and I half close the window because of the dust coming in off the unsurfaced road. Susan slows the car as we come to an old stone house tucked away between a rock face and some trees.

"Look, it's for sale," she says.

"An old bit of Provence." Romain comments.

Bert looks past me. "Rahver 'ave one o' vose noo flats in Kennin'ton, meself." I start to work out the price in sterling.

Susan sees me and says, "About thirty-six thousand pounds. Mind you, it wants a lot done to it. You'd probably have to tear out the whole inside. I love those flat roofs. Even in a building that small they've put in a 'step' and given the roof two levels. Wouldn't that low roof make a lovely place to lie out and sunbathe?"

"It'd prob'ly give way," Bert says.

"Of course it wouldn't, Bert," she says. "The place is built like a fort. And look at those apple trees, simply laden. Let's pinch some."

Three car doors open. I say, "Oh, leave them. You never know—"

"I fancy some apples," Bert says to me through the window. "Mott'at might be bloody clever, but I daht if h's go' at vese."

Romain and Susan laugh and walk toward the house. "Come on, Terry," she calls.

I shake my head and watch them. The poor old ticker that today wasn't going to do more than turn over has got its boots on, and I feel a little sick. Her, £500,000, a place like this, and the rest of my life to turn it into the most marvelous home. Yes, and there by that path there's room for a nice pond. Susan's up on the low roof. She waves to me and stretches out her arms as if taking in the sun. I turn away and look across the rocky terrain on the other side. For a few seconds I lift my sunglasses and the blinding whiteness makes me screw up my eyes. I don't know; perhaps I'm too restless to settle anywhere. Although Susan's right—I'll have to one day. But what do I really want from life? Excitement, change, youth, and although it's asking a lot, a little bit of immortality. I'm not clever enough to be anything in the business world. Orders from others make me choke and I'm too restless to sit around and watch my toenails grow. Bobbie asked herself, "What am I?" Well, what am I? A bit of everything, a mongrel of useless bits. In the whole of my life I've won a handful of worthwhile races, and I'm such an "expert" with women that I've probably put the poor kid in the spud line.

I look back toward the house as I hear the others returning. In the glove compartment I see some newspaper cuttings and photographs of myself that Susan's got hold of from somewhere. They're all recent, for in each one I'm wearing the *maillot jaune*. I pick one up and look at our grim glistening faces: Romain's, van Faignaert's and mine. All those years and no luck. Now, at the very last knockings, this happens. But it's come too late. It's like getting an old geezer off his deathbed to have his first woman.

"You wouldn't believe it," Susan says as she gets in, "but from that little roof you can see the sea quite clearly. Here, Terry, have an apple."

Susan keeps enthusing about the house, but I wish she'd shut up. I know what's in Romain's mind. He's thinking the same as I was, that £36,000 is a very good price. Already Susan's got the floorboards stacked in a pile outside and a generator installed in a corner under the low roof. I shut my ears and try not to listen. Instead I think of what Jeff said when I told him about Mottiat.

Apparently Jeff has a relation who runs a cycle and motorcycle business in Marseilles. Jeff phoned him this morning, and it seems he has a good secondhand motorcycle that we could borrow. Last night I went to the Tour director and told him about Mottiat's threats. The director and his colleagues assured me they would watch Mottiat and Harich as closely as possible, and agreed to let Jeff join the team cars and act as my manager-mechanic. Jeff, however, prefers a motorcycle, and today he's gone down to Marseilles to collect it and to get a set of panniers welded up which will carry four spare cycle wheels and other necessary parts. If I had found the right opportunity to chat Susan about going to the Consulate at Marseilles to find the phone number of Bobbie's friend, I would have sent her along with Jeff. But with Romain and I sharing a room I don't get much chance to talk to the girl for long.

I'm bursting to know if Bobbie's all right. Having a worry doesn't affect your riding as much as some people like to make out, but it does affect your sleep. And what with the heat, the boil and the noise—to say nothing about the near-impossibility of stopping your mind churning over the race and how it's going—sleep is a pretty elusive thing.

I suppose one of the biggest of the human tragedies is that we so rarely ever get close to others. We're all so alone, all the time. And it's not a matter of being able to understand people. I understand Paula and Susan yet can't say I feel particularly close. It's only at chosen moments that I can show parts of my soul to them. To me, Bobbie is one hell of a mystery, and yet I felt close to her. If I'd had the chance I'm sure we could have reached that state of closeness that most people try for all their lives.

"What about down there?" Susan says.

I must look a bit stupid, because I didn't even know the car had stopped. "Where?"

"Terry, you're just not with it today, are you? Down there,

where those pines reach right to the beach." She points.

"You know, I'm so tired that I was dozing off. Sorry. Yes, it looks all right. I wonder what it's called? Keep-Out Cove, perhaps. We'll probably be set upon by a cluster of elkhounds."

Susan can't persuade any of us to take along some apples. I noticed that, like me, Bert and Romain ate only two apiece. One of the plagues of racing in this part of the world is that non-local riders are prone to pick up a type of dysentery. Les Runs can knock you out even if the limit of your daily stagger is to the beach and back. It's no understatement to say that racing a hundred and twenty miles a day in such a state is the nearest thing to hell I can think of.

We pick our way over the rocks toward where the pines jut out into the Mediterranean. Romain and Bert have brought their swimming gear, but what with the boil and things I think I'll keep out of the sea. If only I had big trousers and braces I'd have paddled and done my best to keep the flag flying. Susan can't swim, anyway, but is one of these nutters who must always lie in the sun. She's come prepared and is nearly naked, dressed in brief shorts and a blue and white spotted bra.

"Nuffin abaht Keep Aht," Bert observes. He kicks his sandals off but quickly puts them on again when the soles of his feet come in contact with the hot sand. "Christ!" he says, hopping about.

"I don't know about you lot," I say, "but I'm getting under those trees and staying there."

Romain and Bert hide coyly among the pines while they change.

"There's a couple of gentlemen for you," Susan says to me. "You wouldn't do that."

"No, I'd show you all I've got, puce jockstrap and all."

She smiles and says. "I'll strike a compromise with you. If

215

I lie just beyond the trees in the sun, would you lie in the edge of the shade. That way we're both happy and can talk. If you want to talk, that is."

"As it happens, I do." I sit myself down against one of the pines nearest to the seashore, and Susan spreads a towel and stretches out. We get showered with sand as Bert and Romain go sprinting past heading for the sea.

"Well?" she asks.

"I want you to do me a favor."

"If I can."

"Don't laugh, because this to me was very real. I had the most vivid dream I've ever had in my life. It was one night back there before the Pyrenees, and it was about Bobbie—number three. I dreamt Paula had forwarded a letter, which you gave me. When I opened it there was nothing inside but a newspaper cutting that Bobbie's friend in London had sent me. The cutting said that Bobbie had gassed herself and, at the inquest, was found to be pregnant. That's all. It doesn't sound much, does it? Except melodramatic. But that dream is as vivid, even now, as if it had actually happened."

She looks at me for a few seconds, scooping up sand in her and letting it run out between her fingers. "And what do you want me to do?"

"Tomorrow, when we pass as near to Marseilles as we're going to, I'd like you to nip down, find the British Consulate, borrow a London directory, and find the number of Bobbie's friend. When you've done that, phone her and ask if there's any news—whether or not she's seen Bobbie. If you can't find the Consulate, I should think a place as big as Marseilles would have London directories at the main post office. If you don't want to phone, then just get the number and I'll try in the evening, only you know how hard it is to get near a telephone at the end of a stage."

She moves her lips as if going to say something, but appears to change her mind. At last she says, "It's not likely she is pregnant, is it? Not by you, anyway, not after all these years of wild oat sowing."

I shrug. The sunglasses I'm wearing are a cheap pair and the rays are catching them at an angle which makes Susan appear to be surrounded by multicolored haloes. "I can't believe I'd have made a mistake, but of course you never know. There wasn't time or chance to get her on the Pill, and as you know, I've mostly relied on the old faithfuls. In fact, you're the only bird I've ever Pilled-it with. I suppose you've stopped taking them now?"

She moves her shoulders, but the sun's too bright to see if she's gone red, or pale, or whatever color she goes when asked an awkward question.

"Well, have you?"

"I still take them, if you must know. Probably through habit. Anyway, I did promise you when we got to Nîmes . . . "

I look out to where Romain is floating on his back and Bert's sitting like a hairy mermaid on an offshore rock "Not much chance yet."

"No, that's what I was thinking. Getting back to what you asked me—certainly I'll go to Marseilles and do what you want. With only a dream to go on, it does seem a lot of trouble, but I don't object if it'll put your mind at rest. I wonder what she'd do if she knew about all this? Don't men just enjoy their Secret Love, Love Thwarted, Love Denied? I honestly wonder whether you're not stuck on this girl solely because she doesn't want to know you.

I let myself slide down the tree until I'm flat on my back in the sand. "I don't know what it is. Perhaps it's because inwardly I know she's the last attractive teenage bird I'll ever have. Perhaps it's because I felt I could be really close if

217

given the chance to know her properly. Or, as you suggest, it might be because the old charm never worked. I'll tell you straight what I think the attraction is that a young person has for an older one: The older one has discovered at least something and seen some life, and things don't impress and excite as they used to. Only by being with someone young, someone you care for, and seeing *them* discover things, can you yourself recapture some of the sensations that have dulled inside you. You know, I'd have loved to show London to Bobbie. I'm not one of these people who believe in the 'only girl in the world.' When a bloke goes after a girl it's because she's acceptable and he knows he stands some sort of chance. If we all went after what we really fancied there'd be bloody great queues stretching into infinity after every bit of nubility build like a brick whatnot."

She laughs and buries her feet into the soft hot sand. "At least you're honest with yourself, Terry."

"I've got to be. It's all that's left."

For a while she thinks, then says, "There's another way of looking at it. It could be you've got this thing about her because she's young and pretty and mysterious, like some fine possession. A person can have a valuable and desirable picture or antique which does nothing to them *personally*, but they covet it because it's something that gives them status in other people's eyes. In your case proof to the world that you're still an attractive man. Maybe it's merely as near to love as a heartless bastard like you can get." Her hand goes up and she pushes her hair from her face."

"I'll get you a hair grip as soon as we get back."

"My fringe needs trimming. I've noticed you look at me before when I've pushed it out of my eyes. Does it annoy you?"

"Not really." I roll onto my stomach. For a while I lie still and listen to the sea, and when I look at her again she says,

218

"I think Romain has grown up a lot during this past week. And in a way so have you."

"Me? No, not me. If anything I've died a little." I turn my face away again, but look round quickly when I hear her next to me.

"They're swimming right out there now. We'd have plenty of chance to be 'decent' if we saw them heading back."

She's smiling, but it's the sickly smile of embarrassment.

"It's nice of you to break your vow."

"Silly, I'm not only doing it to please you."

"I understand. It's the heat. There were moments back there on the road into Nîmes when I thought about this. Do you know, there were honestly times when I felt I'd never be able to do it, or even feel like it, when the chance came. I didn't want to do anything that would make me hot. Today I could face anything but sweating."

She lies close, next to me, so that her arm is across my stomach. "You won't have to get all hot, Terry. Just get those clothes off and lie still. You've done enough work lately."

◆

When I open my eyes I'm blinded by the sun's rays, which are stabbing their shafts through a gap in the branches above. Susan is lying next to me, quite still, looking out to sea. With the sun behind her I can see the slight down on her face, something I've never noticed before.

"Nice?" she asks without looking at me.

"Paradise. I don't think I've ever enjoyed it as much." I pick up my sunglasses and put them on.

"Coming from you that's praise indeed. It must always be more flattering to the woman if the man seems to enjoy it so. As you do. Terry, you'd better slip your shorts on. The boys are coming out of the water now."

Without standing up, I manage to wriggle into them.

Susan moves away and leans against one of the pines. "Are you phoning Mother tonight?"

"Might do. Beginning to wonder if it's worth it. She never sounds very happy."

She looks toward the two coming along the beach. "No."

"Anyone would think she didn't want me to win."

"No."

"You keep saying no."

"Do I?" She turns her head toward me and I can see something's wrong.

"What is it?"

She shakes her head slowly. "Poor Terry. Of course she doesn't want you to win. She's not that gullible."

"How do you mean? I don't understand."

"Do I have to paint you a picture? Terry with a Tour victory isn't going to find Paula as desirable as would Terry with the odd thousand or two. Is he?"

"But—" I go to jump up.

"Sit still; they'll see you."

I cup my hands over my ears. "Oh, bloody hell! Doesn't anyone want me to win?"

She has her sickly embarrassed smile again. "Offhand I can't think of many. Mottiat doesn't, I don't think the Public do, Romain's doing What's Right, but he more than anyone should want you out, and Mother doesn't."

"Which leaves?"

"Me? Well, I'd be starting married life with a lot of money if you didn't win. But I hope you do, honestly. And I expect Bert and Jeff are on your side. I can't speak for number three."

"Marvelous!" Romain says as he comes up and flings himself onto the sand next to Susan. He kisses her shoulder and

I look away.

" 'Ave a go, Terry-boy," Bert says. "The old salt might 'eel yer bleedin' fumper up. Do it some good, like."

I give a mock stretch. There's nothing I want more than to be on my own and think, so I stand and do a bit more stretching. "I don't know . . . I think I'll take a stroll down the beach." I give the sand a kick and walk away. "See you," I call over my shoulder.

It's still too hot for me out of the shade, so I keep to the edge of the pines, booting the odd fir cone as I go. After about fifty yards I stop and lean against a tree and look up in the direction of the old flat-roofed house. I can just see part of the roof and the tops of the apple trees. Then I look toward where Susan, Romain and Bert are racing about playing football with a fir cone. Susan sees me and waves. "What are you looking at?" she calls.

I wave back and start walking again, saying quietly, "Myself."

Should I not just pull out now and give Romain his chance? I'm tiring, I know; I can feel it. But I might be on a winning streak of luck. Maybe van Faignaert will crack, or be taken ill—with dysentery perhaps. What if I do pull out and then Romain's forced to retire? It won't be any good going to the organizers and saying, "Look, I could have kept going; can we all go back to Nîmes and start again from there?" When I think of all the damn good pros who've retired unnoticed and unmourned. Few people ever notice they've gone. Suddenly their names don't crop up any more. I'm one of these, but now I have a chance to be remembered, which is what most of us really want.

The ordinary bloke settles for kids as a sort of poor man's immortality, but I'll settle for a half-minute lead at Paris. Thirty bloody wretched seconds that flash past on our watches so fast we don't even notice. Even five seconds would do, or two, or one. It's not much to ask from a life made up of so many thousands of seconds, is it? I admit I want to win; I want it so much it hurts. It's an old-fashioned word, but I want a bit of glory. Even the money doesn't mean as much as it should. All my life I've been a nobody, and now, perhaps, who or whatever dishes out Luck has given me this one last chance. I think all men who've been in a position to have striven to be remembered. Glory—however minor—is most people's secret wish. People want to be remembered. It's what makes them paint, compose, scheme, donate, et cetera. Some even settle for infamy.

A shiver goes through me and I walk down the beach to the edge of the water, where I can feel the sun through my shirt. I stand there tossing stones, going over yet again the stages that lie ahead, trying to work out optimistically how much I'll lose on each one. I *could* win, if I don't tire too much and Fate isn't too unkind. After a while I sit on a rock and run through the remainder of the race, only this time throwing a pessimistic light on everything. This way I make it van Faignaert first, Romain two minutes behind, and either me or Butch Cassidy five minutes down on the Belgian. But you can never tell. The pattern of the race has been cast, but I'm the unpredictable one, even to myself. A man on borrowed time doesn't know when he's going to crack. It might be tomorrow, it might be next year.

Unconsciously I've been writing my name with a stick in the wet sand. I laugh. It just shows what conceited apes we are. I'm doing what all people do—carving my name on a tree, signing the visitors' book, scribbling on a wall. Win, and I'll be remembered. I plonk my foot onto the sand where my name's written, and the writing disappears, leaving the sand as smooth as before.

Lose, and my name will never have existed.

11

And I'll Be a Sunbeam
for Him

TODAY'S STAGE IS THE SHORTEST in the race. It is in fact only twenty-one kilometers, yet will probably be one of the most punishing. Mont Ventoux—The Giant of Provence—is an extinct volcano, and the road that winds to its summit climbs to five thousand feet in that twenty-one kilometers.

For the stage, a time trial where each man is started at two-minute intervals and rides against the clock, we're transported to a village called Bedoin about fifty miles from Nîmes.

This won't be the first time I've been up the Ventoux; I've done it twice before in competition and several times at slower speeds on training runs. A lot has been made of this mountain in relation to the Tour de France, for on its slopes riders have ridden themselves senseless, and of course in 1967 Tommy Simpson rode himself to death here. But it's not the gradient or the length of the climb that has made the mountain so infamous. It's the heat. To ride up it in early spring, leisurely, in a low gear, is not particularly brutal. But now, in June, it becomes a dust-choked, rock-strewn, shadeless wasteland, to be pounded up in intense heat from a sun that hangs up there in a cloudless sky like a polished brass gong.

There's only one consolation: van Faignaert won't do a lot better on the ascent than I will. He'll do better, of course, because he's younger, but like me he won't be high on the finishing list. Although only twenty-one kilometers, it's possible for a good climber to ride up as much as ten minutes faster than a man who can't climb well.

The doctor managed to burst the boil early this morning, and it's now in a state popularly known as "weeping." It's left my thigh pretty stiff, so before the start I must ride around for a few miles to try and pedal some of the stiffness out. Susan was disappointed at having to go to Marseilles to make my phone call, especially as Romain will probably win the climb. She intends to hurry back to Bedoin and see the start, and she should make it all right, as riders will be going off between midday and three-thirty. But as much as she'd like to see the finish, it probably won't be possible. The slopes are packed with spectators, most of whom have been waiting there since yesterday, and unless Romain or I can get her a lift to the top in an official car, she's had it.

I sit under one of the official awnings with Romain and Bert. The canvas flaps a little, but there's hardly any breeze. We sip glasses of natural mineral water, slightly chilled. Crowds press against the rope barriers for a glimpse of us and keep calling out to their favorite riders. A woman in a big sun hat has been waving a little Union Jack at me for about ten minutes, and calling out, "*Allez bien. Bonne chance, Anglais.*" If she doesn't shove off soon I'll have to go over and be polite. If this were a normal race it's the sort of incident I'd make use of, and try to arrange to meet her afterwards.

Outside, the riders who are lower on classification are being sent off on their solo climbs. Being number one, I'm off last. Jeff has taken charge of my machine and equipment

224

and slept with it all in his room at the hotel. He sits now in a far corner of the shade, his big hands resting on the crossbar of my cycle and glowering at anyone who comes near. Last night I got round the eating problem by picking at random a high-class restaurant in Nîmes and going in and asking to see the chef. When I explained who I was and why I was there, he and the manager did all they could to prepare exactly what I asked for. For breakfast Jeff went out and did much the same thing, bringing it back on a tray for me to eat. Shortly I'll eat a banana and a rice cake, and this too we have looked over carefully.

The riders who wait are trying to relax, but it isn't easy. Van Faignaert keeps pacing about, sometimes punching his right fist into his left palm, sometimes waving to fans who call to him. Romain fidgets, tapping his glass on the table, biting one of his thumbnails. Bert keeps tying and untying the laces on his racing shoes. He'll walk about, decide they are either too tight or too loose, then sit down and readjust them again.

Sometimes I look at my watch, but for the most part I either go as limp as possible or wonder how Susan has got on in Marseilles.

"It's true, you know," Romain says.

"What is?"

"You English are the calmest people on earth."

I grunt and say, "Don't you believe it. Mostly it's because we're too daft to grasp the real issues. Anyway, look at Bert. If he undoes those shoes many more times he'll be able to step straight into a manager's job with any top booterie."

"No," Romain says quietly, "you are calm. I know what's at stake for you, and so do you know. This next week will be the most important in your life."

Because of what Romain's giving up for me, I find it awkward now to talk to him about the race. I think of a stiff-upper-lip story I recently read, and tell it to him. "Here, talking about being English, I was reading about the Zulu War not so long ago. In this book was a bit where they found two British officers, sitting back to back, quite dead, and they both still had their monocles in."

He looks interested. "No!"

"They did. It's a fact."

"But how did they keep them in?"

I shrug. "I don't know. A good fit, I suppose."

I leave him to ponder on it, and go over to my sole admirer. As I get near I can see it's a bit rough and my internal warning system comes up with no. She shakes my hand and kisses my cheek. Garlic and Chanel jostle to overpower me. I act British and polite and get back to my seat as soon as I can.

They're getting through the list now and there aren't many of us left. Susan arrives in time to wish Romain good luck before he, in tenth overall position, gets called out. I take this as my cue to go for a spin up the road so that I don't start out too stiff. Jeff gives me my cycle and I wheel it out into the sun, where I'm in time to see Romain get pushed off. Apparently Susan has got a lift in the car that's to follow Romain. As she climbs in I ride up and say, "Well, how did you get on?"

She shakes her head. "No go I'm afraid, Terry; couldn't get an answer."

"Oh. Well, thanks for trying. I'll see if I can get through tonight." I see her slap her forehead just as the engine starts. "My God. Terry, I'm so sorry. I screwed up the piece of paper and threw it away. The piece of paper with the number on it." As the car pulls away she's still shaking her head and mouthing "I'm sorry." I watch the vehicle roar after Romain up the easier initial slopes of the Ventoux and disappear among the pines which shade the first part of the climb.

I ride back down the road for about half a mile, then turn and come back at a quicker pace. The crowds that get in my way and shout make no impression on me. All my mind can do is to call Susan all the silly cows under the sun.

I watch van Faignaert go. Still overgeared, to my way of thinking, he pulls away rapidly toward the first bend. Now I'm the only rider left. Messages are being radioed back that Romain is climbing strongly but has not yet hit the "parched desert" where the real suffering begins. For the climb I carry no equipment whatsoever, nothing. Harich voted himself the job of following Romain up, and Jeff on the motorcycle is to tail me and carry anything I might need. Jeff starts his motor and I give him the British Thumb, which he returns.

A minute to go. I get on, take an eau-de-cologne sponge from a helper and stuff it in a rear pocket. You can't over-plan a climb like this, you've just got to get up as quickly as you know how. There can be no hanging about, because in a time trial you can't see how the others are doing. And yet you can't flog yourself too early on; you must keep something back for that last bit.

I tighten my toeclips and glance at my watch.

"*Trois, deux, un, partez!*" The starter's hand comes down and the person holding me gives an almighty shove.

I wind up a steady pace out of the village toward the first bend. My intention is to push it while still sheltered by the trees in the hope that I can perhaps gain on van Faignaert, or at least get him in view. I hate it when I'm alone and have nothing to ride against. If only I can see the Belgian and keep sight of him to the top, it must mean I haven't lost much time to him. But as I say, you can't really plan, you can only do your best.

For miles the trees make it impossible to see far round the

bends ahead. Although the pines give some shade from the sun, they also block any cooling breeze. My stiff leg is giving way to a soreness which, if anything, I prefer. I wonder how I look, and what they're all thinking. "Good for an old un, but . . ." or "Look at him climb! I wouldn't be surprised to see him win this Tour." Maybe they're thinking, "He ought to be at home in bed. It's indecent." You never can tell. They seem a sporting lot and are giving bags of encouragement, shouting and waving me on. Perhaps they've got over seeing Audaire disqualified.

I'd heard they are giving a dope check to all riders and are taking them straight from the top of the mountain to a vehicle parked back in the village. Car after car passes me, coming back toward Bedoin. The riders who have completed their climb sit quite still in the car seats and look dully at me, probably not having enough energy to care how I get on. If it weren't for my yellow jersey, they probably wouldn't even recognize me.

Up now through the trees, the gradient beginning to bite and the shade getting sparser. It seems everyone has a transistor turned up full blast, listening to the commentaries of how riders are faring and what sort of times they're doing. From a distance this mountain must look and sound alive, like a vast crawling anthill, or like a mountain in a Disney cartoon where the pursuer catches the pursued and hammers him so hard that the whole terrain jumps and rocks. I think of the birds and insects who normally live quiet lives among these trees, and of how they must be wondering what's hit them. No doubt they're thinking what a crazy lot we humans are, and to what lengths we'll go to make a crust.

The last of the trees disappear behind me and I'm joined by a television van and a commentator on the pillion of a motorcycle. I try to look relaxed, but I'm sure the limelight steps up the revs a bit on the old ticker. By now, of course, it's the sweat bath and the pounding heart. I look away from the cameras and drag the sponge across my forehead and round my face, then one at a time I do my arms. So far I've stayed in the saddle and used a low gear, but more for a change than anything else I go up a sprocket and stand on the pedals. A change is as good as a rest, and I was beginning to feel sluggish and stale. Even through the very dark sunglasses I can see the heat shimmering off the rocky landscape.

The higher gear begins to pall so I drop back one to the gear I started with. My legs feel a bit jelly-ish and I use the saddle once more. For a while now I've noticed this car up front. It's been holding a steady speed and must be the Belgian team car that's with van Faignaert. It's a good way ahead, but as near as I can make out it's about a two-minute ride away, which means I must be holding my own. Also I can taste the dust its wheels have churned up and which hasn't yet settled.. For a few seconds I feel the most marvelous breeze spring up from somewhere, but it doesn't last and the memory of it only forces me to use the sponge again.

Jeff has fallen behind and spoken to somebody in one of the cars. He draws alongside of me and hands me a bottle of iced water. I rinse my mouth and pour the rest over my head.

"You're almost three minutes down on Faignaert. Romain's done the fastest time so far," Jeff shouts and then drops back. He knows it's not wise to stay at my side for long because some nut will up and accuse him of pacing me.

Ten kilometers to go. The road snakes up in wide even sweeps. Not only can I see van Faignaert, but also the rider in front of him. The heat's appalling; it even smells hot, and as I gasp it in, it seems to aggravate and constrict my breathing. Right on the summit I can see the spectators packed in their hundreds and giving off a dull roar as rider after rider arrives. I try not to look at the road but fix my eyes on the summit and plod on toward it.

Jeff keeps giving me time checks. I can tell I'm going to be well down, but as long as van Faignaert and, to a lesser degree, Butch Cassidy and The Sundance Kid are also down, then it doesn't matter too much. I can't stop asking myself that if Romain puts up a terrific ride, will he perhaps still change his mind and go all out for victory?

On one of the tighter bends I glance up and see van Faignaert climbing on the road above me. Although the distance is too great to be able to see his face clearly, I can tell he looks down at me. He's one of these unsightly climbers who fights his cycle, rocking it from side to side as he stands on the pedals and stamps on a high gear. Not that style counts for much. Today or any day, all that matters is results.

Soaked, and with my heart going like an old one-lunged longstroke motor, I decide it's about a mile to go and time for the supreme effort. My head hangs as I shake the sweat from it, and I catch a glimpse of my leg muscles, hard and prominent under a near-black skin. They look strong enough but feel as if they're made of foam rubber. I couldn't fight a higher gear and my legs are too weary to cope with the increased revs from a lower one. All I can do is try to turn my existing gear a bit faster. I gather by the commotion that van Faignaert has finished. Hundreds of brown faces crane forward and search mine. I screw up my eyes and rivet them on the finish sign stretched across the road ahead, but the faces and sign swim together in a dizzy mist. Experience tells me I'm near to passing out from heat exhaustion and fatigue but that I must keep going at a reasonable gallop and finish without this happening. This sort of thing occurs more often than people realize, and only self-knowledge in keeping yourself that fraction under boiling point stops you from lying down in the road and expiring with a croak and a gray face.

The blurred sign looms up. Suddenly I don't see it any more and stop pedaling. Jeff catches me, tears off the sunglasses, lays me on a blanket on the ground, and wrings the most glorious iced sponge over my face. The doctor, stethoscope at the ready, bends down and asks how I feel.

"Okay, okay," I gasp.

He feels my pulse, hovers, and goes away.

I close my eyes and try to get as much dusty air as possible inside me in the shortest possible time. For minutes I lie there gasping, like a fish on a deck, while people watch.

A hand touches my shoulder.

"Susan?" I open my eyes.

"Yes. How was it? Hard?"

I nod. "Where's Romain?"

"He's coming over. There's someone from the British press with him."

I sit up, my chest still heaving. "Oh, God. Where? Has he got a camera?"

"Yes."

"Here, lend us your comb. Where's that sponge? Oh, it's him—that boob. Here to ask Sensible Questions."

Romain gets to me first and shakes my hand. "Your time's not up yet, but you weren't too far behind van Faignaert."

"Good. I hear you slaughtered 'em."

He smiles. "Wasn't the last bit murder? It's true what they say—it's like a desert up here."

Boob bobs down and sticks his face between Romain and myself. "Mr. Davenport?"

"The very same: the well-known white-slaver and rapist."

"Ha, ha!" He shows teeth like cubes of sugar. We've met before but this sort always make out they've forgotten, so as to hammer home the point that you're so insignificant they can't remember you. He's wearing a starched open-neck white shirt, sleeves down and with cufflinks, and regulation pattern khaki shorts with legs so wide they'd make a good half-scale replica of the Grand Canyon. Just to emphasize he's both a boob and British, he's wearing a paisley scarf, tied cravat-style, round his neck. I mean, you need this; it's only about eighty degrees in the nonexistent shade. And I've no doubt he's one of these people who'll tell you hot tea makes you cool.

"You're doing jolly well here, Mr. Davenport. How do you feel about eventual victory?"

"Anything can happen between here and Paris. I can only do my best."

"And I'm sure you will. How about a few pictures?"

He stands up and starts clicking. I look at him sullenly, trying to check my desire to keep gasping in air like some old lunger gone west for a cure. While he does something to his camera I glance at the time board where the results of the Ventoux climb are being chalked up. Van Faignaert's time is just being written in, and a few moments later comes mine. In my mind I fix the five results that count:

1. R. Hendrickx	1 hr 3 mins 5 secs
6. "B. Cassidy"	1 hr 7 mins 11 secs
8. "Sundance"	1 hr 8 mins 8 secs
9. H. van Faignaert	1 hr 9 mins
22. T. Davenport	1 hr 11 mins 44 secs

For several seconds I daren't look at the board showing overall positions. My arithmetic never was very rapid, but I know that Romain's climb being eight and a half minutes faster than mine will have put him now within reasonable striking distance of both me and van Faignaert. I drag my eyes on to the board and one by one look at the same five names.

1. T. Davenport	84 hrs 10 mins 10 secs
2. H. van Faignaert	84 hrs 20 mins 18 secs
3. "B. Cassidy"	84 hrs 22 mins 14 secs
4. "Sundance"	84 hrs 23 mins 20 secs
5. R. Hendrickx	84 hrs 24 mins 40 secs

Boob squats next to me and starts the same old round of questions: Is this my last Tour? What made me ride again after having retired? How much was I relying on Romain's help? I often wonder how people like him get these jobs. To me they seem capable of thinking only in terms of black and white. I suppose he Knows Somebody.

"I'm sure a British win in the Tour would be like a shot in the arm to our sporting prestige," he says, easing his neck inside the sticky cravat.

It's impossible to answer statements like these. "Huh," I mutter.

"I suppose in a way you must feel proud?"

"No, just hot and tired."

"And what are your hopes here today on the Ventoux?"

"That my luck will hold—or rather that my rivals run out of it."

"I see. Could you say what you hope to get out of winning, assuming you do win, of course. You'll get a lot of money, I know, but apart from that . . ."

"Prestige, I suppose."

"Then you do have pride?"

"Not as you mean it. I want the money to buy myself immunity from others, I want the woman of my choice, and I want the prestige—here in France, where winning the Tour means something."

"Oh. And have you anything further to add?"

"Not a thing."

"Oh. Well, I'll go and talk to Mr. . . . Mr. Throbnostle, is it? Thank you, old boy."

"Don't mention it." I wonder what he meant by "old boy."

Romain's looking at the general classification board. If I said to him, "Go on, win," he'd say, "No, next year for me." But if he knew it was only yesterday that I was belting his fiancée, he'd take off like a bloody hawk. Mottiat, wearing a pith helmet and looking like something from High Street, Ujiji, calls Romain over.

"Well," Susan says, "at least he got something from you that I never managed—a statement of what you want from life. And who is the woman of your choice?"

I drag myself to my feet and pull the yellow jersey away from my body, first from the back and then the front, so that the air can circulate. "I'm blowed if I know. That's the sort of answer you have to give blokes like him. There was some truth in the prestige bit. Do you know, my father died when I was young, so I'm the only person left alive who recalls even the remotest fact or detail about him. And that amounts to only one thing. He used to read labels on sauce bottles and tins of paint, and look inside shoes to see who made them, and if the name was known to him he'd say, 'That's a reputable firm.' Isn't it absurd that a man could live, marry and have a kid, and yet this useless snippet is all that anyone remembers. I want more than that." I look away from her when I hear Jeff calling me. It seems I've got to go back down in one of the official cars, and not on Jeff's motorcycle. They're having this dope test back in Bedoin and if I was with Jeff I could nip off and have a crafty pee.

◆

Stage 19. Carpentras-Gap. 173 kilometers.

The peloton moves out on the road to Gap, through the Provençal olive groves and fields of lavender, on this the first of the Alpine stages. The really big climbs come tomorrow. Today, just to get us into our stride, are three cols, the biggest of which is the Col de Perty. Nearer the end of the stage is the Col de la Sentinelle, lower but harder then Perty.

I'm still able through Jeff to make private eating arrangements, and I have been keeping my cycle and equipment under constant watch. But it's very wearing when all you want to do is relax. Romain, in spite of his win on the Ventoux, has been quiet. In the back of my mind I wonder if he smells victory and will decide to attack. If he does, I know how he'll do it. He'll go after the Mountain title so hard that he suddenly "finds" himself leading the race. And what could Terry say? He'll have to say, "Good luck, lad; it was an accident. Go on and win." Then again his quietness might have to do with his being religious. It'll be on these next few stages that Romain will, or will not, stamp himself a super champion. If he wins the Tour he's In, but in riding a defensive race on my behalf the experts will still be able to judge what he's made of. He tells me that when Mottiat spoke to him on top of the Ventoux it was to offer him double wages for the rest of his contract if only he'd attack my position. Romain says that he turned him down, and to be honest I've no reason to disbelieve him.

Things are now getting so crowded in my mind that it's almost as if I haven't any energy left to think about Bobbie. London seems so far away, and it feels as if it were years ago that I saw her. She's like my boyhood—a dream I once had from which all I can remember are picture stills and snatches of words spoken. Win or lose, I'd better wait until the Tour's over before I do anything further to contact her. In a week's time I'll be able to hop on a plane for London and really track her down. And if I can guarantee her that my income for the next few months will be big time, I shouldn't be surprised if I didn't bring her back with me. All I'll want then is Out—Right Out.

In my time I've morally sided with all sorts of issues, causes and creeds. But really, when you boil it down, they're all to do with people and their viciousness. Which is probably why I'm still a loner. Associate yourself too much and the stench of Humanity gets overpowering. No, I want Out. If you can't beat 'em—quit. Plenty of big bikkies would buy me time to get Bobbie with me for as long as it would take. I used to reckon that given sufficient time, opportunity and the desire, I could get *any* bird to fall for me. For the most part I still believe this, in spite of everything. It's got nothing to do with conceit, even though it sounds like it. It's a matter of applying Nature. With that real money I could, say, spend a third on gold or diamonds—something that would maintain a value whatever happens, barring the holocaust. And the rest I could put to work. Me, living off the efforts of others? It would make a change. My aching limbs and bursting lungs have been entertaining them for all these years.

Some of the press have been saying that, as Romain was nominated leader of the international team in the first place, he should not hold back and should ride his own race. Other sports writers say he is doing the correct thing by helping me, and this opinion finds favor in the Belgian, Italian and Spanish camps. None of them believes I can last out, and that by aiding me Romain is ruining his own chance, leaving it a three-way duel between van Faignaert, The Sundance Kid and Butch Cassidy.

Romain is still asking my advice when it comes to winning the King of the Mountains prize, and in all fairness I can only tell him what I believe to be true. I've advised him to take the mountain primes on this stage and not to push his advantage, but to slaughter the field on tomorrow's big stage from Gap to Briançon. Then, if he still feels up to it on the following day, to do the same again. The trouble is, if he takes me too literally, he'll take the *maillot jaune* as well. Between here and the end of the mountain stages are eleven major climbs on which Romain could, simply by topping each one first, pick up eleven minutes in bonuses alone. His official time is only fourteen minutes and thirty seconds behind me, and I make eleven from fourteen and a half to be three and a half. And if Romain couldn't take three and a half minutes out of my hide between here and Paris, then I'll eat my sweaty socks. He could take double that amount in the time trial. So I know he can beat me if he wants to, but can either of us hold off van Faignaert? The Belgian dealt out a lot of punishment as far as the Pyrenees, so much so that several times I saw Romain finish shaking like a belly dancer. Although Romain appears quite fresh, he is a "delicate" sort of rider, and he's never raced this distance before. I think he's capable of riding one devastating Alpine stage, but no man can race this far without weakening. Tomorrow's stage might take it out of him so much that all he'll have left for the rest of the climbs will be the ability to take the primes. On tomorrow's stage are the two big ones: Vars and Izoard. They're high, steep, long and hard. Of course he'll get away all right on his own, but he's got to descend as well, and ride the rest of the stage alone.

In a way the mountains are a Godsend, at least as far as worrying about van Faignaert's concerned. Going up he can just beat me because he's younger; coming down I think I've got the edge on him. Until the mountains end, the Belgian has got to consolidate and ride a defensive race. I don't believe it's even in his mind to try and win anything in the next few stages. All he'll try to do is not lose too much time to the better climbers. He'll come into his own in the time trial. Normally a more stylish rider like Audaire (if he were still with us), or even Romain, would win this, but after two thousand miles of racing behind us, it's a strong man such as van Faignaert who'll be the danger. And he is strong. I saw him win his first world title. One lap to go and he was about half a mile behind the leading group. As they came round on the last lap he wasn't far from being half a mile in front, his face screwed up in agony but going like a fourpenny rocket.

When I've spoken to Paula on the phone I haven't felt inclined to upset her by asking how her friends are taking the news. I reckon there're a few cynical thoughts churning over in Ghent this week. Each day I get a new yellow jersey. I'm hoping, win or lose, to collect enough to present them with one each. It's a pity they're not actually here so I could wring the sweat from the jerseys over their heads.

It's a funny sort of stage. Everyone seems to be waiting for Romain to attack. Van Faignaert, as I expected, is taking things easy and trying to keep the bunch together. Butch Cassidy's not a bad climber and on the Col de Foreyssasse he has a go, but the Belgian team swoops and soon has him under control. I can see on the faces of the spectators that they are disappointed. They've turned out in their thousands expecting this to be It; I feel like shouting to them to go home and come back tomorrow. We get strung out a bit coming down the Foreyssasse but regroup at the bottom. The ominous threat of Romain taking off, coupled with the strong control of the race by the Belgian team, who're doing their damnedest to keep everyone in one lump, has really put the mockers on things.

I'm just beginning to think that the worst of the stage has passed when the rider directly in front of me punctures, loses control and goes sliding along the loose surface on his side. It's on a sharp descent and the bunch is moving. Although it all happens in a split second, I'm unable to go either to the left or right of the fallen man and I jam on my brakes. With both wheels locked solid I pile into him at about thirty miles per hour. Normally I would have been flung over the handlebars, but my toe straps are sufficiently tight for me to do several cartwheels with the bike still attached to me. For a second everything seems upside down; then pain. I lie there feeling as if I'll never move again. From the front of the group I see van Faignaert and his henchmen pushing forward on the expected break. He leads out and as one the Belgian team groups round him and they're away, the rest of the field chasing.

Romain comes from somewhere, lifts my shoulders and blinks anxiously down at me. My mouth is full of dust and I can taste the blood from where I've nearly bitten through my lip. I spit while Romain holds my head. I can't see Bert, but I hear him say, "Bloody hell." My legs feel so numb that I wonder if my back's broken. I feel down toward my thigh. It's wet and gritty and when I bring my hand slowly up to my face I see my fingers are caked with blood. I don't really faint, just sort of drift away for a few seconds. The sound of my own voice saying "I've had it" brings me, like the popping in a blocked ear when it clears, back to consciousness.

"Terry, there's nothing broken. Can't you get up? Get up and we'll push you," Romain says.

My lips feel as if they've become rubber beach rings. Bert wipes something wet across my mouth. White trouser legs walk past my face and I can feel hands with an expert touch running over my legs and body. I hear Bert say, "Careful or

I'll bleedin' fill yer in."

The doctor peers into my face and says in broken English, "Well, what about it, *Maillot Jaune?*"

Before I can answer, Romain puts his arms under my shoulders and drags me to my feet. For a few seconds I reel and cling to Romain, but then feel better for being upright. I wipe my eyes on the back of my hand while medics paint me with iodine.

"*Vite, vite!*" Romain keeps shouting as he waves an arm at the first-aid team.

I catch his hand. "I'll never make it."

"You will! Bert and I can get you back!"

"Listen," I say, pointing down the empty road. "Listen. Use your head. I'm a beaten-up vet with only two helpers. About a mile away is one of the strongest and most determined roadmen for years, in his prime, backed by an all-star team."

Romain angrily tears his arm away and his usually so quiet voice comes at me with force. "I'll get you back."

I look around in despair. Bert's helping Jeff with my machine. Frantic hands rip at plaster. "Romain, I don't want to be unkind, but you could never tow me back to van Faignaert. I'd need a team made up of Coppi, van Steenbergen, van Looy and Stablinski, all at their best, all dedicated to me. Can't you see? You'd never catch them, and I couldn't stay with you."

He bites his lips together and for a second I think he's going to hit me. Either that or burst into tears. Strangely, he isn't blinking. We stare at each other while the medics finish working on my legs. At last Romain says quietly, as if he's thought it all over carefully, "Perhaps you don't think much of me, Terry. Perhaps you think I'm weak and have no real chance. But I'm going to start this chase with one advantage the others never got. I've had the best teacher in the game."

I can't look at him and I don't know what to say.

He points at my machine. "Get on before you get too stiff."

With a swoop of his right hand he lifts his bike from the ground, plonks it on the road and jumps on.

My left leg feels dead and already blood is soaking through the dressing. One of the attendants hands me a pad soaked in antiseptic, which I hold to my mouth as I walk toward where Bert's holding my cycle.

" 'Ow d'yer feel, Terry?"

"Groggy, mate. Like after a night out down Aldgate."

"Vat's the spirit. We'll catch the sods."

"Ta." Stiffly I get on. It's then that it dawns on me the whole affair has been televised, or at least part of it, probably alternating between my pile-up and van Faignaert's break at the front. A vulture-faced copper on a motorcycle is revving his engine, waiting to lead us. I put my right foot in the toeclip and push off. My left leg feels rigid and the first few thrusts are agony. I come up to Romain. "How long?"

"Six minutes. Don't worry."

A six-minute deficit on van Faignaert, I keep saying to myself. There's only one bloke here who could catch him, and that's the copper on the motorcycle.

The police escort sets off, siren going like an alley cat hit by an airgun slug. Romain streaks ahead, looking back over his shoulder, freewheeling impatiently and waiting for me to get into some sort of stride. I feel whacked and giddy. Bert's hand rests on my shoulder as he tries to push me, but really it doesn't help much. Now that the blood's pumping round me, it's also pumping out—through every available exit, or so it seems.

Romain drops back and rides next to me. "Get dead close to my wheel. Watch it. Don't take your eyes off it. Don't think.

You must stay with me." He pulls ahead and dumbly I obey. My mouth is bleeding and as I shoot a glance back to Bert the wind carries spots of blood from my face and peppers them over my arm. I know what's coming is going to hurt, probably more than anything I've ever done, and almost certainly it's all for nothing.

Romain is doing his best to pace me as Alphonse would on a motorbike. I can see he's trying to feel as I feel, to put himself in my place. A jeep with a TV camera and crew keeps coming up and filming us. I feel absurd and dejected and try to turn my swollen face away from the camera. When you feel all handsome and are winning, no bugger will even point a box camera at you.

This road is familiar. Already it's starting to climb. Not long gradients, but short switchbacks that break your rhythm and take it out of you something wicked. At the first opportunity I leave the saddle so that I can use my body weight to help my left leg with the climbing. It seems that as soon as I've selected a gear that feels like a happy medium, the gradient changes and I either have to change up or change down.

I remember that once out of these short hills the road changes direction, and if I'm not very much mistaken will put the wind behind us. It'll mean that everyone will be able to steam along quicker. For me, the sick man, it will at least be the easiest way to suffer.

Up, down: my legs feel as useless as two bits of rope. I try to do more work with my right leg, but this tires it quicker. Bert keeps trying to push me, but his attempts are getting feebler and intervals between are becoming longer. He rides past me and pours warmish water over my head. His mouth is sagging open and I wish he'd drunk some before tossing it over me. He goes to wink and click his tongue, but he hasn't really got the strength and it comes out as a nervous tic.

I try not to look up at the coming col. I fix Romain's rear wheel firmly in my eye as if I were squinting down a gun sight. The thing to do is to try and imagine that the road is flat. You must forget everything and try to become hypnotized by the spinning wheel. Round and round I turn the cranks, my heart beating its own echo in my temples. I glance at my hands, grimed with sweaty blood, the veins standing black and prominent through the hairs like mountain ranges in a forest. Romain's wheel suddenly seems to draw away. I can't hold it any longer and he doesn't hear me gasp his name. Why doesn't he look back and ease up for a second? I stand on the pedals and fight with everything I've got to close the gap, but I can't make it. Then I look up and see the road twisting upward, and my heart sinks. I don't know how I feel; it's almost as if I were stationary and the world was flashing past me giving the illusion of speed.

He looks round and sees me. He gasps and a stringy length of spittle flies off his mouth and lands on the dusty road. All I can do is nod to him and he turns away and plods on up the col. I know there are spectators and following cars, but somehow they don't exist for us. The limits of our world are made up of aching limbs and hammering head, creaking cycles with frames and bars which strain and whip under our efforts, sweat and pain and gradient and furnacelike heat. These people are watching something they can never understand. To them I'm Davenport, T., number fifty-two, veteran luckily wearing *maillot jaune*, and the way they stare gives you the impression they can't credit you with ever doing anything else other than pounding past on a bicycle.

We turn a hairpin and I see Bert on the road below, doggedly punching his way upward. I tell myself that if we've dropped Bert then perhaps we've made up some time on the peloton.

At last we make the top. It might be fatal to stop pedaling, but stop I do. The bliss of snatching a short freewheel! We're both gasping for breath, both unable to speak. Romain wearily points down the road, meaning that our pause is over. There's no sign yet of Bert, who must be still coming up.

The crowds, as usual, are as thick as they always are at the top of a climb. Our copper sticks a whistle in his mouth and starts to blow; it shrieks in mournful duet with his siren. People lean forward as far as they dare and squint at our faces, hoping to take in indelible impressions of our silent suffering. I don't care now how I look, anyway, because I feel half monster with my drooling swollen face. Mercifully I feel the wind in our backs, and the road ahead looks more level. If we've gained on the bunch at all it would have been on the climb. Because van Faignaert is not a climber it seems unlikely he would have got far from the peloton on the way up. If he's going to get away, it'll be on this part of the stage where the climb levels out. Ahead I see a motorcycle cruising slowly, waiting for us, the pillion rider with a walkie-talkie. At last we can get some information. As we pass, the driver shouts, "*Peloton à trois minutes.*"

"Van Faignaert?" I hear Romain gasp.

The pillion rider laughs and waves his walkie-talkie. "*A trois minutes!*"

Romain freewheels for the first time since we began the climb. Like me, he glistens and drips. His chest heaves in quick time and his nose is bleeding slightly. "How far to the finish?"

For a few seconds I can't get enough wind to answer him. "About twenty-five kilometers."

He starts to pedal again, craning his head forward in the

hope he might see some stragglers. Bert comes up behind us, his head lolling forward, unable to speak.

Romain freewheels again and looks round. "Don't make me do this for nothing. You must keep with me. Ten-tenths, Terry. I mean it. *Allons.*"

"I've gone to my limit!" I try to shout but it comes in a hoarse gasp and he doesn't hear. I know what he means: I should do it because I told him in the first place. Only a few times in his life, perhaps never, does a rider push himself to the absolute limit, or ten-tenths as I call it. Most of the time you ride pretty close to it, say at about eight-tenths. Nine is really suffering. But ten is how you'd ride if to be caught meant dis-embowelment or the torture of the hooks, or to save your mother or your children. It means to ride so that parts you never think of, such as your liver, your whole system, refuse to do any more. I've seen men try it. Sometimes they succeed, but mostly they finish in the ambulance. Usually they faint and crash at about nine and a half-tenths.

I call after him again, but he won't look round. With a clink I see his chain jump onto his smallest sprocket. He glances back, but when our eyes meet he quickly turns his head and bends low over the bars. Faster and faster he turns his big gear. My hand drops to my front shifter and I too am in top, which means I'll travel 106 inches for every complete revolution of the pedals. I'm aware of Bert falling behind as I return to fixing my eyes on Romain's rear wheel. The left side of my body feels as if it's severely burned from ankle to shoulder, and bad though this pain is I'm almost able to for-get it. Replacing it, edging it out, is this great knot inside me, feeling how I imagine you'd be if you had a living bloody-minded octopus inside your stomach with its tenta-cles reaching out at every artery and organ.

We pound on, seeming to go faster and faster, helped by

wind and flatter road. The faces which line our path are so closely spaced that they become an endless gray line flashing past on either side, like crash barriers on a road to hell. I realize now what a great cyclist Romain really is. He'd never ride like this in a bunch, but out here, on an open road and with me in trouble, he's a different person. There's no way I can even guess what speed we're doing or what progress we're making, if any. I don't think my eyes are watering, yet I seem to be looking at everything through a mist. It would be fatal to drag my eyes from the wheel in front. As much as I want to peer round Romain's sheltering body, I daren't.

One physical pain blends with another until I think I must be alight from head to toe. Dimly, like looking through a gauze screen, I can still see Romain's wheel. I have enough instinct left to realize I'm not as steady as I should be, and I keep about two feet between our wheels.

And now we're climbing again. My fumbling slippery hand fluffs a gear change and I stop pedaling while I sort out what gear I want, but when I go to pedal again I find my legs have no strength at all. Gradually I freewheel to a standstill; Romain has seen me stop and has circled in the road. He rides up just in time to catch my arm and stop me falling. For a while he just stares, running his tongue round his lips as he tries to draw enough air to speak.

"Get on. I'll push."

"What, up a mountain!"

"It's still quite flat."

I look, and see that the road in front has only a gradual slope. I shake my head. "Must be dreaming . . . I thought we were climbing."

I sit on the saddle and wearily once more begin the treadmill. Romain's bony slender hand lands in the middle of my back and he starts to push. Almost immediately I know it's not going to work. Athletically Romain might be great, but as a man he's weak, and even after shedding enough sweat to fill the Serpentine I still weigh around twelve stone. And should Bert catch us he'll be in too much of a state to do any pushing. Doing ten-tenths didn't work. We both rode too near the brink, and my age made me break first. I sit up and look round at him. His whole body is heaving and gasping and he looks almost finished. Desperately I try pedaling hard again. At first there's not much there, but gradually the old motor starts to pick up again after its rest. It's a relieved Romain who rides past me and takes his position at the front.

Again we resume the chase, and again it's up and up and up until I think I must have died and am in an everlasting climbing purgatory. I know that Romain's sting has gone, but even without it he'll probably climb as fast as the peloton. Although I've lost all sense of what's happening and am riding by instinct alone, I can tell we're not moving very fast. For all I know we might be an hour down on van Faignaert.

Fully a minute must have passed before it hits me, like the stab of merciful relief you'd get if your doctor said there was nothing wrong and he wouldn't have to operate. The road sign we just passed said Gap.

I suddenly become conscious of a lot of things: that misty clouds blot out the sun, that Jeff's motorcycle is tailing me and behind Jeff a shattered Bert plods on. Again I'm aware of the crowds and of the *Arrivée* banner stretched across the road ahead. Before we reach it I stop pedaling, and as it passes above me I feel I've just ridden through the gates of paradise.

◆

I can still see the word *Arrivée* when I open my eyes and find myself on a bed in the never-changing hotel room.

They're all there: Romain, Jeff, Susan and Bert. I know I haven't been here long, because Romain's covered in dust and his mouth is still open. The doctor, to my left, is putting away his instruments.

Susan takes a step forward and whispers, "How do you feel?"

"On fire, I guess."

"This isn't a race," she says bitterly, "it's a rhapsody in suffering."

The doctor turns and faces me. "You passed out. I have given you nothing, because even if I advised you not to, you would be at the start tomorrow. Lie perfectly still and later a nurse will see to your cuts."

I thank him and he goes.

"Well, say something!" I gasp. "This is getting to look like a scene from *Doctor Kildare*."

Jeff shrugs and sits on a chair next to the bed. "You lost five minutes five seconds to van Faignaert; Romain lost the same. As it stands your lead is now down to five minutes three seconds, and Romain is still fourteen-thirty behind you but back to nine-twenty-seven down on van Faignaert. I take it this is what you're waiting to hear?"

The news seems to put on army boots and run around inside my head. I lie still and listen while it dances a reel and kicks home the implications into every corner of my mind. To be beaten is one thing, but to lose half my lead on a silly accident is almost more than I can cope with. Well, I've had it now.

Hoarsely, I lisp through my swollen mouth, "Listen, Romain. Tomorrow you forget all about me. And the day after that, and the day after that, you forget. If you really go now—you might just scrape home. And thanks for helping me as you did. 'Thanks' is a meaningless sound that could have been given to anything, but right now it's all I can say."

He comes over to the bed. "That's all right, Terry." He works the peak of his racing cap nervously in a rotating movement, like a peon up before the boss. "After today's ride I don't think I could win now. I'll probably be able to take off tomorrow, but after that—Phtt!" Wearily he sits on the bed. "There's such a long, long way to go yet, isn't there? I never realized it was so long. I know our plans got altered when you took the lead, but I see—oh, so clearly—what you meant about planning a race. I'm sorry to say this, Terry, but I don't think either of us can win. Van Faignaert played it right; throughout he's kept within a stone's throw of leadership without actually taking it. I think now he'll take over when it suits him."

He looks really dejected and Susan puts her arm on his shoulder.

"Have your bath first," I say. "I can't even move." He stands up and goes toward the bathroom.

I say after him, "I'm sorry I messed things up for you."

He half smiles as he gets to the bathroom door. "All we can do is keep trying. Perhaps tomorrow, or the day after, our luck will change. Tonight I'll pray hard so that tomorrow, maybe, you'll go with God."

"I would, if there was one."

"There is. He's up there in the mountains."

I sigh. "Put in a good word for me then as you pass."

◆

Gap-Briançon. 165 kilometers.

It's really something to see, a climber waiting to attack. Any other sort of attack can be neutralized, but when a climber goes there's little the non-climbers can do.

Already my new yellow jersey and bandages are blotting up the sweat and my aches and pains starting to thump. I doubt if I'll even finish the stage. It's goodbye to independence, Bobbie, fame, the old house near Nîmes. Goodbye to me, in fact. Still, we come into the world with nothing. No longer do I have any plans. To carry me through today my only plan is to get over the two big cols with as little suffering as possible, and to try and keep up by making a fast run down. On both Vars and Izoard I can clock some fantastic speeds on the runs down, and in a spiteful sort of way I look forward to slaughtering van Faignaert on these two big descents. And if I go a bit too fast or misjudge—what the hell? A yellow jersey makes a good mini-shroud.

The peloton is tightly grouped. Romain rides near the front, a little to one side, away from the rest. Van Faignaert, Butch Cassidy and the other leaders are trying to make out he's not there. When Romain goes, a few outsiders might attempt to hold him, but the leaders know it'll be no use killing themselves to stay with him on the big climbs. And so today, for once, we're all wanting the same thing—not to lose too much time.

Romain drops back and joins me. "Good luck. Something might happen to save you," he says.

"I doubt it. Slaughter 'em. Make 'em suffer, make them pay."

He's blinking. "I will."

"Pretend you're stamping on the banker's wife's head. Nothing like a drop of hate to make you go."

He smiles and rides back to the front.

I've told him what do do. Rather than ride away and string out the field, I suggested that he hit them in bursts. This will have a very demoralizing effect, because time and again they'll think he's cracked or that they've caught him, only to see him draw away once more. And to do this on the early part of the stage will give him a number of needed rests. Later, of course, he'll have to stay away and keep going.

I know Romain well enough to know when it's coming. We're getting up toward Vars now. It towers in front of us and I can see the dusty road winding up into a bank of low cloud. Even the wind is against us. People often think that hills and mountains are the worst obstacles in the way of cycling, but really the wind is the worst, topped only by wind combined with gradient.

He won't go just yet, it's not steep enough. On these long drags through the foothills he'd be likely to take some of the better climbers with him. No, he must wait a bit so that when he makes his move there's no doubt who's boss. Although yesterday's stage took it out of him I believe he'll do a good ride today.

There he goes. Small spurts of dust come off his wheels as he stands on the pedals and gives a real lung-bursting effort. The best of the Belgian climbers is Loncke—the man whom I just beat in the pouring rain on my "comeback" race to impress Bobbie. Loncke gets in front of van Faignaert and does his best to pace his captain up the col. The rest of the Belgian squad forms itself solidly around the World Champion to act as a buffer against the wind. They know they won't catch Romain but want to keep van Faignaert as fresh as possible.

Romain has a hundred-yard lead now. Suddenly he looks round and sits up, waiting to be caught. But he's made it too obvious; an expert like van Faignaert won't fall for that one. Gradually, in our own time, we draw near and then off he goes again.

The peloton is beginning to break up, the better climbers going away in small groups. Although it'll kill them, most of the Belgian team manage to keep their leader toward the front.

I keep watching Loncke and remembering that day at
Bruges. I should never have let her go. If only I could put
the clock back to that day. I wonder what she's doing? In
bed with some bloke, I suppose. Still, every bird I've ever
had is probably in bed with some bloke. But I mustn't
believe the worst of her. Maybe she's tearing along on her
scooter thinking of me. I can't see her ever becoming much
of a whore, yet when she got going she was no prude either.
Don't they say that inside every prude there's a whore
shrieking to get out? And vice versa? My feelings for Bobbie
make this side of things seem not quite so important, but I
harp on it a bit because for me and blokes like me there's
not much else. The Act is something Man has always had,
however primitive he's been, to help him hang on to his
sanity. For me, everything eventually palls, or turns out a lie
or a trap, but with you-know-what one can be sure that the
next time is going to be pretty well as good as the last.

I'm finding it harder and harder to keep up with van
Faignaert. Between us now there's a definite gap. That
bloody idiot Beach Boy grinds slowly past me, looking down
his nose as he passes, as if to say, "If only I'd had your luck."
I can't even be bothered to get angry when he joins the
Belgian squad and goes to the front of it to help pace van
Faignaert. Beach Boy keeps turning his head so that the
Belgian leader gets a good look at him. With a team of
blokes like Beach Boy you wouldn't need opponents.

I pass riders and riders pass me. The going's so slow that
I'm able to keep closing my eyes, shutting out the sun and
dust and faces and everything.

When I finally top the Vars I can't see a sign of van Faignaert. All Jeff has gathered over the radio is that the Belgian
is going down like a statesman heading for his fallout shelter.
As soon as I feel the cycle rolling without my pedaling, I

ease up and snatch a rest. The machine begins to gather momentum, but for as long as I'm able I keep sponging my face and arms. Then it's the sponge away, into top, and some real concentration.

One by one, and then in groups, I catch and overtake riders. When you get up into the really fast speeds that go with descending, cycle hubs give off this odd whine, which now hits my ears in increasing volume. I'm as low on the bike as I can get, knees and elbows tucked well in, top gear in case I have to pedal, hands ready on brake levers. Soon the nervous gropers who are feeling their way down are left behind, and the riders I'm beginning to make contact with are harder to pass. Several press vehicles latch on at various times but can't stay with me. It's rather a nice feeling to drop motorcycles and cars.

The air pressure is terrific. My still swollen face must be putting up a lot of drag. The long white road rushes to meet me as I throw the bike into bend after bend, riding as near to the edges as I dare, sending spectators scurrying for cover. As the bends get less frequent I'm able to give it everything, and with hubs literally singing I mold myself to the machine and hurtle downward. I can see now for miles ahead and have spotted a strung-out group which must be van Faignaert's. There aren't enough bends left to make the effects of my descending felt, but as the road begins to level out and my freewheeling speed drops off, I thrash my big gear in an effort to close the gap.

As I approach what must be the last slight bend, I see a girl standing at the roadside, quite alone. She has long blond hair. The rested ticker gives a jump and I sit up in my headlong chase and mouth her name. I've even grabbed for my brakes before I glimpse her face. It's plump and spotty— and not Bobbie's. Self-preservation makes me forget the incident for a second as I lay the bike down and just get round.

In front I can see the Belgian's group. With a supreme effort I could catch them, but it would mean arriving exhausted just in time to climb the Izoard—a bastard even higher than Vars. Next time round, when I'm reincarnated, I'll pick an easy way to make a living. My sponsors will be from the hookworm industry, my team the Cold Norton Pensioners' Karate Club, and my job to push a golf ball across Waterloo Bridge with my nose on Christmas Day for a million bucks. Cash. Tax free.

12

Better to Die on Our Feet than Live on Our Knees

I STARE AT THIS FLY ON THE BEDROOM ceiling. Even the effort of moving my eyes is too much. I close them. The bedside light's on because I'm trying to fool myself into falling asleep. It must be about one o'clock. Romain's got a room of his own tonight. That's the way it works out sometimes.

What a day. I never caught van Faignaert; nearly did, but not quite. For what it's worth (which is nothing) I now have a lead over the Belgian of two minutes forty-four seconds. Tomorrow, officially, the dream ends. I knew my chance was only a slight one, but in spite of the pessimism we adopt, basically I'm like most people—a fairly optimistic animal. If we weren't we'd blow our brains out at puberty. Romain gained seven minutes, putting himself on overall classification about two and a half behind van Faignaert and five behind me. At one point he was near to being twenty minutes up, but he lost his nerve coming down the Izoard. Van Faignaert's team car immediately informed him of Romain's trouble and the Belgian went after him with everything he had. This evening I saw both Romain and the Belgian, and I know who'll win. Van Faignaert looks much the same as he did when he started, whereas Romain looks like a bloody wraith.

There's more. Loncke was killed descending the Izoard. He was just ahead of me when it happened. We'd got over the worst bit and were nearing the bottom of the run down. He hit a stone in the road; it wasn't a big stone but at sixty miles per hour it was enough to burst his front tire. It shook me something wicked to see it all. For about fifty yards he fought it and all I could do was keep going and watch him, hypnotized. He would have made it except for this bend. It seemed he couldn't turn his bars. Rather than plow straight into the rock wall, he more slid along it, filing himself away as he went. What can you do? They say prayers and have a big ceremony for his wife and print nice things in the papers. But in a couple of years some follower of the sport will ask, "What became of Loncke? Haven't seen his name lately." Loncke, Davenport, what's the difference.

I saw Susan alone for about quarter of an hour. The race is wearing her out as well. I think that girl, although she'll make Romain a good wife, will always be somebody's mistress. She said a funny thing to me tonight. She said I was Everything—conceited, modest, muddled, certain, old, young, honest, dishonest—and odd. We were interrupted and she never explained herself. I suppose I can be a bit odd, but I don't know why Susan should suddenly say so. I know that if I go into the Gents and there's someone else there, I can't do anything until they've gone. And I can remember when, some years back, I had a craze for making illiterate applications for Top Jobs advertised in the posh papers, using phonetic spelling and putting S's the wrong way round. Maybe a lot of people would think this odd, but as far as I was concerned it was done for a laugh.

Perhaps it's odd to want Out, but to me those who want In are either the trouble causers or their worshipers. I've given up trying to find out the truth about anything. One lie merely conceals another, and the deeper I dig the more disgusted I get. With big money I could have kept it all at bay. Neither is it that odd to fancy a bird eighteen years younger than yourself. She was bloody lovely—it's as simple as that. Dead nubile, even if her phobia did get a bit wearing. When a man thinks he'll try for a particular woman, and vice versa, it's nothing more than a less obvious form of cattle buying. The romantics and those who think we're some kind of High Being (after all Christ's got two arms, two legs and a head) would be horrified to hear me compare the Great Chemistry with cattle buying. But even at my low level it's a subject I've thought about and practiced.

Toward the end of today's stage we ran into damp mist, then rain. Now it sounds as if it's getting worse and turning to hail. I always do better in bad weather, but really if I'm going to lose the *maillot jaune* I might as well part with it tomorrow. No kidding when I say I feel completely exhausted. I repeat, the difference between age and youth is that youth recovers from a beating so much quicker. All I'm doing is getting tireder and tireder. The night's rest between stages isn't long enough for me.

Romain too has had it. In future years, with trade teams, when he'll have a strong backing such as van Faignaert's got, he'll win. He's had to ride a negative race, throwing away his reserves to help me and getting no time gains in return. If he could choose when to make the attacks and have behind him the whole T.B.H.-Aigle team, only real bad luck could stop him from winning. Without strong support he's too frail and nervy, and there's not much room in the Tour for people like that. He's too meek and I'm too old. Right up to where I took the *maillot jaune*, his only team was me and Bert. The rest of the internationals have ridden for themselves. You can't get anywhere with flash yobs like Kimber, or with Swiss Herrenvolk. Other than Romain, Bert and myself, the remaining internationals left in the race are Kimber and the Portuguese. The only other team to take a bigger pounding was the French national team, which lost half its riders with the Audaire caper.

I'll try it for a while with the light out and give that fly up there a bit of peace. The forecast is bad. I hope it's snow up in the mountains and not rain. I'd rather do the Skater's Waltz than plod through Flanders Fields.

Odd, am I?

◆

I put my fingers on my eyebrows, my thumbs on my cheeks, and force my closing eyes to stay open. "God, I'm tired," I say to Susan. She continues to pour the coffee and shoots me a glance.

"I've just given Romain his coffee. He looked rough. Neither of you is going to win, are you?"

"No. Coffee's supposed to be on our banned list; did you know that?"

"If you're not going to win, what does it matter?"

"It doesn't. Why did you say yesterday that I was odd?"

"I'll have to ask you a question first."

"Go on then."

"How would you describe fear?"

"Fear?" I have a little think. "It's a funny sensation. It gets you right here, just north of the bellybutton, like a sort of tight sickness, and no matter what you try to think about it won't go away. Perhaps it's the real you, your soul showing itself, right here in your stomach. Why did you ask me that?"

I see there are tears in her eyes as she picks up the cups

and coffee jug. "It's how you feel, isn't it?" She walks to the door and looks round.

"Yes."

"It's just that it's odd to see you scared. Is it because of Loncke, or because you've lost?"

"It's because of everything. . . . I don't know."

I listen to the cups rattling as she goes away, and then I close my eyes and lie back, resting my head on the pillow. Outside it sounds like the end of the world, and I've got to ride through it for 222 kilometers and over four cols to Aix-les-Bains. Perhaps that's all I'm scared of—the physical suffering. There was a time when it wouldn't have mattered and I'd have taken it in my stride. In the iris of my mind I can see myself at about twenty-five riding through similar conditions in a hundred races, untroubled and holding my own with the best of them. The picture's so clear that I feel I could put my hand out and touch, as if I were standing at arm's length in front of a painting.

I hear the door open. "Wotto," Bert says. His hair's standing on end and he's wearing a crumpled dressing gown.

"Hello, Bert. How do you feel?"

He sinks onto a settee and runs a hand through his hair. "Rough, mate, rough. I've 'ad it."

"How d'you mean, had it?"

He shakes his head. "I'm pullin' aht. I can 'ardly bleedin' stand. Buggered, I am."

I don't know what to say to him. I let go a big sympathetic sigh.

"Well," I say at last, "it'll be my turn tomorrow. Believe me, I know how you feel, so I won't try to talk you out of it. You've been a good mate, Bert, and I appreciate how you've helped."

"Fanks. I was finking I might turf it in altogevver, like. Sling me 'ook, go 'ome, you know."

"Oh, don't do that, Bert. You're good for a few years yet. How old are you?"

"Firty-wun. Soon be over the 'ump."

"What about me, then?"

"You! Gawd, you're all cock 'n' courage. I don't know 'ow yer do it, my life I don't. I can't face vose marntins agin, not in vis lot. It's pissing dahn. Chay-os. Brass monkey wevver."

"Yes," I say and look at the rain running down the window. "What will you do when you get home? Or will you stay out here?"

"Nar, go 'ome, I specs. Me bruvver's got a little number on a rar-way stachun near Sarfend. Reck'ns 'e kun git me in as a port'r. 'E's 'appy. 'Andy f' the Eliminations ev'ry aut'mn; runs a Ford Fiesta. And it'll all be in English. When I first caugh' a train for Paris I fort all ver bleedin' stachuns was called *Sortie*. 'Ere." He leans toward me. "On me bruvver's stachun 'im an' 'is mates 'ave got vis 'ole drilled froo t' ver ladies' bog. One day, when me bruvver was 'aving a gander, 'is mate nipped rahnd, inter the bog like, and stuck 'is eye on the uvver end. Me bruvver fort 'e'd been tumbled. Shit blue lights, 'e did." He starts to laugh, but the effort seems too much and he leans back on the settee, coughing.

I ask him if he'd like to ride in the car with Susan, but he says he would rather catch a train back to Paris.

"Good luck, Terry-boy. Yer never know, yer might still pull it orf. 'Specs I'll see yer sometime." He shakes my hand.

I watch him shuffle out flatfooted, back to pack his things. I hope he gets something on the railways, even if it's only when they get around to using gangs of unemployed to pull the trains. He'd have been all right for a few quid if I'd won.

Thank God there's still Paula. I couldn't go back and take a job. I'd go round the bend. I suppose Paula will be pleased when she hears I've lost. Poor cow, I don't hold it against her. I can see her point of view, and in a way she's right. If only I'd have had some chances when I was a kid I'd be all right now—a house with stone balls on the gate posts and a couple of hundredweight of polished tongue-and-groove nailed across the front to prove it was architect designed. When I was a kid I used to want to grow up to look like Kirk Douglas and have a buckskin jacket, and every time I kissed a girl to have Leonard Bernstein in the background conducting a cool piece by Burt Bacharach. The only job I ever had that I didn't mind was in a car factory. I remember there was this enormous pile of tires, and some of the men had removed the tires from the middle, leaving the pile hollow. By shifting a certain stack of tires you could get inside, where they had half-inflated inner tubes to lounge on. It was like a club where all the laziest met to play cards and hide from the foreman.

◆

The sleet plops as it hits me, and the wheels send it up from the road, stinging, into my face. It's getting colder all the time, just as the forecast predicted, and already low clouds cover the peaks around us. If I feel too bad I'll ride without trying, so that van Faignaert will easily get my two minutes forty-four seconds. Then I can quit.

Romain took the Col du Lautaret and then waited to be caught. He's got the King of the Mountains title in the bag but is still taking the primes for the sheer pride of it. In order to collect the money for the Mountain prize the rider has to finish the Tour, and so Romain isn't going to extend himself too much. Other than wearing short transparent plastic jackets over our racing vests, we wear the same clothing as on a hot dry stage. I've ridden in some cold races before, and

Jeff's carrying for me some woolen arm warmers, gloves, light-weight goggles, and some newspapers that I can stuff up my jersey to protect my front from the cold. Another accessory that I use, and others don't, is a racing cap with a larger peak. Nowadays the peaks are short and useless, like on guardsmen's caps, but I think a bit of peak out there does wonders in keeping the rain from your eyes.

The roads are so slippery that I shouldn't be surprised if we didn't all stay together and fight it out on a sprint. Myself, I wouldn't mind seeing the field break up and spread out. With a bunch this size, it only takes one to fall and we could all come down.

The descents are the worst. Nobody will give an inch or drop to the rear. I ride as far to the outside as I dare, hoping that no one falls and pushes me over the edge.

We're halfway to the bottom of the Col du Luitel-Chamrousse when this heavy blackness which has been pressing down decides it's been bottled up long enough. The low clouds have made visibility bad since the stage began, but now the hail comes so thick and fast that it's almost impossible to see. What was previously wet slush now becomes icy, and on top of that the sleet and hailstones set-tle like a comfortable old dog in an armchair. One by one—mostly the Latins—they begin to dismount, unable to go on. Team managers rush about issuing hot drinks and additional clothing, and mechanics brush the caking slush from the derailleur gears. While Harich attends to Romain, Jeff props his motorcycle against a tree and I pull in next to him. I tear off the plastic jacket and roll on the arm warmers, then put on a thicker longer jacket and push the newspaper up the front of the yellow jersey. My gloves are made of PVC and are lined, and before I get back on I slip plastic bags over my feet and secure them with rubber bands around my ankles. I have to grin to myself; I look anything but a professional cyclist leading the Tour de France. Jeff gives me a flask of hot tea, which I drink, then I pull down my peak and, peering out from beneath it like a village idiot, I set off.

Soon I pass some others who had got themselves ready before I did. They have stopped by the roadside and are arguing with their team manager. I gather they want to quit and he's trying to talk them out of it. The wind and the falling sleet make it impossible to hear much and I'm mildly surprised when I look back and see a fairly large bunch sitting in behind me. In it are Romain, van Faignaert and three of the Belgian team, and some others. I notice that quite a few of them are without such luxuries as gloves and arm warmers.

Slowly we grind on, toward the cols de Porte, du Cucheron and du Granier. The first one, de Porte, is the worst, and although I see a sign announcing that we are about to hit it I can see nothing of the col itself through the blizzard. Only the pull of gravity and the firmer slush tell me I'm getting higher.

We pass two riders from a French provincial team who had decided against stopping for additional clothing. They huddle together like a pair of drowned rats while a better-protected third member rubs hot tea from a flask into their legs.

The slush is thick enough on the road's surface to hide large stones and ruts. At the slow speed we're traveling this need not necessarily be dangerous, but I think ahead to the descent on the other side. For this time of year it's a freak storm, and possibly on the other side of the col the sun will be shining. But right now it's not, and one by one, blue and chattering, riders go off the back of the group until there are only four of us left: van Faignaert, one of his team, Romain and myself.

We come to a lay-by where a group of holiday makers are

stranded in a Volkswagen van that's been converted into a mobile caravan. As soon as they spot us they dart out from the vehicle with hot drinks in their hands. Van Faignaert ignores them and keeps riding, but his teammate and Romain gratefully shed their machines and take the drinks. I go to stop but decide against it and keep riding. As I turn my head I'm just in time to see Romain and the other Belgian go into the van.

13

Lazarus, or The Big Hammer

IT CAN'T BE ANYTHING TO WATCH, two men on bikes plodding through a storm at about ten miles an hour. Normally van Faignaert would drop me, but then these aren't exactly normal conditions. I glance at him; he looks like a yeti. Sleet clings to his eyebrows and a sort of slush seems to have frozen over the rest of his face, the only bare patch being round his mouth, which his tongue has cleared like a windscreen wiper. No doubt I look much the same.

We approach an official car, its back wheels spinning and its rear end swaying from side to side like the behind on a big bird doing the rumba. Finally it slews round, nearly blocking the road, and I see the driver throw up his hands in despair. Van Faignaert and I go past in single file; flashbulbs pop and temporarily blind me.

And now there's nothing: no spectators, abandoning riders, or cars. Just the two of us. I can't feel much except the cold. As I peer out from behind sleet-encrusted eyelids I believe that the only thing left alive inside me is a crafty animal-like brain that knows it has to watch both the road and van Faignaert.

Painfully slowly we push toward the summit. I can sense we're getting near. If only I could see. I wonder about van Faignaert. Here we are together, yet I know nothing much about him. A tough Flandrien, probably with a background much like my own. A nobody who wanted to be a somebody. For a second the wind drops and I hear my chattering teeth keeping in time with the stinging plip-plop of the sleet and the swish of tires on the road. If I puncture now I've had it. I could never change a tire in these conditions. In fact if I do puncture and the road behind is temporarily blocked to vehicles, I'll probably croak up here from exposure.

It's getting steeper. Probably we'd do better to get off and push. I think it would be quicker. We're still side by side, up-down, plod-plod. He drops behind for a few yards, then comes up again. I think we'd both quit if we could see some shelter to quit to. He falters again—just for a few seconds—then rejoins me. It would be no good my increasing the pressure. In the first place I couldn't, and I don't think I could tell if I did.

The gulps of cold air burn my throat. I try to stop my chattering teeth, but my jaw keeps hammering uncontrollably like a trip-hammer. I think for a second of all the great Tour men who've plodded this col, and glimpse in my mind's eye some of the oldtimers from the twenties and thirties who must have stamped this same route. Men with goggles, long shorts, and sloping gearless bikes. I wonder if they're sitting safely at home listening to Radio Tour and speculating on what's happening up here.

Van Faignaert begins to drop back. I imagine I increase the pressure, but I can't be sure. For a brief moment I glance round at his face, but can only see his eyes staring at me as if through slits in a mask. It's for no more than a flash that our eyes meet, but I know he's beaten. His chattering mouth drools as he fights back, trying to close with me. Once he almost makes it. I pray we won't suddenly reach the top and find ourselves descending. Still the road goes up and still I keep plodding. This isn't cycle racing—it's me, everything I am and have ever been, beating a man named Hendrik van Faignaert. It's not one of the current best riders in the world being screwed by a veteran, it's everything that's me beating everything that's him. You can't call five miles an hour cycle racing. I've read of people "finding themselves" on a mountain, and I wonder if in a remote sort of way it's not what I'm doing now, just like a bloody fakir. I can't tell you why, but I suddenly feel I know myself, as if I've stepped out of my body and sat next to a blazing fire to watch myself on a TV screen. If Susan could read my thoughts now she'd be right in saying I'm odd.

I'm alone—I'm in the lead. Hope and despair wrestle for a soapbox, but I don't know which one to listen to first. Any second I expect to see him come through the sleet and go straight past me, or to hear one of my tires explode. Away from the road I can see parked cars and I realize I must have reached the top. I go into top gear and my chain makes heavy weather of climbing from the largest sprocket to the smallest, it's that bunged up. If I can get down this col a bit sharpish, without trouble, and the next two cols are the same for weather . . . See, Hope has got the soapbox. But if I crash? Well, I'd got used to the idea of losing, anyway. But then van Faignaert might crash or puncture and be right out of the race. I've got to try now, with what strength I have left.

It's only for a second, but I have this sudden vision of all these Bank of England fivers stacked high on the table. Talk about counting your chickens before they're hatched. Money's like crumpet—it's there around you all the time. You're tripping over it and yet very little of it's yours and for the most part you can barely get enough to survive.

I grope my way downward, mostly without seeing, and chancing to luck. I've taken the precaution of substituting a quick-release nut for the ordinary nut that adjusts my saddle height. A quick turn on the release device and down goes my saddle so that I can remain seated and yet get my feet on the ground, when needed, which is often. I want to think about things, about ifs and buts and possibilities, but too much concentration is needed as I hurtle through the slush and send it up in tacky spray all around me.

The cold bites deep. My legs are paralyzed by it and my upper clothing feels no more than an aertex vest. The brakes are useless and the forlorn truth is that if I can't get down without them then I don't get down at all. If it were possible to slow up I'd get off and walk round the dodgier bits. The farther down the col I get the warmer it becomes and the sleet gives way to heavy rain. At last I make contact with the second Italian team car, which had gone on ahead before the storm broke as part of a plan for an attack by their team. They tell me this as I ride along—as far as they can make out there's hardly any of the Italian team left. They know nothing of what's happened to van Faignaert or Romain.

I'm getting a bit steamed up and dive under some trees to remove the arm warmers, newspaper and gloves. It's possible to stick the gloves into a rear pocket, but the other items I have to abandon. As I start the climb of the next col I'm met by Tour cars and officials that have driven out from Aix-les-Bains. After I've gasped out the bones of my story, they carry on back in the direction of the rest of the field. Some local press men, seeing their chance for an exclusive, tag along behind me in a little Peugeot.

Still the rain blinds down, and again it reverts to sleet as I go upward. Am I tireder than on Ventoux? Or in the Audaire break? Or when I crashed? I don't know. The memories of them blend into one long hell. At least this time it's not hot. On go the gloves again and the press men give me some brown paper to stick down the front of the yellow jersey.

◆

From doorways, cars and beneath umbrellas the spectators of Aix clap, whistle and shout. Car hooters blare and men run alongside photographing me through the rain. Of all the vehicles that have passed me going the other way not one has come back with any information.

There's just one thing—the usual thing—that I want to know.

When I get off at the finish my legs are too weak to support me, and two men help me as far as a waiting car. I sit inside trembling, weak and soaked. Although I keep asking, nobody seems to know anything of the Belgian. It seems fairly certain that, after persuasion and waiting for the worst of the storm to pass, most of the field kept going. Romain is among them. They will all have lost so much time that if only van Faignaert's out of the running, I've won the Tour by a mile. The times you think you can't ride another yard and then something like this happens you know that from somewhere you'll find the strength to keep going. Perhaps Romain's prayers have worked and kept alive my up-down dream.

I sit with a blanket wrapped round me, staring through the car window back down the road that leads to Briançon. The driver—I haven't a clue who he is—asks if I mind his smoking. I barely answer and he lights up with a shrug. I watch the clock on the dashboard. Two minutes must have passed before I notice it, and I've been watching it now for four minutes. Then through the gray rain I see cars and in their midst a lone figure. At first I'm sure it's a motorcyclist, and then I think it's not van Faignaert because he's crouched too low. I reason that if the Belgian crashed or retired and this is some other rider, I could still be safe.

But it is van Faignaert. He's crouched so low because he has no alternative. I've never seen a man so shattered. As he gets near to the finish the Belgian team car accelerates ahead so that the manager and his helpers are there to catch him as he collapses into their waiting arms.

I look at the clock. Say I finished six and a half minutes ago, plus my original two minutes forty-four seconds-that gives me about a nine-and-a-half-minute lead.

I give the nod to the driver and he takes off toward the hotel.

◆

"An epic! That's what they all say!" Jeff slaps the back of his hand against the pile of newspapers he's holding. "They're all for you now. All of them! Suddenly van Faignaert has become the Big Bad Wolf."

As Mottiat has disappeared from the scene, we decided it was safe to eat the as-issued grub. Since arriving at the hotel I've been literally besieged, and have had no chance at all to think about time, distance and van Faignaert. And these are the things I dearly want to think about. Jeff managed to get our meal served in a private room. This is not usual, but it appears I'm something of a hero in the proprietor's eyes and if I sign his autograph book many more times it'll be full. In the seven hours since I finished, I've been filmed for cinema newsreel and for television, have given my life story several times over to the press and have been interviewed for just about every radio station in Europe.

Of course they all love this sort of thing—blizzards and underdogs who prove themselves. It smacks of the heroic. But really, looking back, the day I crashed and Romain helped me was the hardest of my life, yet it passed almost without mention. I believe it annoyed most people to think I was still in the running. Of course I feel the cold, but compared with the heat it represents to me the difference between being shot and slowly tortured to death. Years ago, back home, we used to have an old woolly hound named Trolley, and I remember how she was always whacked in the summer. She'd flop about the house with her pink tongue hanging out, and the Old Lady would say, "That dog's getting old, she's slowing up." And I used to believe it. But as soon as the winter came she'd take off and chase her tail all round the yard.

Romain had come in with the whole field, which had kept together for shelter. Unless van Faignaert and I both pull out, Romain hasn't a chance. His only thought now is to get to Paris and collect his prize money.

Jeff sits down and passes the evening newspapers around the table. Bert's gone home and now there are only the four of us: Susan, Romain, Jeff and myself. Susan looks at me over the top of the paper she's holding and blows me a kiss.

I watch my companions as they read the newspapers. Their eyes click along the words like the carriage on a typewriter, and then snap back to the beginning of the next line.

"Iron Man, they call you here," Jeff says to me excitedly.

"Huh, at the moment there's more rust than iron."

"This paper reckons van Faignaert won't be at the start in the morning." Romain looks at me questioningly over his paper.

"He'll be there," I say dryly.

Romain puts the paper down and leans anxiously across

271

the table. "Well? Can you still pull it off?"

The million-dollar question. Three pairs of eyes fix on mine. For a long time I don't answer. "Three stages to go. I can afford to lose three minutes a stage and still just beat him. The mountains are over, which, while neither of us are climbers, helped me more than they helped him. Now there's the time trial and two flat stages: three chances for him to excel, and he's still got seven of his team to help him." I bang my fist on the table. "If only to God I had a couple more minutes! Say eleven or twelve in all. Then I'd say yes. But with nine minutes fifteen seconds—I simply don't know."

They look at me awkwardly.

Jeff says, "The time trial will be the worst. Ninety kilometers, stuck out there alone. He might beat you on this stage alone by nine or ten minutes. He could do."

"Don't I know it," I say wearily and run my hand round my face.

"Unless he really is shattered," Susan suggests.

"Oh, he's shattered all right," I tell her. "But not half as much as I am. He's so strong he'll recover quickly. The press—everyone—is fooled by the fact that he arrived at Aix in one hell of a state. But this was simply because, when he knew he was over the worst bit and getting toward the finish, he gave it all he'd got."

"Well, then he's shattered!" she persists.

"No! He was shattered *at that time*." I thump my chest and slap my thighs. "I'm shattered here—and here. It's been building up. It's *in* me. Don't you see? Dear God, to be twenty-five again!"

She looks at me, believing what I've said but trying to find an argument that will give me comfort. I wish she'd find one; I wish any of them would. It'd be nice to hear even if I didn't believe it.

"Anyway," she says at last, "when I phoned Mother tonight she said she'd close the shop and drive down right away in case she can be of any help."

"In for the kill," I sigh.

She looks angry. "Yes, if you're going to make the killing. You know she'd be proud of you. None prouder. But you didn't mean it like that, did you?"

Jeff and Romain shuffle and read their papers.

"I'm sorry," I say. "I shouldn't have said it. I'll be glad to see her."

Romain breaks the silence. "Your mother isn't actually going to get that great car out of mothballs and *drive* it?"

Susan tries to smile. "It seems like it."

One of Paula's earlier admirers had been a car dealer. Not the sort with a snap-brimmed felt hat who lounges against the bargain of the week, but a Purveyor of Horseless Carriages. In a blinding fit of passion (I suspect he wasn't getting anywhere) he gave Paula this renovated-regardless-of-cost 1930 Minerva. It's so big I can just about see over the bonnet. Paula's very timid about driving and to put her in such a vehicle is akin to giving a baby a hand grenade. If she ever gets this far in it she'll be in a worse state than I was today on the Col de Porte.

When the meal is over, Susan and Romain go for a stroll. Jeff cocks his head to one side listening to their footsteps growing fainter in the corridor outside which leads to the lift. He gets up and sits next to me. As I put down my newspaper he grips my arm. "What is it?" I ask him.

"Listen, Terry." He takes a small bottle from his pocket and flashes it at me.

Before he can say anything I shake my head. "No, no dope. You need time to experiment with the stuff. It might

273

make me worse. Don't think I hadn't thought of it. And after the time trial there are sure to be checks."

"I know! I know!" He says excitedly. "Don't you take any. Let me slip some to van Faignaert and then he'll be disqualified!"

I look at his closed fist and he opens his hand suddenly so that I can see the bottle again. "No," I say.

His grip gets firmer. "Why not?"

"I don't know. Perhaps it's a bit low, even for me."

"Don't be so daft." He holds up the bottle. "In here is your future—everything. I can easily slip some in his food when I see to yours. With van Faignaert out of the way you can ride as slow as you like and still win." He holds the bottle between his thumb and forefinger and brings his hand in front of my face.

"No," I say again.

"What is it with you? Standards? Ideals? You want to wind up like me? A poor forgotten nobody? What is van Faignaert? A Flandrien pig. I rioted in Paris for ideals, but they are nothing. Nobody really cares. In the long run money is everything. Win, no matter how. Get the money and get out. Buy your freedom. I know it's a rotten world, but I didn't make it. Of course I'd like things fair and honest. Once I fought for what I thought was justice, but it's only a word, an illusion. Even if you can get it, it doesn't last. Along come the vultures and the jackals, and the people who care get pushed into the background again. How can it be too low for you? You care about this rotten world? The only people who are worth considering spend their lives giving out pamphlets on street corners or running a cats' home or looking after lepers. They die unnoticed, unwanted and poor. The innocent have no chance at all. I have even seen dogs wag their tails at vivisectors. What is it, Terry? Fear?"

I look hard into his gray eyes set like two currants in a round steamed pudding. I know he's thinking of me and means well. "No, not fear, Jeff. Pride, perhaps. Maybe my pride won't let me do a thing like that. I don't mind winning with luck because it's been luck that's caused me to lose so often. Put the bottle away, Jeff. Forget it. Thanks for the thought, but I'll chance my nine minutes."

14

The Final Solution

I SIT IN THE LOUNGE OF THE HOTEL, dressed and ready to go, and listen to the riders being individually started outside. Other late starters sit around the room, thumbing magazines, waiting for their number to approach. Van Faignaert sits by the window, quite still, staring out without seeing the rubbernecks and nose pressers.

I feel as if I've just walked across London on a hot day wearing shoes with composition soles and nylon socks and carrying two heavy suitcases. Like a ton weight this overwhelming desire presses down on me to crawl upstairs and sleep for a week.

This morning some self-consciously starry-eyed London girls here on holiday called in to wish me Lots of Luck, Luv. There were big implications that if it wasn't for the pressing need to conserve my energy, I'd have been All Right. They make me laugh. I went along with leers and nudges, but I learned long ago, when they were on five fingers of gripe water, that there's no harder nut to crack than a Cockney bird. They roar with the loudest at dirty jokes and remain worldly and poker-faced right up to the Hard Word, but then, and only then, does the prude show itself. Why? I don't know. I've never fathomed it. The nearest I've come to a nympho was a Welsh schoolteacher in some posh private school. It wore tweed and rode an upright bicycle with a basket on the handlebars. And yet she really cared for me. Fanatical, she was. I've got a bent toe, and one day she made a splint for it out of a hair clip. She bound it all up and as I was wearing sandals at the time I was able to keep this thing on for several days. Although the old toe creased up again with the splint off, it really pleased her to think she'd straightened it for a while. "I like you perfect," she said. It just goes to prove the old saying that where there's culture there's crumpet.

It looks like being a side wind for the stage, and a strong one at that. On a hotel balcony opposite I can see two men standing, their trousers flapping and pressed tightly to their legs.

Romain, who is sitting by me, says, "I don't like the look of that wind. If it moves round much more it'll be dead against us."

"I know. God help us if that happens."

"You feel pretty rough, I expect?"

"It's almost an effort to stand. Yesterday I thought my lead would have stoked the old fire a bit, but at the moment the thought of one stage—let alone three—makes the bone marrow melt."

Romain wearily stands up. "I'm not going to chance it with the gearing I've got." He turns to Jeff. "Will you help me, Jeff? I'll put the other wheel in, the one with closer gears."

When they've gone, Susan puts down her magazine and says, "Isn't there anything you can do, any fiddle you can pull? Surely nothing matters now except to win."

I shake my head. "He's off two minutes ahead of me. If I

could catch him I could ride on the far side of the road, next to him. Officially this doesn't count as being paced, but the public wouldn't like it. To catch him and then sit behind him would get me disqualified."

"Can't you do that? Ride next to him?"

I look at her and then turn my head away. "I'd have to catch him first. Two minutes is a lot of road. He'd never let it happen."

"Do you honestly believe you've had it, then? Don't forget you've thought this before and things have come right."

I sigh from the depth of my stomach and peer out of the window. "If that wind turns against us, I don't know what I'll do. The big cols are finished, but it's still plenty hilly."

She joins me in another sigh. "Of all the rotten luck, having these carrots dangled before you when—as you've said yourself—you're a bit past biting them. First you met this girl and then got two lucky breaks in the Tour." She puts down her cigarette and touches my arm. "I really am sorry, Terry."

"Don't be. It's the oldest and most pathetic story in the world: the roué and the nymph."

She wrinkles her nose in a mock-think. "It's not sad really."

"It is. If only one's real self would age with the rest of you; but it doesn't. Oh, it's all over with her. I shall marry your mother and live happily ever after. As for this marrying lark, I reckon your generation—yours and Bobbie's—is the last one that will even contemplate it. It'll die out, probably in your lifetime."

"Do you really think so?"

I don't answer, because Romain comes back. "Nearly time," he says.

"Hark at him! Still eager. If only I could borrow your body for three days."

"Don't think I'm not tired," Romain replies.

"Tired—you don't know what it means. Again I'm sorry you're out of the running. I'm sorry for everything."

He taps my shoulder. "And sorry for yourself, by the sound of it. Perhaps it's just as well I'm so far behind now. It's clear cut, we know where we stand. Come on."

The loudspeakers are calling for the last five riders. I walk out behind van Faignaert, hoping against hope I can detect some weakness. But he strides along, the muscles beneath the dark skin on his legs looking powerful and rested. I draw myself up and put on a purposeful walk. Cheers and applause greet us. A group of about fifty young people carrying a large cardboard Belgian lion chant, "Van Faignaert! Van Faignaert!" A smaller group starts up in opposition. They have a big cartoon of me, the wheels of my cycle being circular Union Jacks. It gives them all plenty to photograph and write about.

Van Faignaert rides up and down among the crowds, unloosening his legs and his ego. Romain gets on and the countdown begins. "He's up the road this time," he says.

For a second I don't know what he means, then I laugh. "Let's hope so. You were right about Him being in the mountains."

I watch him go. He won't win the time trial, but he won't be far down either.

Two minutes later van Faignaert is sent off. I remain sitting until there's only a minute to go, and then I get on my machine. Jeff holds me and I put my feet in the toeclips and pull tight the straps. The wind is still a side wind, but given a few more degrees it would be what I call a three-quarter head wind.

"Good luck!' says Jeff.

"*Allez!*" roars the crowd.

I'm off.

For thirty kilometers I forge on as hard as I'm able. If I could catch van Faignaert I'd ride next to him and sod what people said. Once on a long stretch I saw him and his following car, but that's all. As each rider has a vehicle in attendance, I've managed to get Jeff and Susan to tail me in my own car. Although I feel physically rough, the sensation of spiritual uplift I got back in that storm when I dropped van Faignaert hasn't left me. I seem to be able to look inward as well as outward and see myself for what I am. What I see I don't like very much, but at the same time it doesn't seem to matter. Nothing, somehow, appears as important as it did yesterday.

The wind doesn't change, but the direction of the road does. It becomes a battle, alone, into wind and gradient. About the only advantage of a time trial is that you're kept better informed on the progress of rivals than you are on other stages. First I'm told van Faignaert's three minutes up, then four, then four and a half. Because there's still a long way to go I begin to panic. I go at this hill with everything I can muster and by the time I've reached the top the looking-through-gauze sensation has come back and my legs shake uncontrollably. On the short run down I grab what rest I can, but I'm soon back on the level and having to pedal hard again. At first it doesn't worry me that there's little sensation in my legs; you often experience this after a knee trembler. Jeff, who I thought was driving about fifty feet behind, suddenly appears next to me looking very worried. Susan's harassed face peeps over his shoulder.

"What's wrong?" he shouts.

I look desperately down at my legs, and even through the gauze I can see they're barely turning. They don't seem to belong to me, and although I will them to work they feel as if they've been grafted onto me from a five-year-old kid.

My speed is now about walking pace but there's nothing I can do. I grope for support against the car and I hear Jeff saying "Don't touch the car, they'll disqualify you." Like a fool I lean for support in the other direction and fall heavily onto the road. I'm conscious that I lie there without moving; the next thing I'm aware of is Jeff pulling my feet out of the toeclips. He rubs and slaps my legs and drags me to my feet, but I hold on to him for support. "My God, my God" is all he keeps saying, over and over again. He sits me on the grass border and straightens my handlebars, then grabs my hand and pulls me toward the bike. I try to get on but fall across it, then my foot slips on the one pedal I've managed to find and I go sprawling on top of the machine. Jeff lays me on my back in the road while Susan awkwardly sponges my face. I tell her to stop crying, but it makes her worse. To my left I see Jeff walk toward the waiting ambulance, making horizontal movements with his hands as if to say Finished, All Over.

Attendants come toward me and stand waiting. Susan's voice doesn't match the movement of her lips; it's like watching a dubbed film and I find I'm lip-reading her. "No, not in the ambulance, we'll take him in the car. Just leave us here. He'll be all right in a few minutes." No one speaks while the doctor examines me; then he goes elbowing his way through the crowd that has gathered around us.

Jeff lets down the back seat, the one I'd seduced Bobbie on, and puts a blanket under my head. "Let's get out of here, huh?" I say to him. "I don't want to give anyone a cheap thrill."

They drive me to the next village and pull into a side road. I sit up and Jeff hands me his jacket. "Here, put this on. Hide that yellow jersey or we'll have a mob here in no time."

"Don't cry, Susan. It was just a dream. They can't hurt you."

She doesn't look round at me although our eyes meet in the driving mirror.

"Look," Jeff says, "Tour vehicles are still coming by. I'll go and grab a lift to the finish. Leave it to me. I'll take care of everything at that end. If I know you, Terry, you won't want to be seen arriving in a car. Come in later, by another road."

When there's nobody looking I open the back door and go and sit in the driver's seat next to Susan. She takes my hand and squeezes it.

"No questions, no inquest, please," I say.

"All right," she mutters, and I can see by the look on her face that she doesn't want to talk about it either. She winds down a window. "Mother should be along soon when the road's opened." She forces a silly laugh. "There'll be no mistaking her in that car!"

"No."

"As soon as we see vehicles passing, we'll go and park up the road a little way. Shall we? When I see her coming I'll wave her down."

"Okay," I mumble.

"Cheer up."

"Huh."

"You did all you could."

"Maybe."

"Listen." She tries to look as if she's perking up, but is too tense to fool me. "Tomorrow's another day, a new day. Try to make a fresh start and put yourself back to a few months ago, when Bobbie was unknown to you and you'd have laughed at the idea of riding in the Tour. You were reasonably happy then and had a settled future with mother. Nothing's changed. Perhaps today it has, but tomorrow you can have things as they were, as you once wanted them."

As she finishes speaking I look at her. "Back in my place, in my own depths. A failure marrying someone his own age for the comfort she can supply."

She screws up her face in despair. "But was it so bad? Surely in a lot of ways it was better? Anyway, you might as well have everything today, so that when you get home you can put a big black circle round the date on the calendar and call it Terry's Day or Bad Day at Wherever-this-place-is, or something." She tries to keep her eyes on mine, but I can see it's getting increasingly harder for her. At last she looks at her fingernails and says slowly, "I drove to Marseilles as you asked, and went through the motions of phoning that woman. I did all this in case you quit the race and went to try for yourself. All I didn't do was to actually phone. You see, there was a letter. Funnily enough it came for you the day the Tour started. I was going to give it to you that same night, but you were hot and flustered and tired. I guessed the letter was from that woman, but at that point in the race Romain was leaning so heavily on you for support that I thought bad news would upset you and you'd quit. However, to make certain the news was bad I steamed open the letter. When I read the contents I knew you'd get all despondent, so I resolved to give it to you as soon as you quit. But of course you didn't, not until now, and with your leading the race I had even more reason not to give you the letter. I'm sorry. Like you, I've tried to do what I've thought best."

She looks up and blinks several times, and without actually moving she seems to draw herself back.

"And where is the letter?" I'd held my breath while she was talking and have to gasp the question at her.

She pulls her bag from the glove compartment, opens it and holds up a dogeared envelope. I take the letter, glance at the postmark and take out a single sheet of ruled airmail paper.

Dear Mr. Davenport,
    I am writing as promised, to tell you that Bobbie is engaged to some man, so I should not hold out hopes if I were you. Sorry if this comes as a blow. She called round to see if there were any letters and I put my foot right in it. This man followed her in and do you know he looks just like you. I said to him Oh so you found her then, and he looked at me as if I was daft. When he spoke I knew it wasn't you though, if you know what I mean. It looks as if she's done all right for herself. He looked loaded and had a big car outside. Seeing as Bobbie had this man with her I thought it best not to mention you'd called.
    Sorry about the news and hoping you are well,
                                        Doreen Moore (Mrs)

I close my eyes and wish Susan would open the car door and go away; I'm vaguely aware of breathing deeply through my nose as I try to check everything that races inside me. When Susan takes the letter from me I open my eyes.

"At least it can't get any worse. From now on you can only go up."

Through my teeth I say, "Up? Down, you mean.'

"No, it'll be all right, you'll see. Some cars just went past; traffic's coming through. We'd better not miss Mother."

Dumbly I start the motor.

She kisses the side of my face. "I'm so sorry, Terry. Does it hurt?"

"Only when I laugh."